THE LONG FALL

TERRY SANVILLE

This is a work of fiction. Names, characters, places, and incidents are products of the author's imagination or are used fictitiously and are not to be construed as real. Any resemblance to actual events, locations, organizations, or persons, living or dead, is entirely coincidental.

World Castle Publishing, LLC
Pensacola, Florida

Hardback ISBN: 9798302643100
Paperback ISBN: 9798891263246
eBook ISBN: 9798891263253
First Edition World Castle Publishing, LLC, December 31, 2024
http://www.worldcastlepublishing.com

Cover: Karen Fuller
Editor: Karen Fuller

To the people of Santa Catalina Island, California, for their friendship, patience, and stories.

We stood on the ridgeline and gazed across the azure channel to the San Pedro coast and snowcapped Mount Wilson. Then she vanished and I scarcely had time to stretch out a hand and grasp at the empty air. My vision compressed and fractured like some crazy kaleidoscope. I followed the arch of her fall, the wind ripping at her clothes, long hair streaming upward like a smoking candle flame. I felt my lungs force breath into a scream that I prayed would haul her back. But I was alone again, with nothing but shattered images and a boundless sense of loss.

CHAPTER 1

Fred Noland is sure his heart will stop. He steers the mountain bike to the edge of Stagecoach Road and clutches his chest. He's been peddling uphill from Avalon for an hour and still hasn't reached the ridge top. The single-lane track winds through Eucalyptus and oaks, cutting across near-vertical slopes to the crest of Santa Catalina Island. He dumps the bike on the narrow shoulder and drinks in deep gulps of air. His varicose-veined legs wobble. But reassuring heartbeats thunder in his chest.

Throwing his helmet down, Fred, a criminal-law attorney from Temecula, bends forward and grabs his knees. Drifting clots of fog hide and then expose the steep mountain slope and the Pacific far below. He tastes bile and vomits into the bushes. Dark spots dance before his eyes, and the landscape swims in and out of focus. But the chest pain subsides, and he pushes himself up, being careful not to topple.

As he stoops to retrieve a water bottle, his eyes sweep the hillside and fix on a patch of chaparral. The lemonade bush has been scraped away, and there's a strip of something white that's far too pallid to be shrubbery. Fred wipes sweat from his eyes with the edge of his jersey and squints but still can't make it out. Dousing his face with warm water doesn't help.

He mounts the bicycle, swears at himself for not renting one with a softer seat, and pedals unsteadily toward the airport, five miles farther along. The fog burns off, and a chocolate smog bank hangs over the California mainland. He remembers how he'd gotten a kick out of phoning his sister in Boise and telling her about Avalon, the only California town where the sun rises over the ocean. It's those small, quirky things that become embedded in Fred's brain. And now it's filled with soft-edged images of the strange downslope object. *Damn, can't get away from that crap, even on vacation,* he thinks.

Catalina's "Airport in the Sky" looks like something found in the Andes. The engineers sliced the tops off two peaks, filled in the saddle, and paved everything with asphalt, leaving a sheer drop at the east end of its runway. A Spanish-tiled terminal squats next to a gravel lot with a WWII-era tanker truck parked nearby. A windsock hangs limp on its pole. Fred dumps his bike under the building's covered porch, yanks back a screen door, and stomps inside.

Tables and chairs crowd a dark fireplace at one end of the room. A lunch counter and gift shop extend across the back wall. The place is deserted, except for a woman with long gray hair perched behind the counter. An aging refrigerator hums loudly.

"Looks like you could use something to drink," the woman calls, her voice bouncing off the Spanish floor tiles.

"Yeah, make it a double," Fred jokes, but his breath catches, and he's overcome with coughing. The woman waits, stares at him with pale eyes.

"I'll have a Crush," he finally gets out.

Gnarled fingers adorned with turquoise reach into an old Coke machine and pull out a dripping Orange Crush. Popping off the cap, she slides the soda across the counter. Fred grasps the bottle, tilts it skyward, and lets the sweet liquid pour down his gullet. From his stool, he studies the room. Huge black-and-white photographs adorn the walls: Grumman seaplanes wing-over and flying low, the Moorish-styled Casino under construction at Avalon Harbor, and sportsmen brandishing rifles with carcasses of wild javelina and long-horned sheep at their feet. The whole place feels like the 1930s. There's not a video game in sight.

"You're the first one up the hill this morning," the old

woman says. "Should be pretty riding now that the fog's lifted. My Pop used to rent bicycles at Descanso Beach before the War. Every summer, he'd get hundreds of 'em, headed for Blackjack Camp, and they weren't riding fancy mountain bikes or electrics."

Fred grins. "Yeah, well, I need every gear I can find."

A sage-scented breeze blows through the screen and warms them. The old woman goes back to reading her *Country Living* and nods when Fred lays crumpled dollars on the counter and shuffles toward the exit.

Outside on the porch, he lowers himself carefully onto a bench, leans against the wall, and stares at the windswept airstrip. He's in no hurry to get back on the bike. The thickening smog bank drifts across the channel toward Catalina, the product of millions of Los Angeles motorists fighting weekend beach traffic.

With a grunt, Fred stands and stretches. He shakes his stone-cold muscles to get the blood moving, which starts his brain spinning again about the torturous ride that's brought him here and that strange object on the hillside. He pulls his cellphone from his jersey, thumbs 9-1-1, and is immediately connected to a sexy-sounding Lucille at emergency dispatch. He speaks precisely, being back on familiar ground.

"Get me the Sheriff's Department."

CHAPTER 2

Sergeant Paul Saldano returns from his rounds. He walks them five times a day. In Avalon, no one's in a hurry. It's November, and the tourist season is over. Saldano slumps in a swivel chair with feet up on the desk and gazes lazily through Venetian blinds onto a palm-shaded plaza. The morning's antique tour buses have departed, but it's too early for the brotherhood of old Mexicans to take up their station, play checkers, and sip sweet wine from paper bags.

The telephone's buzz breaks the Sergeant's reverie. He presses the cell against an ear, pencil poised over a notepad. "Where was this? …. uh huh…and you think it looks like *what?* …. right…where are you staying? …. cell number? …. I'll also need your home address and phone…right…thanks, we'll check it out."

The Sergeant pockets his cellphone and smiles as he catches himself using the term *we'll.* Back on the mainland it had made sense, with him one of hundreds that patrolled the suburbs and rolling canyons with their posh hilltop homes scattered throughout Los Angeles County. But during the off-season on Catalina, the Sheriff's Department deploys only a handful of officers. And with Frank, the Station Commander, off island, Saldano's in charge. He telephones Lucille.

"I'll be up top for about an hour; let County Fire know."

"No problem, Sergeant. I will," Lucille says in a low, lazy voice.

Saldano wonders what else she's willing to do. He's never met her, having been on-island for only a month. But her voice is seductively smooth, like just-shaved legs, and he envisions an un-tethered halter-top and a wine glass tilted toward full red lips.

Buckling his gun belt, Saldano slips from the station and climbs into the Explorer, records the odometer reading, then heads up Stagecoach Road, the SUV humming in second gear. He pulls off halfway up to let the gearbox rest. The fog has vanished. The eucalyptus trees are whipped by a strong Santa Ana wind, a kiln-heated breath off the Mojave Desert that carries the scent of sage mixed with LA's chemical soup.

Topping the ridgeline, he drives slowly, scans the gravel shoulder, and pulls over when he sees the knobby tracks from a mountain bike. He grabs his binoculars, pops open the door, and eases toward the edge. He stands on a part of the ridgeline the locals call the China Wall, a 1,200-foot near-vertical drop to the ocean.

Through the binoculars, the mountainside appears as a dusty green texture, nothing unusual, except for a few bare spots where the brush has been torn up. The week before, maintenance crews had cut down some dead eucalyptus that lined the road and rolled the trunks over the edge - angering the Island Conservancy folks. Saldano inspects each disturbed plot. He sweeps across one and freezes. The red sandy soil has been laid bare at the edge of a drop-off, exposing the bones of a human forearm and hand. The phalanges are fanned out against the ground as if waving to someone on the faraway ridge road.

Saldano scans the surrounding areas, but the brush hides everything, and there's no obvious disturbance trail leading to the spot. He returns to the SUV, takes an electronic notebook from the console, and begins roughing out his report - time, date, location, physical setting, approximate angle of the site from the road, and odometer reading. He snaps digital photos with his Nikon. The two-way radio crackles, and Saldano reaches for the handset.

"Y'all okay up there, Sergeant? Should we respond? Over." The slow accent of Phillips, the Fire Chief, comes through clearly.

Saldano smiles. On the mainland anyone radioing in such a casual manner would have been chewed out. But here on Catalina, none of them pay much attention to the ten code.

"No problems, Chief. Does that one-ton of yours have a winch? Over."

"Sure does. Over."

"Join me at the east end of the China Wall. No need to hurry. Over."

"What's goin' on up there, Saldano? Over."

"I think I found what's left of a body. Over."

"A what?"

"A body, as in human."

Phillips's voice shifts to business mode. "Copy that. ETA in about 30. Base clear."

This should be fun, Saldano thinks. *The fire boys have been itching to use their fancy new truck.*

The Sergeant hears them coming miles away, and when they finally appear around the last bend, three guys dressed in yellow fill the cab while another hangs off the back. The truck pulls up in front of the Explorer, doors pop open, and the crew joins him at the edge.

"*Que paso, hombre,* what da ya got?" Phillips grins.

Saldano hands him the binoculars and points. "About 300 feet down and forty-five degrees from the road."

The Fire Chief sweeps the hillside. "Yeah, I see it. Looks like the bones of a human arm and a hand. *That's* what ya dragged us out here for?" Phillips gives the binoculars to his crew, who take turns checking the hillside.

"You've been watching too many Internet movies, Chief," Saldano says. "They can't all be bloody crime scenes. Do you think the winch on your truck could lower me down?"

Phillips laughs. "My cable isn't more than 150 feet, couldn't get ya close. But I got an idea. Those Verizon guys still have their truck parked at Pebbly Beach. We could wrap their spool with wire. But it'll take me time to set up."

"Good idea...and nobody's going to mess with anything down there. Just call me tomorrow when you have it set, and I'll meet you here."

Saldano climbs inside the Explorer to finish his initial report. He has completed hundreds. But this is his first on Catalina and the questions that require answers are no longer second nature. He stares at the notepad, hoping for inspiration. The bell chimes sound twelve o'clock from their perch above Seven Moons Bay. He abandons his report and fires up the SUV. The image of bleached white bones tugs at his concentration as he carefully wheels down through the torturous turns of the old Stagecoach Road into Avalon.

CHAPTER 3

It's late the next morning before Saldano hears from Phillips. The communications people hadn't been anxious to volunteer their cable truck for a potentially hazardous investigation. Only after Phillips offered to help with encroachment permits for underground cable work had they let him spool up five hundred feet of wire and drive their truck to the China Wall. When Saldano arrives just before lunch, the fire guys have coned off the road and backed the truck to the edge. A half-inch steel cable dangles from its spool. Saldano straps himself into a harness, pulls on a helmet, heavy boots and gloves, and clips the cable to the attachment ring.

"Y'all don't have to do this," Phillips says. "I can lower one of my guys. Or we can call Headquarters Rescue from Long Beach."

"I'm not gonna miss this much fun," Saldano says, grinning, "and it'll take HQ a week to get here. Let me at least check out the site before they screw up my hillside."

Saldano edges down the slope, half suspended, half rappelling through hip-high sugar bush and toyon. The first fifty yards go easily, with no trees or clumps of prickly pear cactus to maneuver around. But twenty yards from the site, Saldano drops over a rocky shelf and dangles in thin air against the cliff. The harness tightens around his groin and armpits. A flash of white catches his eye, and he signals the fire crew to stop lowering.

The skull grins at him from under the sagebrush, with only a small section of its frontal bone missing. It reminds Saldano of the skeletons that adorned his Texas neighborhood during the celebration of *Dia de los Muertos*. But here on this precarious mountain face, there are no joyful fiesta sounds, only mournful blasts from boat horns.

Maneuvering a roll of yellow plastic tape from his coat, Saldano cuts off a strip with his jackknife and ties it to the brush, marking the spot. He signals the crew to continue lowering. A toyon branch rakes across his face but doesn't penetrate his helmet's wire screen.

After dropping a few more yards, Saldano edges onto the clearing. The skeletal remains of the hand and lower arm are bleached white, with the forearm, wrist, palm, and digits intact. No skin or flesh remains, and, given the lack of insects, it has been that way for a long time. Under the brush near the clear patch, bone fragments litter the ground.

Saldano struggles to maintain balance and drops to his knees. *It's going to be one hell of a collection job. The island foxes have probably scattered the remains over half the mountain.*

Tying another piece of crime scene tape to a clump of lemonade bush, Saldano gives the signal to be hauled upslope. The fire crew reels him in like a lunging tuna. In ten minutes, he stumbles through the last phalanx of sagebrush and unclicks the cable.

"Had enough fun playing mountain goat?" Phillips asks.

"More…more than enough."

"You goin' down again?"

"Hell no! I'll call the Coroner…and see…how he wants to handle it. It's way too big…a job for us."

"You'd better do some fancy talkin'. Those yahoos don't ever wanna come out here, and with the budget mess…."

Saldano gasps when he pulls off the heavy helmet and tugs at the gloves. Deep scratches crisscross his wrists, and the crease of his neck burns where the helmet failed to protect him.

Phillips frowns. "Better let Larken treat those – plenty of

poison oak out there."

The descent and climb back up the China Wall has taken less than an hour. But Saldano already feels the ache of muscles long unused, and he thinks about how good a soak in the Catalina Hotel's hot tubs will feel. He grits his teeth as the EMT smears foul-smelling cream over the wounds.

"Christ, man, what's in that stuff, grain alcohol?"

"Yeah, pretty much – but it costs a lot more." Larkin pastes ugly bandages over the injured areas. The fire crew roars off to town, leaving him alone with a throbbing neck and the job of adding more pages to his notes.

Saldano types furiously until his hand cramps, and he's forced to stop. The Explorer's hot interior stinks of sweat and chaparral. He leans back and shuts his eyes, remembering his college days at UCLA as a pre-law student on a scholarship from the Knights of Columbus. Paul was stuck in the library on a Saturday night, piecing together a research paper, when he'd met Julie. She sat at an oak table near him, a handful of open texts spread out before her and scribbled into a dog-eared workbook. She'd caught him with pen poised over a blank tablet page.

"That first sentence is always the hardest," Julie said.

Saldano glared at her, his precarious concentration broken. Julie looked startled and ready to flee. Paul quickly apologized. "Sorry, didn't mean to frighten you. For me, writing is like inventing every word."

Her face relaxed. "Just jot down your thoughts. Worry about the sentences later."

"What are you, a Lit major?"

She nodded.

They'd talked about school, about what they would do afterward, and about why they were stuck in the library on a Saturday night. She was Irish, with red hair and constellations of freckles, from a rich Philadelphia family. He was *Tejano* and tan, like the color of dilute butterscotch pudding, from Cuero, Texas. Both were Catholic.

Six months later, they got married. Nine years later, they got divorced. These events were separated by two daughters, an unsuccessful writing career for Julie, three failed bar exams, and several twelve-step programs for Paul.

He did well at the Police Academy and got a job almost immediately with the Los Angeles County Sheriff's Department. But this minor success wasn't enough to save them, and their season of unhappiness stretched into years. Neither could figure out how to get past it. Finally, Julie took a lover, and Paul stayed late at the bars or volunteered for a third watch.

The blare of a tour bus's horn shakes Saldano from his memories. The old vehicle squeezes past his SUV on the narrow mountain road. A hand waves from its driver's window. But that raucous noise only takes him back to the last time he fought with Julie.

It had been a hot June afternoon when she found him passed out, lying naked in twisted and stained sheets, the nightstand upended.

"Get up, you son of a bitch, and GET OUT!" she roared.

"Get off my fucking back." Saldano heaved a half-full beer bottle at her. It exploded against the wall. He was too late to notice his daughters nearly hidden behind his wife's sundress. The youngest sported a black-and-blue cheek and wouldn't look at him.

In a daze, he escaped, collecting a few personal things from the front lawn and sidewalk where Julie had heaved them. He felt like the starring actor in a B-rated movie. The neighbors watched his performance in silence. He flopped at a Motel Six just off the 405, knew he had to get away, get straight, and somehow gain forgiveness from his little girls. The alternative? Become one more drunk, handcuffed in the back of a black-and-white rolling down the 101 to Men's Central Jail. He needed a fresh start to get off the booze and feel good about himself - it had been so long. Six weeks later, his transfer came through, and with only a suitcase full of clothes, Paul caught the night boat to Avalon.

The mournful hoot from a ferryboat's air horn mercifully drags Saldano back to the present. "That crap follows me everywhere," he mutters to himself.

Switching off the notepad, he gives the Explorer's keys a twist and winds down the canyon to his afternoon rounds, but not before contacting the Chief of Coroner's Investigations, Dr. McKinney.

"Jesus, if those bones are bleached as white as you say, they could be Native American," McKinney grouses. "We might have to send an observer from one of the local tribal councils."

They agree that a four-person team should take the Thursday barge from San Pedro and meet Saldano at Pebbly Beach.

"Better e-mail me a map that shows where you found the remains," McKinney says. "I'll get our GIS people to produce an aerial that we can grid off to record where we find material."

"Whatever you do, don't send any indoor types out here," Saldano says. "The terrain will eat 'em up." He rings off and busies himself with arranging for the coroner crew's lodging.

They arrive on schedule, driving two trucks loaded with boxes of equipment. The Sergeant has cleared out the back Station office and they set up a temporary morgue, complete with layout tables, microscopes, audio equipment, lights, and cameras. He's glad that the Station Commander won't return for a few more days. If he's lucky, the coroner's team will have cleared on out before Frank McCluskey comes back and directs their every move.

The forensic team calibrates their equipment and studies an aerial photograph of the hillside that's divided into grids. The next day, they ascend into the early morning mist. A pretty blond, whose bulging chest threatens the binding capacity of her work shirt, hooks up to a cable and lowers herself over the threshold. Another crewmember does the same twenty yards farther along the road. Each carries a canvas sack, plastic bags, and an iPad for describing each find and establishing its GIS coordinates.

It's slow going, and by the second day, the crew has worked only a fraction of the way downslope. They've found only beer cans, used condoms, and splintered ground squirrel and gopher bones left behind by the island's foxes and kestrels.

On the third day, they hit pay dirt. At the lunch break, Saldano examines the bone chips and larger pieces hauled upslope in numbered plastic bags. By sundown of the fourth day, they're done and half the crew boards the evening barge for San Pedro. The remaining two members, unfortunately not the blond, stay at the Sheriff's Station and catalog the finds.

"What's the story with the two tables?" Saldano asks Charles, a mustached guy who smokes a pipe.

"You have two skeletons here. Looks like a man and a woman. We're still sorting things out, but we'll know more in a day or two."

"You mean *two* people went over the side?" Saldano asks.

Charles nods impatiently.

Slowly, the skeletal jigsaw puzzles take shape; one with an almost intact skull, while the other has only a fragment of the jawbone to indicate where a head had once rested. Finally, Charles and his assistant take hundreds of digital photos, carefully catalog then bag each bone, and pack up for good.

"We won't know how long they've been lying on your hillside without more tests," Charles says. "My guess is seventy to eighty years. Based on the structure of the skeleton's pelvic bones, you have a man and a woman here. The length of their femurs and tibias suggests that the male was about six foot two inches, and the female maybe five foot three with broad hips. But that's not the interesting part. Look at this."

Charles hands Paul a flat, nondescript bone with a neat dime-sized hole bored through its center. The Sergeant turns it over in his hands. "What is it?"

"It's the female's sternum…with a bullet hole…looks like from a high-powered rifle." Charles puffs on his pipe and stares at Saldano.

"Good God, that pretty much rules out an accidental COD."

Charles nods. "We'll check the diameter of the hole and compare it with our database, but it looks like it's from a 30-calibre, maybe more."

"So you're sure a gunshot killed her?" Saldano asks.

"No, I can't say for certain until we examine the remains for other trauma or disease. But years ago I worked the Topanga Canyon Sniper Case - saw a few skeletons with neat holes drilled in them, just like this one. You'll get the final path report in about three weeks. It'll include a write-up from our forensic anthropologist."

Saldano groans to himself and knows that it will be a month, maybe more, before the paperwork hits Frank's desk. *Christ, eighty-year-old homicide…. Frank could kill this thing before my investigation gets started…. I wonder what she looked like…and what the hell were they doing up there so long ago?*

CHAPTER 4

The wrinkled blue channel stretched to distant bluffs that framed San Pedro harbor. The sun had just come up over Mt. Wilson. Flavia enjoyed the freshening breeze that brought with it summer smells of mainland sage and mesquite. She felt bright, clear-headed, and, for the first time in a long while, hopeful.

Flavia lived in one of two dozen Quonset huts off a back canyon that opened onto Pebbly Beach. Three years before, she had lived in Avalon with her mother, father, and older brother in a tiny clapboard cottage. But then President Roosevelt gave a speech about "a day that will live in infamy" and World War II came to Catalina Island.

Flavia was astonished at how quickly the military took over. The gringo Yacht Club had been seized by the Merchant Marines and turned into a seamen's school. She missed the summer crowds and beach parties at the Hotel Saint Catherine that now housed a dreary cooks' school and officers' barracks run by the U.S. Maritime Service. But she missed her family's home on Descanso Avenue most of all. Flavia frowned, creasing her smooth brown face, and remembered her father shaking her awake in the darkness.

"Come on, Flavia, we must go."

"What's happening, Papa? I have to go to school in a while."

"Not today. We must move back to the barrio."

"But this is our home. Why must we leave? It is not right."

"The gringos want it for their officers and families. The landlord says we must go. So hurry, and no more questions."

The town's Mexican tenants had been *relocated* back to one of the island's original barrios, to a cluster of cabins and Quonset huts near the power plant. The constant whine of the plant's turbines never let them forget their misfortune.

But this morning, Flavia felt hopeful on her way to the Seafood Grotto Restaurant to speak with Señor Burke about a kitchen job. Her cousin knew the girl that had been fired. With the town awash with seamen, every open eatery hummed with customers. Burke would need immediate help.

Two weeks after Pearl Harbor, the military had stopped tourists from coming to Catalina, marooning a thousand families and tying a tourniquet around the island's economic lifeblood. Most island folks searched for work constantly. But while the restaurant job held promise, Flavia's mother had shaken her head, "You don't know what...what those men are like...and Señor Burke can't be trusted."

"But Mama, only the sailors have money. Besides, Papa already works too much. It's not like before when we could live off fees and tips."

"You think you're so grown up. But it's dangerous for island girls. You must be careful."

"I am strong and can look after myself, Mama. I know you worry - but you will see."

Flavia's father, Eduardo, used to work as a paid guide for mainland hunters. He'd lead them into the back canyons and wait patiently for them to take their first shots before he slammed an ancient Enfield to his shoulder and brought the charging javelina down with a single well-placed round. But that profitable world had vanished along with the American fleet, and the military forbade civilians from discharging firearms anywhere on the island.

Flavia wore her cleanest white blouse, the one that showed off her ample figure. Green ribbons held her long coffee-brown hair in check. She walked toward Avalon along Lover's Cove and used the time to select just the right English words, just the right sense of pleading while retaining her composure. She didn't want to sound desperate. Too many desperate girls plied their charms on the upper floors of back street hotels. Flavia knew some of them were from good families whose fathers and brothers had worked in Avalon's tile factory alongside her own father. Flavia was ten when the factory closed. But time and circumstance had created new channels to cross, especially for the island's poor.

Near the restaurant's entrance, Flavia found a boy flushing out garbage cans with a hose.

"Excuse me," she said in Spanish, "can you tell me where I can find Señor Burke?"

"Si, Señorita, he's inside his office." The boy grinned, eyeing her shamelessly. "Go up the stairs and look to the left."

Flavia climbed to the second floor and entered a narrow hallway that led into the dining room. She looked to the left through an open door. An enormous man with a drooping mustache sat in a closet-sized office, belt undone. He sorted through a stack of paperwork. Flavia knocked quietly on the doorframe.

He glanced up. "What…what da ya want?" His purplish lips shook when he spoke.

"Beg your pardon, Señor Burke. But a friend of mine says that you have a job in the kitchen. I know a lot about kitchens, and I'm a hard worker." Flavia rushed her words.

"Yeah, I need somebody that can work breakfast through supper. You think you can handle those hours?" Burke looked at her like most men did, which made her shiver.

"My…my back is strong, señor. Ask any *pescador*, ah, fisherman, in Avalon. I used to unload and clean Yellowtail when they ran off San Clemente."

"Yeah, but *I* need somebody to clean my pots and pans."

"I can do that, *muy bueno*. Just give me a chance, Señor Burke."

"I pay 20¢ an hour. You eat between meals and only leftovers. You want the job or not?"

"Si, I mean, yes. Thank you, Señor Burke." Flavia tried to smile but only managed an upward quiver of her lips.

"Well, go see Ramón in the back kitchen, and he'll get you started."

Flavia edged sideways out of the tiny office, not ready to turn her back on her new boss.

In the back kitchen, a tall and lanky Mexican boy bent over a cast iron sink. He looked close to her age.

"Excuse me, are…are you Ramón?" she asked.

He turned and wiped his dripping hands on his white smock. He wore a green rubber apron.

"Si, senorita."

"My name is Flavia. Señor Burke hired me to wash pots and pans. He said you'd get me started."

Ramón smiled shyly. "I will…and welcome to hell."

Flavia noticed the room's steamy heat, their workstations were separated from the food prep area by a pair of swinging portholed doors.

Ramón showed her the storage bins full of smocks and aprons. As a dishwasher, he stood on a rubber mat over three iron tubs where he scraped, scrubbed, and rinsed the dishes, then placed them in drying racks. Flavia had a similar setup, but instead of plates, she cleaned the pots, pans, and any other kitchenware used to prepare the Grotto's fine bill of fare.

To retrieve the dirty pots, she had to venture into the food prep area where the white-hatted cooks bobbed and weaved. Catcalls and whistles announced her first visit. The young men chattered in Spanish and English.

"I'm in love. Come here and give me a kiss," one of them called.

Flavia answered, "Ah, *muchachos,* don't you know? I'm saving myself for a rich gringo."

They laughed and grinned at her. Flavia worked hard and fast. The cooks weren't careful about how they prepared the food because the pots Flavia scrubbed were caked with burned-on fish, chicken, or other foods. She scratched at each with a steel-wire scrubber or attacked it with an assortment of scrapers and knives that hung on cords from the wall.

When she returned to the kitchen with the gleaming pans, she chided them. "You're supposed to cook the food, not destroy it," she said firmly. "Pay more attention and talk less."

"Oh señorita, you're just like *mi madre,*" a tall brown man crooned. "I'll try, I promise."

After the lunch crowd disappeared, the kitchen staff broke for their mid-afternoon meal of albacore, greasy chicken, and mashed potatoes. They greedily attacked the food set out on a splintery picnic table in back of the restaurant and chattered about their families, sweethearts, and how Señor Burke was one *pendejo grande.*

"Why don't the waitresses join us?" Flavia asked.

"Those gringa think they're too refined for us hooligans," a red-haired cook named Jimmy complained. "They eat at their own side table up front - only talk nice when they want some special order."

"Don't worry about those want-to-be movie stars," Ramón said, "you're as pretty as any of them."

The rest of the crew hooted and whistled.

Ramón muttered, "I'm sorry, señorita. I didn't mean anything by it." His face darkened, and he grabbed his plate and bolted for the restaurant.

"It is all right, Ramón..." Flavia called after him.

"He's shy - but he's got a good heart," Jimmy said.

"I know. But I wish the waitresses would join us so I could talk with them. I'd love to earn the tips they make." *If I was a waitress, I could pay for my schoolbooks and clothes,* she thought.

Flavia had lasted longer in high school than nearly all of her friends, mostly because she'd forced herself to learn English. She didn't want to give up school with the end so near. Flavia also knew that her chances for finding a prosperous husband on Catalina were slim and that she'd likely end up on the supply barge bound for San Pedro and fade into the great metropolis of Los Angeles with its two million people. That's what her brother, Pastor, had planned before the Selective Service sent him his "greetings" letter. He'd enlisted in the Navy and served as a deck gunner on a destroyer somewhere off Subic Bay. He'd returned to Catalina on leave from the Philippines, dressed smartly in white bell bottoms, a sailor's cap jauntily cocked to one side. But he'd lost the playfulness in his eyes, and it made Flavia sad to stare at other young men and know that the same would happen to them.

The dinner rush continued past seven o'clock. It was almost nine before Flavia scrubbed her last pot. Ramón told her to go home. Trudging along the oceanfront, the cold night wind dried her body. A dull pain stabbed the small of her back from bending over to reach the bottoms of the tubs. But she'd earned more than two dollars. Flavia smiled to herself in anticipation of telling her mother about the job, about her friendly co-workers, and that Señor Burke wasn't as much the lecher as everybody thought, at least so far.

The summer became an exhausting routine of pots and pans, scalding water, and cold walks home. The strange wartime season without tourists wound down as Labor Day approached. Flavia looked forward to school and going to dances, although the number of boys had dwindled as the older ones got drafted or enlisted.

The Labor Day weekend at the restaurant proved the most hectic yet, and Ramón moved like a high-stepping dancer, gliding between tubs and flinging plates into their racks. Before the lunch rush began, Jimmy stuck his head through the back door: "Flavia, Señor Burke wants to see you, pronto."

She looked at Ramón with raised eyebrows, but he shrugged. She removed her rubber apron and went to the office.

"They say you know English," Burke said before she cleared the doorway.

"Yes, I've studied hard and can speak it as well as Spanish, well, almost."

"Look here. Mary came in with morning sickness and couldn't finish her shift. I had to let her go - which sort of puts me in a bind. I need you to waitress for the rest of the day - and if you do okay, you can keep the job."

"Gracias, I mean, thank you, Señor Burke, but I've been working in the kitchen, and I'm a mess." Flavia felt sweat trickle between her breasts.

"Don't worry about that - go see Laura, and she'll give you lipstick and show you where the uniforms are stored. And comb that hair out - the customers will like it."

Burke leered at her, and she disappeared into the back kitchen. Pepe, the garbage can boy, had already taken her place at the tubs, a promotion for him as well.

Ramón's shoulders sagged. He bent over the dirty rinse water but stiffened when Flavia touched his arm gently. Whirling, he picked up a rack of dishes and heaved it across the room. The plates smashed against the wall, shards flying. She stared open-mouthed into his sullen eyes, then backed away slowly. Jimmy pushed halfway through the kitchen doors but stopped when Pepe waved him off.

"It's all right, Ramón," Flavia whispered. "I'll still be here."

Ramón ducked his head and muttered. "You be careful of those seamen, Flavia."

"I will, Ramón, and I'll still be here," she repeated and escaped to the dining room.

Laura was everything that Flavia was not, a pale blond with short-cut hair and more angles than curves. She seemed glad to see Flavia and gave her dark red lipstick to apply, helped pick out a uniform, and found her a fresh order pad and pencil.

"Have you ever waitressed before?"

Flavia shook her head and tried to control the tremor that threatened to shiver her body apart.

"Well, remember to listen carefully to the orders, write everything down, and above all, keep smiling. And if you unbutton that blouse a bit, you'll get better tips." With a laugh, she vanished, leaving Flavia panic-stricken at the order window.

But her first customers, two painfully shy seamen, caused no problems, and she stared at the menu posted on the wall and recorded their orders. Jimmy snorted when he pulled the ticket from the spindle, then showed it to Leonardo, who giggled.

"It's okay to write sloppy," Jimmy said, "we'll get it." She smiled at him from her new vantage point.

By the end of the day, Flavia had learned most of the menu and could talk a little with the customers without becoming flustered. By the end of a week, she'd settled in and had patrons asking for her. Flavia's memories of the hot kitchen and impossible-to-clean pots were replaced by young men staring at her cleavage, teetering plates loaded with food, and mad dashes between tables and the order window. But she always took her mid-afternoon meal with the kitchen staff, and they kidded her about it, especially Ramón, who called her the next Mexican movie star.

Those first nights, Flavia returned home exhausted, her

pockets full of silver. She carefully counted her tips and gave most to her mother along with her pay.

"Flavia, we can buy tamales from Señora Rosalia for your father's birthday," Dolores said excitedly.

Flavia shot back, "Better also buy *cervezas* and invite Papa's friends if he's going to stay happy." Seeing her mother smile was worth the backaches and sore feet.

But Flavia always held back some of the coins, stowed them in a carved wooden box kept in a bottom dresser drawer. The box also contained road maps of the mainland that she studied at night while her parents slept. She stared at the names of strange towns and dreamed about what it must be like to live in the big cities across the channel. *This new milagro job can pay for my ticket over town. It will be my salvation.* Flavia decided to ask Señor Burke if she could continue working weekends and the dinner hours when school started.

"Jesus, it'll make scheduling a royal pain in the ass," Burke whined. "Nobody's gonna want to work just breakfasts and lunches."

Flavia purred, "But Señor Burke, look at all the men that come back just to see me. You don't want to lose them, do you?"

"No, of course not. But there are plenty of other pretty girls more willing than you…." Burke's voice trailed off, his eyes affixed on her chest.

Flavia controlled a shudder and stared him down. "If I say one word to *mi padre,*" she hissed, "he will shoot you, and we'll have you for supper."

"All right, all right. No need to get uppity."

Flavia escaped the office and barely reached the bottom of the stairs before exploding into hysterical laughter at the image of Señor Burke's rotund body laid out on her mother's table, trussed up like a pork roast.

Much later, after closing, she walked home in the moonlit

night. The faint glow of Palos Verdes beckoned from across the silver channel, calling her to a better life, to a chance at something beyond Avalon.

CHAPTER 5

At least now I've got something to work on. Sergeant Saldano hovers over the computer keyboard, index fingers stabbing in a hunt-and-peck rhythm. Two skeletons, one bullet hole, a man and a woman, and eighty years of history have recharged his brain and given it focus. Logging onto LA County's Criminal Data Base, Saldano types in the code for missing persons, cross-references it with the town of Avalon, and queries all known listings arranged in descending chronological order.

The computer pauses for a count of three, then displays a list of forty-two names and case numbers. The entries go back to 1963. When he queries an earlier date, the computer instructs him to contact the *Records and Identification Bureau* in Norwalk. He taps their phone number.

"You want station reports for where and when?" a bored voice mutters.

Saldano repeats, "For Avalon…anything you've got before 1950." He hears computer keys clicking, followed by a long pause before the records clerk speaks again.

"Looks like you're out of luck, Sergeant. Before '63, a private police force patrolled Catalina. Their records are not in our system."

"Well, they wouldn't have thrown that stuff out, would they?"

"Of course not. They're around someplace…probably in hard copy."

"Just effing great. So I'll have to phone up all thirty station houses and ask them to check their back closets?"

"You could send a query e-mail," the clerk suggests. "But I would contact the Pico Rivera Station first. It's in your operational region, and they have a pretty good-sized barn out back."

A phone call to Pico Rivera tells Saldano that the records *might* be there, but nobody's sure, and he'll have to dig the files out himself.

He leaves the station to complete his mid-afternoon rounds and stops at Avalon's living-room-sized Library. Saldano approaches the head librarian.

"Good afternoon, Señora Estella." Saldano smiles and tips his hat.

"*Buenas tardes, Pablo*. You still looking for some of those interesting magazines?" Estella grins.

"Not today, Señora," Saldano croaks, hoping his embarrassment doesn't show.

During his first week on Catalina, Paul had gone into the library late on a Friday night. As a new patron, Estella had given him the grand tour, all the while pumping him for personal data: Was he married? Did he have a family? A place to live? A girlfriend? Did he like girls? All questions came in hushed tones as she'd herded him around the room. Her eyes gleamed through huge bifocals. Exasperated, Saldano had finally asked her if the library had any interesting magazines. The old woman blushed and told him that he'd have to purchase them at Ed's Book Emporium on Sumner Street. Since then, Estella kids Saldano about the magazines. It makes him feel like a naughty schoolboy. But tonight, he's all business.

"Señora, do you keep old copies of the *Catalina Islander*?"

"Well, Paul, how far back do you want to go?" she asks.

"I'm looking for anything before 1950. You have them in storage?"

Estella laughs. "We did. Had every weekly edition going back to 1914. A few years ago, I shipped ten boxes of those old newspapers to the main library to get microfilmed. Never got anything back, not the newspapers nor the microfilm. They're probably stored in a basement somewhere. You want to do some investigating for me? Track them down?"

"Maybe later this winter." Saldano smiles, tips his hat, and backs out of the library before the Señora can pin him down on the particulars.

With no available records, all Paul's got to work with is a "potential" crime scene. *I'll take one more crack at the Wall in case the coroner's team missed something.* He telephones Phillips of his intentions.

"Jesus, I thought y'all had enough of that the first time."

"Yeah, well, ya know, anything to break the boredom."

"Take a long rope and tie it to the bumper of that Explorer. I'll check on you around noon to make sure you're not hangin' by your privates." Phillips chuckles and rings off.

Saldano is at the top of the China Wall and over its side before the first morning tour bus grinds its way uphill to the airport. He's done rappelling before and has the right kind of harness. But there's no crew or cable truck to pull him up the near-vertical slope. After a gradual descent, Saldano begins to haul on the rope, climbing a yard at a time. He thinks about his last New Year's resolution to diet and get more exercise. His arms go numb, and rest breaks become frequent and prolonged.

At a hundred feet below the road, he's blowing hard. A congregation of black ravens has crowded onto the Explorer's roof, watches him advance, and discusses his progress. He reaches for the base of a red-berried toyon to pull himself up. A fragment of pewter-colored metal rests next to his hand. It looks like a thin rectangular slice of stone but with a small hole drilled into one end. Working with his left hand, Saldano seizes the fragment and drops it into his shirt pocket.

Phillips greets him when he finally hauls himself over the

edge and staggers to the truck. "Just couldn't get enough. Was it worth it?" he asks.

"Well…I found this." The Sergeant hands him the metal fragment. "Who knows what else the coroner's crew missed - but I'm not gonna try finding out." He sighs, arches his back, and tries to relieve the ice-pick-like pain that stabs him between the shoulder blades.

"This thing looks a lot like a military dog tag," Phillips drawls and hands it back.

Saldano nods. "Yeah, that's what I thought too. Looks like it's been down there a long time." Saldano turns the piece over in his hand.

"Too bad it's corroded to hell," Phillips says.

"Ah, give me a chance. I am a skilled investigator," Saldano quips.

Phillips waves him off and drives away.

Saldano sits in the Explorer, adds a few new paragraphs to his electronic file notes, and then motors back to town to walk his mid-morning rounds. It's afternoon before he has a chance to telephone the Sheriff's Technical Services Division.

"Tech services, Roberts."

"This is Sergeant Paul Saldano at the Avalon Station. I'm working on a homicide case and need your help."

The line stays silent. Saldano forges ahead. "I've found an old military dog tag that's badly corroded. I'd like you to clean it up and tell me who it belongs to."

The male voice finally responds. "Have you contacted the military?"

"No, not yet. I figure they can't help me unless I know whose tag it is."

A long sigh comes over the phone. "Fill out an Investigation Request slip and mail it and the dog tag to our Physical Evidence Section. You should have results in a few weeks."

"I'd really appreciate it if you could do it sooner – it's only a small item." Saldano keeps his voice smooth and encouraging.

"Listen, Sergeant, everybody wants stuff by yesterday. Next year, pay attention to something other than your uniform allowance when budget time rolls around. We've got only three lab techs working the entire county, and I've got requests coming out my—"

"Jeez, sorry I asked, buddy." Saldano hangs up.

On his way back to the office after rounds, he stops at the corner drug store to see Leo, the pharmacist. "This medication should bring that blood pressure down," Leo tells a stout gray-haired woman in a pink muumuu. "But you need to stop smoking."

"I know, I know," she murmurs in a sultry voice. "But thanks, Leo, you always know best." The woman turns to leave, smiling at Saldano as she passes.

"Have a good one, Lucille," Leo calls after her. Saldano fights to keep his jaw from dropping. He remembers where he's heard that sexy voice before and how her reality collides with his love-starved fantasy…but he recovers quickly.

"So what do you think might clean this thing up?" Saldano gives the dog tag to Leo. The pharmacist tilts his bald head back to stare through Coke bottle glasses.

"Haven't seen one of these in years. Where'd ya find it?"

"Up on the side of the China Wall under some brush."

"Was this all ya found? Was there a metal necklace with it?"

"No, just that."

Leo removes his glasses and slumps onto the stool behind the tiny counter. He massages his bum knee, then tugs at the tight neckline of his high-buttoned smock.

"My first job in the Army was making dog tags for new recruits at Fort Ord."

"I thought you went to pharmacy school?"

"That was afterwards on the GI bill. For nearly two years, I sat behind a big typewriter-like machine and stamped these things out. My eyesight was too bad to get a combat assignment, so they stuck me at Headquarters doing clerical jobs."

"So, what do you know about dog tags?"

"Well, before World War II began, they were made of nickel and copper mixed with manganese. But they changed 'em to steel 'cause copper and nickel were scarce. And it wasn't until near the end that they used those metal beaded necklaces. I bet this tag was made in the early '40s."

"Jeez, I didn't know they'd ever changed. My own set from Desert Storm was like my Dad's from Nam." He retrieves the dog tag from Leo and turns it over in his hand.

"To answer your question, Paul, I wouldn't use any harsh cleansers on it. You could destroy what's left of the metal." Leo bends painfully to snatch a plastic bottle from a bottom shelf. "Soak it overnight in a one-in-five solution of this. If that doesn't work, your lab boys will have to figure it out."

"What is this stuff?"

"Acetic Acid, like what's found in vinegar. Just don't soak it too long. Your dog tag could turn pink or green."

"Thanks, Leo – I owe you."

That night, before turning over the station to the third watch, Saldano places the dog tag in an orphaned coffee cup, pours in a twenty-percent solution, and leaves it to soak. The next morning, he finds that the corrosion has partially dissolved but still clogs the indentations. On his mid-morning rounds he retrieves a soft toothbrush from his garage apartment and spends his lunch break gently scrubbing at the tag under lukewarm tap water. Finally, the corrosion melts away, and the metal reveals its fragment of history:

Stanley H DeVaul Jr
39632592 T42 43 B+
Stanley H De

CHAPTER 6

He awoke. He walked. He slept. He awoke again. Sometime in between, he ate, read, and drank. Maybe today would be different. Maybe not. But it wasn't just this place. It was his whole situation, and he had to wait it out.

Not that Stanley DeVaul's life before the war was any less banal. His friends liked predictable Stan, with slick blond hair and no rough edges. But then, who were his friends anyway? Well-heeled college cads, the stuffed shirts on the debate team, or his clinging cousin Betty? Their tryst in the family's tractor shed proved him pathetic, although Betty's response to his lovemaking showed that he could at least do a creditable job in that department.

Uniformed men now filled Stan's world. He was billeted on the top floor of the Saint Catherine Hotel with nine other Army privates. All of them had been drafted from the Los Angeles area, had finished basic training at Camp Ord, then shipped directly to Catalina Island. No one gave them a reason for their assignment nor issued work duties. But Stan had learned one thing about the Army: it's better not to ask questions because some fool will feel obliged to come up with answers, often undesirable ones.

For two years, they waited, drew monthly stipends from the quartermaster, roamed the streets of Avalon and Catalina's back canyons, and drank themselves silly. They read newspapers, wrote letters home, and hoped that the war would fizzle before someone discovered their lost platoon.

In the fall of 1943, the residents of Saint Catherine got a break from their tedium. Warner Brothers filmed a movie about the battle of Guadalcanal on Catalina and hired on-island extras. Stan's entire platoon signed on, and so did a lot of seamen from the Atwater Hotel, along with local townspeople. Mexicans played the parts of Japanese soldiers.

Stan used the money he earned as an extra to take evening meals in Avalon. Most nights, he walked along Bachelor's Cove with the island palms thrashing in the winter wind and ate supper at one of three restaurants. He drank a bottle of red wine, often more, and stared across the dark channel to where the twinkling lights of San Pedro should have been.

But coastal cities were under *brownout* conditions with smaller communities under strict *blackout* orders. The Busy Bee Café, John's Diner, and the Seafood Grotto used heavy curtains to block off their kitchen areas; dining rooms stayed dark with only shielded candles on the tables and windows looking out onto a black ocean.

Stan ate alone. Afterwards, he'd return to the barracks staggering drunk, ready to write the long-overdue letter to his parents. Over the past year, he'd mentally composed this particular communiqué. With time, its detailed paragraphs compressed into a string of disjointed phrases that he recited to himself, like a good Catholic recites the litany of the Saints:

"I'm not cut out for business…father forgive me…but that's George's life, not mine…father forgive me…it was my idea, not hers…father forgive me…you can't protect me forever…father forgive me…I'll see you when it's over…father forgive me."

On a Saturday evening in February, Stan felt like eating fish. He took the longer walk eastward past Avalon and around the point to the Seafood Grotto Restaurant. From his darkened second floor table, he could just make out the albacore boats nudging their way into the harbor, trailed by seagulls and pelicans fighting for scraps the fishermen cast into the channel. Stan longed for his paints, wishing to capture the beauty of the winter seas at sunset. But then he'd have to write his parents and ask them for supplies - way too high a price.

As he sat stoop-shouldered and stared across the darkening cove, the waitress delivered his dinner and a second bottle of wine.

"You sure you're okay, Señor?" she asked.

"Whatdayah mean - do I look sick?" He slurred his words. The pretty Mexican looked startled.

"Please excuse my intrusion. But you have been staring at the sea ever since you came in."

"It must be this good wine, makes me want to paint these beautiful things." He broadly gestured with his glass. The waitress either missed or ignored his sarcasm.

"Ah, you are an artist." Her eyes grew wider, and Stan noticed how large they were. "*Mi padre* was one of several who painted clay tiles before the factory closed." She smiled easily, then disappeared behind the curtains. Stan turned to his dinner and swept the plate clean of swordfish and sliced fried potatoes.

The waitress returned to clear his service.

"So, what type of things did your father paint?" Stan asked.

"Mostly *pajaros*, birds, sea birds, but also the black ravens and parrots. You can see his designs on buildings around town."

"I'll have to pay more attention." An awkward few seconds passed while the waitress rummaged for his bill. He reached unsteadily for his wallet and almost knocked over the wine bottle. Stumbling from the restaurant, he leaned against the shoreline rail and sucked in cold sea air. His head cleared somewhat, and he practiced taking straight, measured steps all the way back to his room.

During the following week, Stan made the rounds of Avalon's streets and alleys and found glazed tiles everywhere: on the walls of the Casino, the plaza fountain, the cornerstones of restaurants, the houses of the rich, churches, hotels, and small mural insets in out-of-the-way alcoves. They used primary colors and bold forms to give the plainest building a touch of color and a distinctive Mexican flare. When he returned to the Grotto for early dinner, Stan showed the smiling waitress his sketches of the tiles.

"You draw very well," she said and stared at the linen sheets held loosely in a leather-bound portfolio. "You should show these to my father. He would be impressed with your detail."

Stanley gazed out the restaurant's darkening windows at waves crashing against the sea wall. "Actually, what…what I want to paint is…is your portrait, but I don't have my paints. Do you think it would be all right if I draw you sometime?" Stan felt surprised at his own boldness but glad that he could ask without stumbling too badly.

The waitress took a step back and glanced toward the kitchen, the smile frozen on her face.

After a moment, she answered. "I…I don't know. I must ask my father." She dipped her head. "But it's probably all right, especially if he is there to chaperone."

Stan didn't quite know what to make of her answer. He'd drawn figures all his life, even nudes in college art classes. *Most people feel flattered to be asked*. "Well, I can show him these sketches at the same time."

The waitress relaxed, blinked rapidly, and nodded. "If my father approves, we could meet next Sunday afternoon at my family's house in Pebbly Beach. Do you know where that is?"

He laughed. "After all the wine, you'd better draw me a map. I'm Stanley." He offered a hand.

"Me llama Flavia." She lightly touched her warm brown fingers to his palm.

Stan left the restaurant with directions to her home sketched on the back of a paper placemat. He worried about whether he could successfully draw this girl and capture her strong yet comfortable grace. He'd have to practice sketching people before their date, think about an attractive composition. But her father would be there, an accomplished artist, a chaperone. Stanley grinned to himself. *At least I'll have a good excuse for staring at her. If I can just….*

CHAPTER 7

Sergeant Saldano hates phone trees. He's been climbing one most of the morning and finds himself caught in a do-loop between individuals who don't answer and have rerouted their calls to someone who also isn't available, whereby his call is routed back to the base of the tree, and he starts all over again. Finally, there's a click, a slight buzz, and a woman's voice:

"Fourth Army Records Division, Specialist Spencer."

The phone call sounds like it's coming over chicken wire from Singapore rather than from San Francisco. Her voice sounds intelligent but flat.

"My name is Sergeant Paul Saldano, Badge Number 471, with the Los Angeles County Sheriff's Department at the Avalon Station on Santa Catalina Island. I need information about a serviceman named Stanley H. DeVaul Jr." He gets it out in a single rush of words.

"Is this person on active duty, or have they been discharged?"

"I'm sure he's been discharged."

"I'm sorry, Sergeant, but you will need to request that information from the National Personnel Records Center in St. Louis, Missouri. Let me give you their e-mail address. They will send you an SF 180 to complete along with a signature verification form and will respond within ninety days."

Saldano sighs. *Everything's slowing me down, and nobody gives a rat's ass about this case. When Frank gets back tomorrow, it could go even slower.* "Listen, I'm investigating a homicide that might involve Serviceman DeVaul. Is there any way that *you* can help me that takes less than three months?"

"Do you have DeVaul's service number?" Spencer's voice softens.

"Yes, I've found a piece of his dog tag. The number is 39632592." Saldano hears computer keys click, then a long pause.

"Sergeant, from the number you gave me, I can tell you that DeVaul was inducted into the Army during the early part of World War II and stationed in the Ninth Corps Area on the West Coast. But there's something very strange about his record. I can't access his 201 Personnel File, and the few ancient Morning Report entries in the system don't make much sense. Can I call you back?"

"Yes…and I really appreciate any help you can give me," Saldano says in the warmest voice he can muster. "If you could phone me tomorrow afternoon, that would be great." He rattles off his number.

"Will do," she replies crisply and hangs up.

Saldano remembers the female soldiers he had run into when serving with the Military Police during Desert Storm. Some were cute, but when performing their jobs, they were as hard-boiled as anybody in uniform. He imagines Spencer as a skinny white girl in a tight green skirt, flat khaki shirt, and no chin, who stares at her computer screen, answers phones, and does data entry day after day.

The next morning, Station Commander Frank McCloskey arrives on the ten o'clock jet boat from Long Beach. Saldano picks him up at the ferry landing in the Department's golf cart. They never call it a "patrol car," though it's conspicuously labeled "Sheriff's Patrol." He stops at Frank's house on Eucalyptus Avenue and waits while the Commander changes into his uniform, then accompanies him back to the station. The whole time, Frank pumps Saldano for information about what's been going on during his two-week absence.

"So where've you gotten with the two skeletons? Have you got the coroner's report? Checked missing persons? Checked with the Military?" Frank rattles off his questions, and Saldano tells him what little he knows but not what he thinks.

"Sounds like a bad accident to me," Frank says and sighs. "If they've been dead that long, they're probably Mexicans. In the old days most of those families wouldn't report anything. You'll probably never find out who they are."

"Yes, but what about the dog tag? DeVaul doesn't sound like a Mexican name to me."

"So far, you've got zip-a-dee-doo-dah tying the dog tag to the remains. This place was crawlin' with the military during the war…the Signal Corps, OSS, Coast Guard, Merchant Marine. That tag coulda been anybody's."

"No, not really," Saldano counters. "The serial number and its shape are for an Army guy. The other services had different shaped tags. And there weren't many Army personnel on the island. I checked it out on the Internet."

Frank scowls, showing his distrust for anything associated with computers. "Yeah, so what. You didn't find the dog tag near your skeletons, did you?"

"No, you're right about that. It was at least a couple hundred feet away."

Saldano escapes the office for his rounds and leaves Frank to his mid-morning coffee break at the Metropole Café where he chats it up with the locals – "good PR," Frank calls it. Saldano walks the streets. In his mind, he pieces together scenarios, possible leads, and avenues of inquiry. After lunch, he struggles to stay awake in the Indian Summer heat and waits for the call. The telephone's buzz snaps him alert.

"Sheriff's Department, Avalon Station, Sergeant Saldano speaking."

"Sergeant, this is Specialist Spencer, I have information for you." Her nasal voice is lower by half an octave, but it's still all business.

"Thanks again for your help. Go ahead." Saldano grabs his iPad.

"Here's what I have: Stanley H. DeVaul Jr. was inducted into the Army on 17 September, 1942. He graduated basic training from the East Garrison at Camp Ord and transferred to the First Quartermasters Company on Santa Catalina Island."

"Wait a minute. Didn't the Army have advanced training after Basic back then?"

"Yes, they did, but it gets even stranger. As far as I can tell, there were no Army advance-training units on Catalina during World War II, only garrison troops that supported the Signal Corps and Coast Guard. Private DeVaul appears to have been stationed in Avalon for over two years, until 6 December, 1944. At that time, he was transferred to the 1st Army, 106th Infantry Division stationed in the Ardennes."

"Yikes, from sunny California to waist-high snow country. That musta been a shock."

"I can only imagine. But he wasn't there long…reported missing in action near Saint Vith on 4 January, 1945."

"Wasn't that a few weeks before the war in Europe ended? Why the heck would the Army wait so long to ship this guy out?"

Specialist Spencer sighs. "I wish I could tell you more – but we have a major problem with DeVaul's records. In '74, a fire at the records annex destroyed his 201 file, medical records, and any written orders. And that was years before the DOD microfilmed everything."

"Jeez, that figures. Do you at least have a next of kin address?"

"Did you check the bottom of the dog tag that you have? It should be there."

"I only have a piece of the tag. After the serial number is a bunch of codes, then part of what is probably his father's name. Everything else is gone."

"What's left of our records doesn't show an address. But DeVaul is not a common name. I could search the Selective Service records - but it will take time, and I'm not sure my CO will authorize it."

"One last question, Specialist. Wasn't there an OSS Unit on Catalina? My Commander mentioned something about a detachment."

There's a pause at the other end of the line before she answers. "Yes, I checked that out also. All of those men ended up behind the lines in Burma or China, a long way from the Ardennes."

Saldano stayed quiet for a moment. "Jesus, another dead end. I guess I can check out our own database. But I really appreciate any further help you can provide."

"Excuse me for asking, Sergeant, but...ah, how might DeVaul have been mixed up in a homicide?" Her voice tells him that she's struggling to keep her curiosity in check. But he needs her help and tells her everything.

"That *is* odd," Spencer says after hearing his story. "Obviously, something doesn't add up if DeVaul was killed in Belgium, yet you have his dog tag and a nearby skeleton on Catalina. But...those remains could be anybody's."

Spencer's voice relaxes, and Saldano hears strange inflections in her pronunciation of certain words that he hadn't picked up before, a mixture of British and something foreign.

"My Station Commander says the same thing," he tells her. "But listen, I have a coroner's report coming any day now. If I could get some kind of description of DeVaul from you, a photo would be great. I could at least compare it with the Coroner's findings to see if there are any similarities - you know, build, height, that sort of thing."

"I have some ideas. Let me search for a few days, then give me a call." She gives him her direct telephone extension and rings off.

Frank returns from his mid-afternoon coffee and slumps into a chair at Saldano's desk. He talks about his reunion with dozens of his East Coast cousins, aunts and uncles.

"I haven't seen most of those fools since flying out here from Jersey in '80. They all thought I was effing crazy, comin' to California after Vietnam. They never thought I'd leave the neighborhood, shake loose from my dago friends, much less join the police force. But then Nam uprooted lots of folks."

Saldano smiles and remembers his own transplantation from Cuero, Texas, after Desert Storm. He'd freaked out his parents by leaving the family's grocery business for UCLA and the wasteland of Los Angeles, where they said he'd become one more stupid Latino in a sea of millions.

"So, Frank, who on Catalina knows the old Mexican families? Maybe I can talk to someone who remembers the war years and anybody who turned up missing."

"I'm not sure; don' know anybody personally, and they don' feel much like talkin' to me. If you want to turn over a few stones, I'd start with Conrad Gomez. He waits tables at the El Galleon and honchos at the La Mesa Club. That's an all wetback… ah, I mean Latino club that's been around since the '30s."

On his afternoon rounds, Saldano stops at the El Galleon. At a copper-topped corner table, the head waiter folds napkins and sucks on something dark in a tall glass. With arms akimbo, the Sergeant stands before Gomez who peers up at him with coal-black eyes, not offering anything. Finally, Saldano sits, pushes his chair back, and stares at the restaurant's walls. They're covered with enlarged *colorized* postcards from the 1930s that show throngs of visitors just off the steamer from Wilmington being welcomed by the townspeople. Gomez provides no such welcome and continues his silent folding.

Paul clears his throat. "I'm Sergeant Saldano with the—"

"I know who you are, Pablo," Gomez murmurs. "You're the new mainlander who's on the wagon."

"Good. That's good," Saldano says smoothly. "But I'm not here to confess my drinking history. I've been told you know the most about Latino families on the island. Tell me about Avalon during World War II."

Gomez's expression changes by degrees. "I was only *cinco años* when the War ended. Don't know much." He shrugs, a quiver of a smile curls his lips.

"Anything would be helpful."

"My father lived here since the '20s and was a *patron* of the Tremont Street barrio. He told lots of stories."

"Did he ever talk about people who went missing?"

Gomez's eyes narrow. "Back then, people went missing a lot. They'd hop a boat to Wilmington or maybe go back to Mexico. The men got drafted, and their families were never told where the hell they went. *Mi padre* tried to find things out for them."

"I'm trying to find out about a missing young woman who disappeared sometime around 1945. Do you know anything… anybody that might help me?"

Gomez stops his folding for a moment, then shakes his head. "Like I said, a lot of people disappeared…and the families didn't talk about missing girls 'cause some of 'em ended up in downtown hotels and—"

"A red light district? Here in Avalon?"

"*Si, si*. But there might be a few old timers that can tell you more." Gomez rubs his bearded chin and stares into space. "I can't think of any right now. Why don't you come to the La Mesa Club meeting next Tuesday and I'll see if I can connect you with the right people. And Sergeant, if ya want anybody to talk, lose the uniform and gun belt."

CHAPTER 8

After attending early mass, Flavia spent hours washing and combing out her coffee-brown mane and selecting her best clothes and jewelry to wear. She tucked stray hairs behind her ears and stared into the mirror. On her smooth tan cheeks, she applied makeup delicately, painted her lips the color of pomegranates. She emerged from the bedroom and lowered herself carefully into a wicker chair on the veranda.

He will be here any moment. I must look perfect…but why? She knew he was one of many who'd leave Catalina with just a glimpse of her stored behind their eyes. *"I met this señorita who was muy simpatico," they'll remember. But Señor Stanley…maybe he will take more than a glimpse. Maybe I will let him.*

She'd skipped the mid-day meal for fear of spilling food on her good clothes. *I hope Papa's not upset…it's been so long since he's had someone to talk with about art…I hope they can become friends.*

Flavia's father, Eduardo, recoiled from Stanley's request to draw his daughter. He'd listened to the gringos' coarse language when they talked about Mexican women. He'd warned Flavia when she began work at the Grotto, "You watch out for those scoundrels. They want their pleasures and will care little for you."

But she had proved herself capable of dealing with men. Most nights, Flavia told her parents stories about how she deftly sidestepped the advances of drunken mariners with a quick laugh and a smile…that kept the tips rolling in and her customers coming back for more gentle rejection. *But to invite one of them into our home?* Eduardo worried, *and an artist no less!* Yet he had agreed to Stanley's request.

As a young man near La Paz, Eduardo had sketched the señoritas at the surf's edge with their skirts rolled up. They bent to pull in the nets and grab the wriggling fish from the wet sand. Dolores had been one of them. She'd laughed when Eduardo had shown her his first attempt at capturing her ample figure in charcoal. "That's not me…that's only in your head," she'd kidded him. By summer's end, his drawing had improved…and they were married.

From the Quonset hut's front window, Eduardo stared at a tall young man moving up the street toward their house. *Stanley, such a gringo name. I must watch him…. I know what they think.*

Stanley met Eduardo and Flavia on the porch. He opened a black portfolio. It held large sheets of blank linen paper, a box of charcoal sticks, earth-toned *Conté* pencils, and sketches of Avalon's decorative tiles.

"I've brought you these to look at," Stanley said and handed the drawings to Eduardo, who sat and examined them, grunting occasionally.

"Yes, I like this one…the seaplane, one of my favorites. You have drawn it well, strong lines, good detail."

"It is your designs and sense of composition that are strong," Stan replied. "I'm sorry the factory closed. Some day, those tiles will be collector's items."

"Many artists worked there. I was only one. But I enjoyed it."

"Do you still draw or paint?" Stan asked.

Eduardo scowled. "No one buys art now…and I have no money for supplies. Maybe after the war."

"I've never sold any of my paintings," Stan said, chuckling, "but my mother likes my work."

Dolores arrived with a pitcher of lemonade and a tray of glasses. Flavia took a seat, arranged her many-layered skirts and petticoats, and prepared for the pose. Her parents disappeared into the house. After a few minutes, Eduardo peeked through the window. Dolores pulled him away. "Leave them alone. You can see the boy struggles. Flavia is not your daughter now. She is his subject."

Eduardo muttered, "Yes, but I know boys better than you…and these gringo soldiers can't be trusted."

He stayed clear of the window and waited an hour before venturing onto the veranda. Stanley scowled at his latest attempt, hands filthy with charcoal. Balled-up paper sheets littered the porch.

"There's just too much," Stan burst out. "With all those ruffles and jewelry, I can't see her face." He pointed at Flavia and then at the tangle of lines on the cream-colored paper.

Eduardo stared at his daughter, then back at Stanley's half-completed drawing, and nodded. *She's dressed like an expensive doll, and her grace is lost.* He bent to Flavia and whispered in her ear.

She stood. "But I spend all morning—"

"Just go," Eduardo said, and she left the men to their lemonade and the afternoon wind.

Stan crumpled his last drawing and heaved it off the porch. "I'm sorry, I must be out of practice."

"You can't see everything the first time. Be patient. It will be better when she returns."

They reclined in their chairs. The hum from the nearby power plant's turbines got louder as the afternoon advanced; the silence between them grew awkward. Finally, Flavia pushed through the screen door and took her seat. She wore a simple white blouse and skirt that only partially covered her strong tan legs. All her makeup and jewelry had disappeared. She slumped onto the chair, pouting.

"Don't be mad," Eduardo told her. "You don't need fine

clothes to make you beautiful."

Flavia glared at him.

But the scowl on Stanley's face disappeared. Grabbing up a pencil, he instructed her to move an arm just so, to pull her chin up and look at him. He reached forward to arrange her hair gently. Eduardo retreated inside. The only sound from the veranda was the scratch of pencil and charcoal on paper and the wind rattling the screen door. Two hours passed. The light turned golden, then gray. Foghorns blew their low-pitched evening serenade. Eduardo ventured outside. He found Flavia asleep in the chair, her head resting on an arm, long, straight strands of hair cascading down the front of her blouse. Stanley continued drawing, a half-dozen completed sketches scattered face-up across the porch.

Stan paused long enough to motion for Eduardo to sit. "Look at these finished ones and tell me what you think."

Dolores watched through the screen. When Flavia started to snore, she pushed outside, letting the door slam behind her. Flavia bolted upright, embarrassed. She excused herself and hurried away. Her parents sat on the bench and discussed the sketches in animated Spanish.

"You may have that one," Stanley said. He motioned to the drawing that Dolores and Eduardo held, a horizontal view of Flavia sleeping. Stan's use of varying shades of brown and red Conté pencil that he'd rubbed with his fingertips into soft gradated tones had caught her likeness perfectly, too perfectly. Dolores glanced at her husband and winked. Eduardo frowned and turned away so that Stan wouldn't see.

They invited him to stay for an early supper of *arroz con pollo,* rice with chicken.

"Tell us about your family, Senor DeVaul," Eduardo said and poured red wine into goblets.

"They live near Los Angeles, work in banking."

"Do you have, ah, brothers and sisters?"

"An older brother."

"You are a military man, *si*?"

"Yes."

"Are you a seaman?"

"No."

Stan ducked his head and shoveled a huge forkful of rice into his mouth.

This gringo hides much. Maybe he thinks I don't understand English. "How long have you been on the island?"

"It feels like forever."

He's probably part of that OSS unit the whole barrio is talking about. Those men are trained to stay silent…and to lie.

"Flavia tells me that you are an excellent marksman and guide," Stan said.

"Yes, I took hunting parties into the back canyons. It paid well. When the War ends…and the military leaves, I will do it again."

"Do you still go shooting?"

Eduardo frowned. "No. Dolores doesn't want me to waste money on bullets…and she's afraid the Shore Patrol will arrest me."

Dolores smiled at Eduardo and rose. Flavia helped her mother clear the table while the two men sipped their Cabernet and gazed through broad windows at the wind-whipped channel. In a few minutes, the girl rejoined them. She wore a shawl and carried a small purse.

"I'm sorry, I have to work the dinner shift at the restaurant."

"With your father's permission, I can walk you there," Stanley said, looking at Eduardo, who nodded curtly.

Stan gathered his artist's equipment. Without speaking, the two walked down the darkening road lined with Quonset huts and attached bungalows built from scrap. Mongrel dogs serenaded them with a chorus of howls and barks. They passed out of the eucalyptus-shaded canyon and joined the path bordering the sea. The wind tore at their clothes. The pounding surf made speaking impossible until they stopped near the bottom of the stairway leading to the Grotto restaurant.

Stan clutched his portfolio with both hands, shivering. "Thank…thank you so much for posing, Flavia. You are beautiful…to draw."

"It was my…my pleasure." She glanced toward the restaurant, then leaned upward and kissed his lips.

Stan retreated a step. "I'm the one who's supposed to do that," he said, blushing.

Flavia giggled and hurried off.

"Can I sketch you again? At the restaurant?" he called after her.

She waved, not looking back, took the stairs two at a time, and disappeared through the carved wooden door.

Stanley set out for his barracks at the Saint Catherine. He broke into a run, rounded Casino Point, and raced down the palm-lined promenade to the hotel, his leather shoes slapping against the pavement. On the dark fourth floor, only a sliver of light from under PFC Brigg's door faintly illuminated the checkerboard linoleum. Stanley passed quickly down the hall to the end room. Inside, he dumped his portfolio on the bed and slumped into a chair at the desk. His rapid breathing filled the space with animal sound. He stared out the window at the frothy row of combers rolling into Descanso Bay and tried to sort out the onrush of thoughts and feelings.

When his breathing slowed, he pulled the blackout curtains across the window. Clicking on the desk lamp, he reached into a drawer and brought out an unopened box of writing paper, a gold fountain pen, and an ink bottle. His hands trembled as he filled the pen and leaned forward to stare at the blank sheet of pastel paper. The litany of his long-rehearsed letter came to him, but he wrote nothing. Finally, he began:

> *23 August 1944*
>
> *Dearest Mother and Father:*
>
> *I have been on Catalina Island for almost two years and have just found something worth painting. Please send an easel, paints, brushes, and canvas as soon as you can. I will explain later.*
>
> *Your Son,*
> *Stanley*

He folded the sheet in thirds, the ink barely dry, and slipped it into an envelope with airmail-colored borders. He scribbled his parents' address on the front, then strained to remember his seldom-used military return address. In stocking feet, Stan slipped from his room and deposited the letter in the mail drop at the end of the hall, anxious to get rid of it before something changed, not realizing that it already had.

CHAPTER 9

A foggy wind blew through Jose Guiermo's hair as he steered the heavy Schwinn bicycle around the driveway's steep turns. He loved the morning rides to the mailbox three miles down the canyon. But the return uphill trips to the mountaintop estate left him weak in the knees. Parts of the road were so steep that automobile tires slipped on its macadam surface.

Jose had worked for the family ever since emigrating with his parents from Mazatlan in 1924. The DeVauls had moved into their newly constructed home in Malibu Canyon and needed laborers to plant and tend orchards and gardens. His father spent fifteen years hacking the rough clay soil and transforming the estate into an unnaturally green oasis in the brown Santa Monica Mountains. When he died, Jose took his place.

As the estate's chief caretaker, he managed an outdoor crew of six Mexicans. But only he was entrusted with certain chores, such as retrieving the mail. Jose learned a lot from the letters and packages the DeVauls received: what organizations they belonged to, the businesses and agencies they associated with, the locations of friends and family, and how well they got along, measured by the frequency of the letters. But it surprised him to find the lone small envelope from Stanley Junior among the legal-looking documents in brown envelopes. *I wonder what he wants? Maybe that woman is causing trouble again.*

Stanley Jr. had always been the odd one, painting huge oils of the gardens and the rolling hillsides overlooking the Pacific. Jose would catch him exploring the creases of the canyon estate while the old man and George, Stan's older and much stubbier brother, holed up in the study and pored over paperwork into the wee hours of the morning. Neither of those men looked happy either.

For a while, Jose thought Stanley Junior was queer. Then he'd discovered Stan and that woman in the tractor shed, naked and making love like wild horses. Jose's opinion of the gangly youth improved, but then Stan disappeared back to college in San Francisco, then into the Army, and the family never talked about him, at least not within earshot of the outdoor crew.

Jose tossed the mail into the front basket and walked the bicycle most of the way up the mountain, contemplating his age and how his legs took an hour to stop trembling if he tried to ride the entire distance. Once on top, he mounted the balloon-tired beast and coasted along the cypress-lined road and around the circular driveway to the hacienda's front door. He yanked the doorbell chain from inside the Spanish-tiled portico. The sound of Juanita's leather sandals advanced along the interior hallway. She opened the door wide enough to extend a smooth brown arm to take in the mail, then shut it immediately without any recognition for Jose. It had been that way between them for five years.

Juanita turned and walked to the cathedral-ceilinged study, where she quietly deposited the mail on a silver tray next to DeVaul Sr. and waited for further instructions. He sat at a table in the far corner with papers spread before him. A thin twist of blue smoke from his pipe curled up past silver-framed glasses that blended with oiled and neatly combed hair. The old man still wore a morning robe and slippers, having announced that he wouldn't be going to the office. A service of coffee and Mexican sweet rolls dusted with cinnamon sat half finished on the table. DeVaul Sr. sorted the mail quickly but paused over the lone personal letter. Inserting a gold opener, he slashed the envelope with a quick flick of his wrist, extracted a pale sheet, and scanned its contents.

"Juanita, could…could you ask Constance, ah Señora DeVaul, to join me for a moment."

"Si señor." She hustled out of the room and climbed the stairs. *La señora doesn't usually rise before eleven,* Juanita thought. *She will be mad as hell when I wake her.* But the señora surprised her at the bedroom door, clad in a violet housedress. Grumpily, Mrs. DeVaul lowered herself down the stairs, always leading with the good leg, and accompanied her to the study. Juanita left them.

Without prelude, Stanley Sr. shoved the letter at his wife. "What do you make of this?"

Constance studied the page, then clutched it to her breast. "I'm not sure…it's been so long…and he said he despised his paintings before he left for the Army."

"I know. I know. We don't hear from that ingrate all this while, and now all he wants is his art crap. Something's changed." DeVaul Sr. drew deep on his pipe and exhaled a cloud of sweet *Imperial* smoke.

"Maybe so. But at least he wrote," Constance replied. She scanned the room surreptitiously, searching for the thick cut-glass bottle filled with amber liquid that had been there the night before. But it had been removed.

"I'll have Juanita gather up his supplies and tell Jose to send them parcel post in the morning," she said.

Constance escaped into the hallway before her husband could repeat his long-standing complaints about Junior's aversion to the business world and his simplicity of heart. Neither trait was tolerated in the DeVaul household…but Constance's drowning them in fine cognac was. She hobbled into the gunroom, filled a snifter half full with Hennessy from one of many bottles clustered on the sideboard, then called her servant.

"Juanita, bring one of the wooden crates in the shed over to Junior's studio. Have an outdoor man help you."

Juanita's eyes widened, but she disappeared without hesitation.

The art studio hadn't been opened for two years, and cobwebs blurred the corners of its windows. Constance keyed the padlock and pushed open the heavy wooden door. Floor-to-ceiling windows on two sides offered vistas of the Pacific and the surrounding ochre hillsides. The heat and stifling odors of turpentine and mold attacked her. Primed and stretched canvases leaned against easels that supported half-finished portraits, still lifes, and landscapes. Paint pots and palettes with caked-on remnants of mixed colors littered the floor. A model stand supported a huge vase of long-dead roses. And sketches, painting studies, and bits and pieces of things that Junior had found while roaming the coastal canyons leaned against the walls.

Juanita arrived with Reynaldo and a wooden crate. Constance ordered them away. She spent the morning digging through the studio's artifacts, carefully selecting her son's favorite brushes and palette knives, rolled canvas and stretchers, tubes of oils, and cans of turps, contemplating each selection in the streaming sunshine. She missed his gentle spirit, his awkward sincerity, and his refusal to kowtow to her husband's will. Without Junior, their lives resembled one of his half-finished paintings, waiting for the absent artist to complete them, with the outcome uncertain.

DeVaul Sr. abandoned his paperwork, so angered by his son's obvious self-centered snub that he couldn't concentrate on completing the complex loan forms spread before him. *The war will be over soon…just what the hell does Junior think he'll do to make a living… painting for women and will never pay…and besides, he's not that good,* ran and reran through the old man's brain until he could no longer sit quietly.

He dressed and escaped the house, taking a favorite path down through the hilltop orange groves to the edge of his property and a bench that overlooked the canyon below. He rested for over an hour and watched crows chase away the circling hawks, unable to purge Junior's letter from his brain. Giving up, he tramped upslope toward the estate. Its cream-white walls and red tile roof glowed softly in the sun. He walked between rows of orange trees. Jose hailed him from where he worked to prop up a limb weighted with golden globes. They talked about the upcoming pick, and Jose estimated what the orchard would yield. But the conversation faltered, and they stood in silence for a few moments.

Damn, I gotta find out what the hell's going on, DeVaul thought. "You have relatives on Santa Catalina Island, don't you?" he demanded.

Jose took a step back and hesitated before answering. "Si, in Avalon…mi Tia Rosalia and three cousins."

"I have a box of art supplies that I want delivered to Stanley Junior…and since you have relatives there, they'll let you on the boat. You can take a couple of days and visit with your people."

"But Señor DeVaul, I can ship those things without going there myself. And besides, I'll have to write and get permission from the authorities to visit her."

The old man sighed. "Yes, yes, I know all that. I'll write the damn letter for you. But while you're there, I want you to check on Junior, see how he's getting on, meet his friends, see what conditions are like…and come back and tell me everything, and I mean everything. *Comprende*?"

"*Si,* I'll leave a week from now on Saturday's boat. But I promised the Señora that we'd replant the flowerbed with azaleas, and that won't get done right if I'm gone."

"Just leave Constance to me. I'll tell her you're visiting

relatives in Ventura. I don't want her to know I'm checking up on Junior."

They talked more about the arrangements, where to buy the tickets for the great white steamer, and how to get to Wilmington in time for the sailing. Jose remembered visiting Avalon when he was twelve, a town crowded with gringo families on holiday. But he worried about how his Catalina relatives survived after the military had shut off the tourist trade and stopped all but mainland family members from visiting. Jose turned to resume his orchard work.

The old man extracted a twenty-dollar bill from his wallet and handed it to him. "That should get you there and back. Don't spend it all on the señoritas," he said, grinning.

Jose tried to smile back, his face stiffening with the effort. He'd never liked the old man and his isolation on the estate made it hard to get away from the *patron's* tactless control. But he liked the comfortable cottage where he and his aging mother lived and he earned more money than he could in Los Angeles working as a gardener. Jose had stayed on with the DeVauls even though his prospects of finding a wife diminished with each passing year and with the advancing angle of his stooped back. *A trip to Catalina will be wonderful. Such a voyage…. I can almost feel the channel swell roll under the steamer as she steers toward that mountain of an island.*

CHAPTER 10

Early Monday morning, Sergeant Saldano leaves his hillside apartment and wanders the back streets of Avalon. He listens to families getting ready for work and school, thinks about his own daughters in their mainland penthouse, and remembers what it's like to wake up next to someone warm. When he checks into the office shortly before eight, there's a thick brown envelope on his desk waiting for him. It's been opened and gone through by Frank, he's sure, and it's from the County Coroner's Office. Saldano leafs through the forms, pulls out the summary report and studies the terse paragraphs.

Subject #1: The postmortem examination of the remains concluded that Subject #1 was a male of approximately 1.9 meters in height, moderate build, of estimated mass of 91 kilograms, and between 16 and 24 years of age based on the incomplete fusion of the epiphysis at the sternal end of the clavicle. Estimated year of death is 1945.

Remains exhibit no evidence of disease. Cause of death cannot be positively established. However, given the fragmented nature of all but the large bones and the characteristics of the recovery site, trauma associated with a fall from a height in excess of 50 meters is a leading candidate for COD.

Subject #2: The postmortem examination of the remains concluded that Subject #2 was a female, likely Hispanic given the span of the ileum but inconclusive, of approximately 1.6 meters in height, moderate build, of estimated mass of 54 kilograms, and between 16 and 21 years of age based on the incomplete fusion of the epiphysis at the sternal end of the clavicle. Estimated year of death is 1945.

Cause of death judged to be trauma caused by gunshot wound. Remains exhibit a 1.30 centimeter hole in the sternum consistent with that created by ordnance from a weapon of 0.30 caliber or greater. (Ballistics Report, to be transmitted under separate cover, will provide more detailed information concerning possible ordnance used.)

Based on fragmentation studies of the breastplate and recovered vertebrae, the bullet appears to have entered subject from the rear, shattered the fourth thoracic vertebra, and exited through the breastplate. Given the precise definition of the exit hole and its path through Subject, estimate that ordnance was from high-powered rifle. Given the length of exposure of subject's skeletal remains, no conclusion can be drawn concerning the location or range from where ordnance may have been discharged. Due to the length of exposure and incomplete nature of the remains, no other conclusive findings can be made at this time.

Saldano lays the summary report aside and studies an aerial photograph that depicts the location of each bone fragment from the two subjects. They appear as two small constellations of white dots on the dusty green hillside. The female lies about 300 feet downslope from the ridge road. It must have been her remains that the bicyclist saw because a clear sandy patch marks the center of her constellation. The male's remains rested farther downslope, which makes sense to Saldano, given the man's greater mass.

"Well, at least ya got yourself a homicide." Frank sticks

his head in Saldano's office and grins. "But good luck solving that one. I was barely out of diapers when those two bought the farm."

Saldano nods and tries to erase the mental image of Frank as an infant needing changing. He continues to sort through the contents of the brown envelope. But it holds nothing more that's useful. If anything, the coroner's findings raise more questions about the identity of the dead man. The remains are located hundreds of feet below where Saldano found Stanley H. DeVaul's dog tag. *It might have come off during the fall, but I doubt it.* Back in Desert Storm, the Sergeant had an APC blown out from under him after it ran over a land mine, and while Saldano had gone flying, his tags stayed put around his neck.

But at least now the case is legit…and Frank has to let me go on a fishing expedition over town. Even seventy-five-year-old homicides aren't shelved without some investigation. Paul compiles a list of things to check on the mainland. He scrawls his ideas on his iPad and stares at the watch schedule. His phone rings.

"Sergeant, this is Specialist Spencer calling. How are you this morning?"

Her voice comes across as cool and slow. Saldano hears a definite accent that he can't quite place, sounding Eastern European but with way too much modulation. When Paul worked out of the Lost Hills Station, he and the other deputies used to bet that they could determine the race or ethnicity of the people who called in. It's a habit Paul has never shaken.

"Good to hear from you, Specialist, since *my* investigation seems to be going nowhere. What have you been able to find out?"

She hesitates before answering. "Since we've been calling each other often, why don't we dispense with the ranks. My name is Barbara, and yours is….?"

"My family back in Cuero calls me Pablo, as in Picasso. But

you can call me Paul." Saldano smiles as they exchange names. He has a hard time remembering the last phone conversation he had that didn't follow law enforcement protocol, except the occasional stilted exchanges with Julie and the girls on birthdays or holidays.

"Well, Paul, I've been able to query the old records of draft boards throughout Southern California and got a hit straight off. Stanley H. DeVaul Jr. got drafted into the Army at the Los Angeles County Induction Center."

"Yeah, I remember that place," Saldano says with a chuckle. "It's an old office building off Wilshire with colored lines painted on the floor that new recruits follow…listen to your heart here, drop your drawers and cough there, and raise your right hand and swear allegiance at the end of the line."

"Sounds familiar, except for the coughing part." Barbara laughs. "Stanley's draft records did include a home address. It's a huge estate in the Santa Monica Mountains, up Malibu Canyon."

"I know that area," Saldano says. "As a rookie, I used to patrol it with this old crusty Sergeant named…named…damn, I can't remember."

"Be careful. The memory is the second thing to go,"

"Yeah, and I guess I should watch who I call old and crusty. But those hilltop estates were surrounded by pole vault high fences. We never got inside unless somebody overdosed."

"Maybe that's what happened to the DeVauls because the property is no longer listed in their name…hasn't been for thirty years."

"Huh, yet another dead end."

Paul tells Barbara everything he's learned from the coroner's report, and they discuss various paths of inquiry.

"Barbara, thanks a lot for helping me. What did your CO say when you asked permission to do the work?"

"Are you kidding? I've been hacking the system from my

home computer and haven't told Major Selser anything. Besides, it's a lot more entertaining doing this than watching TV reality shows."

"I really could use a picture of Stanley as a full-grown adult. If his likeness matches the body height and weight that's described in the coroner's report, then it's worth pursuing. If not, then the dead guy could be anybody. Any ideas?"

"Maybe they took graduation pictures at Fort Ord like they did later on," Barbara says. "I'll check with our Records Unit and see if they have any Fourth Army files squirreled away somewhere. If they've been digitized, I can e-mail them to you. If not, I'll take a long lunch hour and tell the Major I'm taking my daughter to the doctor or some other excuse." She laughs.

"Thanks, Barbara, but don't get into trouble on my account. So, ah…you have a daughter?"

"Lisa's twelve."

"Tricky age."

There's a long pause before Barbara asks, "So what about the other skeleton you found on the hillside? Any clues?"

Saldano breathes easier now that they're back to business. "I can't tell you much except what's in the coroner's report. I've got feelers out here in Avalon, but being a newcomer, I doubt the locals will tell me much about a missing *señorita*."

"It was wartime, and our man Stanley might have been looking for love," Barbara says, her voice tinged with bitterness.

"Yeah, I know something about failed…"

Saldano notices Frank standing impatiently at the entrance to his office with last month's staffing reports in hand.

"I'm sorry, specialist, but I've got work I need to finish."

"Specialist? What happened to Barbara? Ah…is your boss listening?"

"Yes, yes. Thanks again for your help. We'll chat later this week. Thursday would be good."

He hangs up as Frank settles into the chair next to his desk. Saldano fantasizes momentarily about catching a flight up the coast to drop in on Barbara. But unannounced visits can be disastrous, especially if you only have a voice as a clue to what a person might look like. Paul remembers meeting Lucille, the telephone operator, at the drug store, which puts an abrupt end to his mainland fantasies. *And…Jesus…she's got a daughter? I wonder if there's a Mr. Spencer in the picture? Now, how the hell do I work that into a phone call?*

On Tuesday night after work, Saldano changes into his street clothes, crimps the cowboy hat that his parents sent him last Christmas, and heads downtown to the El Galleon Restaurant and the monthly meeting of the La Mesa Club. Conrad Gomez greets him at the door. He seems surprised that Saldano showed up. Paul follows him through the empty dining room to a banquet hall off the passageway to the lavatories. Two long tables are set in an "L" pattern. A crowd of aging Latino men chatter in Spanish, talking so fast that Paul can't catch much of their conversations. Saldano's the youngest person there and the only one wearing a cowboy hat.

The room quiets. Conrad introduces Saldano. The crowd mumbles their greetings and quietly resumes their conversations. Fortunately, there's a vacant seat next to Conrad at the table, and the Sergeant sits carefully, smiling at his neighbors who ignore him.

"I've told them you might come to the meeting," Conrad whispers in Paul's ear. "They didn't like it, but I said that you just wanted information about the war years. That old guy in the corner is Felipe Vargas, and he's been here longer than anybody. I'll introduce you after the meeting. If I know Felipe, the drinks will loosen him up."

As the night wears on, the La Mesa Club feels to Saldano

more and more like an Elks Lodge meeting, only everything's done in Spanish. There are special opening ceremonies, a prayer led by the Chaplin for family members in Mexico, a discussion of upcoming community events and how the Club will sponsor an entry in the New Year's Eve Dinghy Parade...if they can find enough volunteers that can stay sober long enough to maneuver a boat through the crowded harbor without ramming some rich gringo's yacht.

White-shirted waiters deliver platters crowded with plates of chicken and beans and huge bowls of green salad. The crowd attacks the food, guzzles red wine, and tosses off Tequila shooters. By the end of dinner, most members lean with both elbows on the table or swagger around the room, yelling boisterously to friends and foes alike.

"You'd better ask your questions soon before these *pendejos* pass out," Gomez says, laughing.

Paul stands up at his place and gives his water glass a rap with a butter knife. He's the only one drinking water. The room settles down, and thirty sets of eyes stare at him. Clearing his throat, he begins:

"My name is Pablo Saldano and I'm a sergeant with the County Sheriff's Department stationed here in Avalon." He speaks in his slow southwest Spanish, and the grins on the club members' faces get a bit wider.

"Thank you for letting me attend your meeting. I'm here to ask for your help, and Conrad tells me that if anyone on this island can help, it will be you. Three weeks ago, a skeleton was found on the side of the China Wall. I received the coroner's report yesterday. It said that the remains were of a woman, about five foot two inches tall and young, maybe 16 to 21 years old. They think her bones have been lying on that hillside since 1945. I would appreciate it if any of you who were here during World War II could talk with me. And even if you weren't here, I'm interested in getting any information about a woman or a young girl who might have gone missing the year the war ended. You don't have to talk with me now. I'm at the Sheriff's station most days, and you can call me at this number, or I can come see you."

Saldano takes a deep breath and shows the crowd his business card, and lays a stack on the table. The smiles and grins on the attendees' faces have momentarily frozen. Paul sits down awkwardly, and a low rumble of conversation returns.

Conrad Gomez leans in close and whispers. "You did good, Sergeant. Now, look around at the faces in the room and memorize them. When you're out walking your rounds, approach them *mano a mano*; you might get somebody to talk. But first, let me introduce you to Felipe."

They stand, Conrad unsteadily, and move to the end of the table where a stooped old man with sad eyes sits with his head resting in his hands.

"Felipe, I thought maybe you could help the good Sergeant here." Conrad speaks as if he's announcing it to the world. "You've been here longer than anybody and have been the *patron* of the Pebbly Beach barrio since before Korea."

Conrad disappears, leaving the Sergeant standing next to Felipe, who stares up at him, unspeaking. Paul notices that the old man's hands tremble and his eyes have milky brown lenses. He takes one of his business cards and extends it forward. Felipe doesn't see it. Saldano slips the card into the old man's shirt pocket. Felipe doesn't protest, nor does he say anything.

"Señor, please tell me where you live, and I'll come speak with you another time," Paul says softly. But the old man just blinks and continues sipping his Sangria.

"He's probably too drunk to hear you," the man sitting next to Felipe says. "Go to Pebbly Canyon, and someone will point out his house." The man turns away, discouraging any further queries.

"Gracias, gracias," Paul says into the air and moves toward the entrance. No one calls after him or sees him to the door. Saldano feels that it would take the rest of his life before the La Mesa Club members would consider him one of their own. But then, like most insiders' clubs, they will die out before he reaches their age.

CHAPTER 11

The SS Avalon looked out of place. It ever so gently rose and fell with the tide, a pearl gray swan surrounded by clusters of slab-sided liberty ships and destroyer escorts taking on bunker oil and supplies before setting course for Hawaii and the Pacific Theater. Everywhere Jose Guiermo looked, the war had changed things, with the most innocuous vessels sporting fore and aft deck guns tilted at crazy angles toward the heavens and armor plating around their wheelhouses. Near the steamer, along Wilmington's backwater docks, a flotilla of battered landing craft crowded a barge. A Navy Sea Bee crew busily welded patches over rusting holes in the ships' steel bow ramps.

On that gray-skied Saturday morning, Jose smiled when the tiny queue of two dozen civilian passengers finally escaped the drafty terminal building and boarded the steamship. They climbed the gangplank and moved to the upper deck…the main lounge being reserved for the hundreds of freshly-shorn Merchant Marine recruits on their way to Avalon for training. Jose found a vacant deck chair near the stern and sheltered from the wind by the lifeboats. He set his suitcase and wrapped presents for his cousins down on the recently scrubbed deck and stretched out in the moist morning air. Without fanfare, the dockside crew let go the hawsers, the pilot gave a long blast from the air horn that echoed down the cold steel canyon of victory ships, and the steamer slowly pulled away, black smoke pouring from its single stack. They approached the Angels Gate lighthouse at the harbor's mouth. The steamer paused while an oil-spattered tugboat pulled back the underwater cable curtain, strung there to protect the port from Japanese submarines.

The crew had loaded the crate of Stanley Junior's painting supplies long before Jose and the rest of the mostly Mexican passengers boarded. He worried that it would get lost or damaged. But one of the mates assured him that he would take special care of it. The man had spoken Spanish in a dialect similar to what Jose and his mother spoke, and he wanted to ask where he had come from but felt too awkward and embarrassed, his isolation at the DeVaul estate putting him out of practice with even the simplest of conversations.

The Catalina eddy clogged the channel with fog, and within the first hour, Jose lost sight of the mainland. They steamed westward toward the gray mountain that rose out of the sea. Only the island's ridgeline was visible along with the radio tower on Blackjack Peak. The SS Avalon aimed for its mid-section and, after several hours of dead-smooth sailing, came within a hundred yards of Catalina's leeward coast. She turned southeast and passed Descanso Beach and the Saint Catherine Hotel before entering Avalon Harbor. A blast from the steamer's horn echoed up the canyon. A pilot boat motored out to meet them and guided the ship into the terminal. Gone were the cavorting speedboats, waving tourists, and welcoming brass bands from before the war. Avalon seemed to doze in its mid-morning stupor.

At the pier, Jose and the other civilian passengers waited while the recruits disembarked, clumsily formed into companies, then marched up Sumner Street to their Villa barracks. Finally, after much delay, they came ashore. A small crowd waited to greet them. Jose recognized his Aunt and three cousins, two young men and a tall, striking girl that he hadn't seen for at least ten years and couldn't remember, but he pretended to anyway. Rosalia had gotten old and large, just like his mother, but his handsome cousins made Jose feel old by comparison. The five of them gossiped in low tones about family and the war, with Jose doing most of the listening. The crew lowered a bulging cargo net to the dock. Jose moved toward it with his claim check. His cousins helped wrestle Stanley's crate onto the pushcart that they'd brought with them. At the head of the pier, a Shore Patrolman, clad in immaculate whites with a .45 automatic strapped to his waist, scrutinized Jose's travel permit. The patrolman checked each of his relatives' identification cards before letting them pass. Their little caravan slowly headed into town and up canyon toward the Tremont Street barrio.

They passed shops with boarded windows and signs that read "Closed Until War Ends." The family had stopped talking as they passed through the hushed business district. Rosalia reminded Jose that they weren't supposed to speak Spanish downtown, although the remaining merchants and proprietors didn't much care anymore. His cousins, including Margarita, took turns pushing the cart with its precious gringo cargo and wouldn't let Jose help. They wound up canyon to Tremont Street and the cluster of whitewashed and mission-tiled bungalows tucked against the chaparral-covered canyon wall.

Old and young women swept the streets or tended lush and immaculately maintained gardens. In small side yards, goats bleated, and chickens cackled from their coops. Everywhere, children laughed, yelled, or cried. Jose shied away from this friendly chaos, heightened by Rosalia's shouted greetings to everyone she passed. She stopped to chat with her neighbor women sitting on their front stoops sipping strong coffee and gossiping. They eyed him with poorly concealed interest.

"So who is this strong man, and when can I introduce him to my daughter?" a gray-haired woman with missing teeth yelled to Rosalia from across the street. His cousins laughed. The entire compound smelled of roses mixed with the scent of spices - cayenne, cumin, and cilantro - from the nearby tamale factory that fronted the main street.

Inside Rosalia's bungalow, the cousins deposited the crate against the front room wall and instructed Jose where to sleep on a cushioned mat inside the screen door. They disappeared to their own rooms to open the presents he'd brought them, leaving Jose and his aunt alone.

"So, I don't see you for *muchos años,* and now this mysterious visit. How is your mother? Does she still have that trouble breathing? And you with no wife all these years, what she must be thinking to have a hulking son with no prospects. If you stay here I could marry you off quick, but then there's no real work until after the war. The Army has taken most of the men and those that haven't been drafted or enlisted work in downtown cafés or on fishing boats. Most boat owners signed contracts with the military to catch albacore off San Clemente. It's the only way for them to fuel their boats. But without the tourist…." Rosalia sighed and stopped complaining.

"I'm not here to find a wife, *mi Tia.*" Jose grinned. "Tomorrow, I must deliver that crate to Señor Stanley at the St. Catherine Hotel. It's his art supplies." Jose motioned to the mystery box. Rosalia looked puzzled but said nothing. "And the following day, I'll be on the return boat to Wilmington. I don't like leaving Mama by herself too long. Her spirit is strong, but her body is slowing. You should visit her in the autumn if you can. We have plenty of room."

"I remember your mother when we were children. She'd race me down the beach outside Mazatlan and always win. And she got married first."

Jose smiled. "You should come see her and remind her of those times."

"We would probably do nothing but cry…both losing husbands and having to struggle to make a living. I work in the tamale factory while my children work downtown at restaurants."

"Margarita also?"

"Si, in the kitchen at the Boos Brothers Cafeteria." Rosalia lowered her voice. "But I've heard stories..."

"What...what kind of stories?" Jose asked.

"About gringo seamen, stories a mother never wants to hear."

Tears leaked from the old woman's eyes, and Jose felt embarrassed as he tried to comfort her.

"I'm sure it's nothing but idle talk, *mi tia*. Margarita's a strong person."

"I'm sorry, Jose, for telling you all of this. But I have no one to talk to, and the barrio women are such gossips. Rosalia dabbed at her eyes with the sleeve of her dress and smiled brightly. "Well, I don't often get a chance to entertain my big-shot nephew from the mainland. We'll take our meal up canyon in the grove next to the training field. You know the Chicago Cubs have stopped coming here for spring practice during the war. But when they're here, the owners let us watch them play from the trees for free."

Rosalia hurried into the kitchen to pack the picnic of newly made tacos and cold *cervezas* reserved for the occasion. The family passed the afternoon in the quiet shade of palm and eucalyptus trees that surrounded the baseball field. They lazily sipped their beers and watched the Merchant Marine recruits go through close-order drills. The cousins quizzed Jose about what it was like to work at the DeVaul estate and if he ever saw any movie stars that frequented those hilltop mansions.

That night, lying on his mat, Jose thought that after the war, he should bring his mother to live with Rosalia. *At least she'd be closer to family and could help take care of her sister's house.* Jose fell asleep to the sounds of goats mating in the yard next door and awoke with the cock's crow. His cousins had already left for work. Rosalia offered him a breakfast of coffee and a stale piece of Mexican sweet bread. He remembered the money in his pocket from old man DeVaul. *I'll fill her pantry before I leave,* he thought.

She's been so kind and has so little.

He shouldered the crate of art supplies, gently lowered it onto the pushcart, and, with a wave to his Aunt, headed down canyon and the mile trek to the St. Catherine Hotel. The town remained quiet. But a flotilla of wooden lifeboats, each with ten seamen straining at the oars, crowed Avalon's harbor. A huge gray ship blocked its mouth. A seaplane climbed over the roof of the Casino with its twin engines roaring, buzzed the marina, then settled into Seven Moons Bay, heading toward Pebbly Beach. In no hurry to find Stanley, Jose paused along the palm-lined promenade to admire the richly ornate Casino that stood guard at the harbor's entrance. He continued along the walkway next to the ocean. He saw golden Garibaldi swimming among the kelp fronds and wondered if these fish would be worth catching for sale to the mainland estate owners.

Rounding Casino Point, the deafening crash of rapid cannon fire forced him to his knees. Along the curved seawall that defined the point, clots of merchant marine recruits and their trainers clustered around gun emplacements. Each recruit took his turn, leaning into the harness and aiming at targets being pulled across the sky by very brave pilots. Farther out on the point, others strafed the targets with large machine guns. The barrage lasted only a few minutes but long enough to set Jose's ears ringing.

When the firing stopped, he rose and hurried forward. He soon reached the St. Catherine Hotel, an impressive white plaster building with Spanish-tiled towers at its corners and a huge entrance courtyard surrounding a pool. Flags of the Merchant Marine and Coast Guard flapped lazily from the tower's poles. But the cabanas and changing booths at the water's edge that Jose remembered from his childhood had been replaced with a row of military launches that stank up the beach with diesel fumes.

He entered the hotel's main door and walked toward what

used to be the reception desk. A bored-looking seaman dressed in blue denim sat behind the counter, reading a magazine and smoking. When Jose approached, he put the magazine down and stood.

"If you're making a kitchen delivery, go around the back and see the cook. Don't bring that crap in here." The seaman had yelled at Jose before he could ask anything or introduce himself.

"No señor, I am not here for that. I have a delivery for Señor Stanley DeVaul. He lives here, no?" Jose handed the seaman a scrap of paper with Stanley's address scrawled on it.

"Yeah, he lives here. Take the elevator to the top then turn left and go to the end of the hall. It's room 47, *comprende*?"

Jose nodded and moved off.

On the quiet fourth floor, he pushed the squeaky-wheeled cart across the black-and-white-checkered linoleum, stopped in front of Stanley's room, and gave the door a quick thump. No sound came from inside. He banged hard but still got no response.

A door two rooms down popped open, and a half-naked man stuck his shaved head out and stared at Jose. "Hey, hombre, I'm PFC Briggs. Who're ya lookin' for?"

"Señor Stanley DeVaul."

"Stan probably won't be back here until late. He's out with his art stuff. Saw him at breakfast…said something about going up canyon, but I'm not sure." The man yawned and then ducked back into his room.

Jose listened to distant building sounds and tried to decide whether to wait for Stanley or flee. Finally, he tried Room 47's door and, finding it unlocked, passed quietly inside. Dirty clothes littered the floor. A collection of empty beer bottles crowded the desktop under the window. Drawings of buildings, boats, the ocean, hillsides, and people, including one particularly pretty señorita, papered the walls. Jose recognized the style and knew he'd got the right room. He wrestled the crate off the pushcart and then quickly escaped. The Saint Catherine felt more like a prison, and Jose was not surprised that few of its inmates hung around during the day.

A cool morning breeze bent the palm trees at the harbor's edge. Jose pushed the empty cart through the quiet town and back up canyon to the barrio. His Aunt had gone to work at the tamale factory. Rather than spend time in the empty, wind-swept cottage, Jose headed up canyon toward the famous cactus gardens planted by the Wrigley family. Señora DeVaul had been pestering him to start a similar garden, and Jose wanted to study how this might be accomplished. But instead of the dusty chaparral-covered hillside at the head of the canyon that Jose remembered as a child, there now stood a concrete and marble memorial to William Wrigley Jr. Its towers and terraces overlooked the cactus gardens, with open-mouthed gargoyles decorating the walls from which jet-black ravens stood watch. Jose climbed toward the edifice. The ravens called to him. They seemed to be saying, *"Why are you here? For God's sake, leave the boy alone!"* Jose smiled to himself, thinking that these black sentinels knew more than his Aunt or cousins.

"Be quiet…and help me find Stanley," he muttered.

Jose climbed the memorial's curved concrete stairway to the upper terrace, wandered across the landing, and found a heavy bronze door. A passageway led upward to a circular courtyard faced off with bluestone walls and an inner crypt where the old man of the island lay entombed. In that cold and quiet place, Jose sat on the edge of a portal overlooking the valley and watched ravens fall silently from the canyon rim, legs outstretched like the landing gear of airplanes.

But Jose's stiffening muscles urged him to keep moving. He climbed a switchback trail through oaks and toyon until reaching Catalina's central ridge. Turning westward along a dirt road, he admired the fine views of deep canyons and rocky coves. The wind blew hard. He planted a callused hand on top of his straw hat and gazed across the wrinkled sea toward San Clemente Island. Below him, on a sloped terrace overlooking the shore, a man and a woman stood in the center of a huge burn scar, their backs to Jose. The man aimed a rifle at some unseen thing below. A puff of smoke, and the rifle cracked. The woman pointed down to the sea. The man turned, laid the weapon on the ground, and spread his overcoat across the burned tufts of grass. At two hundred yards, Jose had no trouble recognizing Stanley.

CHAPTER 12

Stan felt overcome with lust and love. For two weeks he'd taken every evening meal at the Grotto, flirted with Flavia, and she with him. His portfolio overflowed with drawings of her rebuffing half-drunk meriners, bussing tables, passing time with the other waitresses…nothing more than quick charcoal sketches that captured the curve of her breasts, the angle of her legs, the gentle slope of her cheekbones. After her shift, while the kitchen crew cleaned up, they sat in a dark booth and talked. She laughed at his use of Spanish words he'd learned from the servants and grounds people on his family's estate. By candlelight, she critiqued his drawings. Afterwards, she'd let him walk her home. But they always stopped before reaching the mouth of Pebbly Canyon, in case Flavia's father might be watching.

On the second night, as they passed Pelican Rock, Stanley gathered Flavia quickly in his arms and kissed her full on the mouth. Her body molded to his contours, and their arms encircled each other. The kiss left both of them trembling and Stan with the memory of a silky smooth cheek and the sweet smell of lavender. It scared them so much that for the next couple of days, they kept up an amicable conversation all the way to Pebbly Beach, never touching.

On the fifth day, Stanley took Flavia roughly into his arms and kissed her hard. She responded by covering his face and neck with kisses and caressed his hair and shoulders until he begged her to stop. They breathed billows of white steam into the cold night and had just enough time to rearrange themselves before the car carrying the power plant's night crew rounded the bend, catching them in its meager, mostly blacked-out headlight beams. The ancient Ford rumbled past, letting the darkness envelop them once again.

After that night, Stanley and Flavia became like many lovers, catching moments of passion between passing cars and nosey stares. But on a Saturday afternoon when Flavia was scheduled to work, she thanked Laura for covering her shifts and walked into Avalon. She turned onto a side street and headed up canyon to Bird Park. Flavia found Stanley waiting for her, pacing back and forth while macaws and talking mynas complained from inside their huge octagonal cage. The couple watched the bird's antics, too excited to admit the purpose of their rendezvous.

"Why did you bring this?" Flavia asked, pointing to Stanley's M1 rifle.

"I thought I could show you what a good shot I am."

"You don't need to be a marksman to prove you are a man," she said, grinning.

"I need to do something. When people find out I'm an artist and paint flowers, they…they sometimes think I'm queer. I've gotten strange looks."

"And to fire your gun will prove what? That you can hit the target?" Flavia's face slowly darkened, and she turned away.

A myna bird began to squawk: "Fire your gun, hit the target, fire your gun, hit the target." The couple ran from the aviary, laughing.

They continued up Avalon Canyon, through the botanical garden with its threatening forest of dragon trees, prickly pear, and elephant bush, up the mountain, along the ridge road, then down the far side of the island. They walked fast, not talking or stopping. They stood on the bluffs overlooking the Palisades and the rocky shoreline below, catching their breaths. Stanley loaded a round into the chamber of his M-1, aimed at a piece of flotsam bobbing in the surf, and squeezed the trigger. The sound jolted both of them.

Stan laid the rifle on the ground and spread his long army-issue coat across the tufts of burned grass. Three months before, he and others from St. Catherine's had been called out in the dark morning to fight a brush fire at that remote spot. A Navy blimp from the Del Mar Station had misjudged the height of Catalina Island, crashed into its ridgeline, and splashed burning diesel fuel across the hillside.

They sat holding hands, feeling in each other the fine tremor of desire. The wind had been cold on the shaded side of the ridge. But on the island's seaward side, facing the infinite Pacific, the sun warmed Stanley's bare arms and neck. His white skin contrasted with Flavia's golden hues. She looked natural in that landscape. Flavia kissed him on the mouth. When he finally pulled back, gasping, her open eyes seemed to beg for his love. He pressed her gently onto the ground and kissed her, his hands caressing her breasts. She moaned and kissed him deeper. He slipped a hand underneath her skirt, and she caught his wrist, holding it steady in her strong grasp before guiding it upward to that place where women's pleasure lies. They struggled with undergarments and trousers. Inside her, he moved slowly and rhythmically until their cries echoed down the slopes to the pounding surf below. They lay spent, not trying to conceal their nakedness nor move from their lovers' embrace.

But finally, they arose and slipped on their clothes, smiling to each other, not needing to speak. Taking Flavia's hand, Stan led the way down the narrow trail, along the crease in the mountainside, to the rocky beach below. He undressed quickly. She slipped out of her skirt and blouse, her nipples hard in the cooling afternoon air. They ran laughing into the green ocean to wash, embrace, and further explore their bodies.

High on the lonely ridge above the burn scar, a solitary man adjusted his straw hat and turned to go, once again reminded of his desperation.

CHAPTER 13

Almost a week has passed since the La Mesa Men's Club dinner meeting. Sergeant Saldano feels he's the only one on the island who cares about solving this case...and with the mainland's homicide clearance rate at less than 50 percent, he knows he'll get no help from HQ. By now, Catalina's entire Latino community knows what he's looking for, but no one has come forward. The old Mexican men he recognizes on the street avert their eyes and pass by, leaving Paul's greetings of *Buenos Tardes* to die without response.

He's about to brave a trip to Pebbly Beach to look up Felipe Vargas when he gets a large envelope in the mail from Barbara Spencer. It contains Xerox copies of an old photograph that portrays a basic training graduating class, with the head of one recruit circled in red pencil. The boy wears a pained expression and sports a boot camp haircut with ears sticking out below a baseball cap. He stands at the left end of the rear row, supporting an American flag on a wooden staff. The photo's caption reads: "D Company, Fourth Army Infantry, East Garrison, Camp Ord - December 1942." Across the photograph's bottom, the soldiers' names are hand printed, with "Stanley DeVaul" corresponding to the awkward-looking kid in the back row. Other names are underlined.

Saldano leans back in his chair and studies the copy. He figures that Stanley is six feet one to six feet three, maybe 175 pounds, with blond hair, although that's difficult to nail down. Paul scans the other young faces and wonders if he looked that raw as an Army private. D Company appears more like a bunch of high school athletes than trained fighting men. Saldano reads Barbara's note.

> *Dear Paul:*
>
> *I found this photograph but nothing else. I ran the other recruits' names through our system to see if their duty station assignments jibed with our man Stanley's. The seven names I've underlined were all stationed in Avalon at the same time that DeVaul was there. Morning Report entries show that every one of those guys, except Stanley, was discharged right after VE day! None served a single day in the European or Pacific Theatres, which seems weird since their medical records don't show any major problems.*
>
> *When you get a chance, ring me up at home, and we can figure out our next move.*
>
> *Your partner in crime,*
>
> *Barbara Spencer*
> *(415)231-8777*

The letter has a faint spicy odor. Her handwriting is large, with lots of loops and strong punctuation marks. Paul tries to remember his writing analysis class back in college and what this style discloses about Barbara. He continues to stare at the photocopy and the underlined names. There's something familiar about them, details that he's absorbed while patrolling county roads from the Lost Hills Station. Saldano gazes out his office window onto the palm-shaded plaza and allows his mind to drift, letting memory bytes align, separate, and realign. In a half-hour, he's got two of the names pegged: one is the same as a boulevard that crosses a mainland freeway, and the other is that of a famous Southland museum. But his brain will produce nothing more. Paul leaves for his late afternoon rounds. He decides that tomorrow will be the day he hits Frank up for permission to go over town. He'll say he needs to visit his kids and check in with his ex-wife...something Frank should appreciate since he's been married a couple of times and pays alimony to both exes.

That night, Saldano sucks on his water bottle nervously and downs handfuls of Cheese-its before phoning Barbara.

"Hello, this is the Spencer residence. With whom do you wish to speak?"

It's a young girl's voice. In the background, Paul hears instructions being called out: "Listen carefully and don't hang up."

"This is Sergeant Saldano from Catalina Island," Paul says slowly. "Can I speak with your, ah, mother?"

There's a chorus of unintelligible whispers at the other end. The phone is laid down hard or dropped, then a woman's voice comes on.

"Hi Paul, this is Barbara. I'm trying to teach Lisa telephone etiquette...but she needs a tad more practice...and I'm not talking about how they gossip on their cell phones." Barbara laughs, a nice throaty sound.

"Yeah, I know how it is. But since *my* kids only hear from me over the phone, they're real pros by now." There's a quiet moment before he plunges ahead.

"I got your envelope this morning. Where did you find that photograph? It's great." Paul stretches out on his bed.

"I took a trip down the coast to Monterey and what used to be Fort Ord. It's now part of the University of California, you know. But they have a military museum with a lot of declassified Fourth Army stuff. We lucked out because that photograph was hanging on the wall. I just about had to guarantee the caretaker a date to copy the photograph."

"Well, before you date him, give me his name, and I'll run him through our system."

They both laugh.

Paul continues, "The good thing is that Stanley DeVaul fits the physical profile of the remains we found here. But as far as the woman is concerned, I'm going over to the mainland in about a week to check out our department's missing persons files and maybe stop at UCLA to look up the GIs' names. Some of those families sound familiar, and somebody's still gotta be around."

"Let me run the recruits through St. Louis again and at least get their induction addresses," Barbara offers. "But it's been over 70 years. Do you really think anybody's still alive?"

"I don't know, but my boss will give me only one shot at a mainland trip. He doesn't care about this case, and the island Latinos don't wanna know. I've got to make some progress, or it's back to breaking up bar fights and writing parking tickets for me." Paul sighs. Barbara stays quiet for far too long.

"Barbara, are you still there?"

"Yes, I'm here. I was thinking.... I have some leave saved up, and it would be a kick to come south for a few days and... well, meet you and help with the investigation."

It's Paul's turn to be at a loss for words. "That sounds great," he blurts. "We can meet in San Pedro and drive to Pico Rivera. But what about your daughter, ah, Lisa?"

"Her school will let her go and it's been so long since we've been on holiday. Do you think that it would be all right if we visit the island? It sounds so exotic."

Paul thinks, *what the hell, it's about time I take some risks*. "I can get you a room at the Pavilion Lodge, right downtown, with a view of the harbor. It's affordable...hell, even I can afford it." Paul realizes that he's pacing his apartment in boxer shorts and getting more and more excited.

"Okay, let's set a date and place to meet. Any hotel arrangements you make I'm sure will be splendid. Lisa and I are easy to please."

They talk about the details of their rendezvous. All the while, Paul thinks about how he needs to clean up his apartment, who he needs to speak with to get the best hotel room, and how he can convince Frank to give him a couple days off without arousing too much curiosity around the office. He says goodbye to Barbara and tries to rein himself in. *Jesus, she could be an ugly cow; her kid a real brat; maybe they just wanna see Catalina, and I'll be their flunky tour guide.* He gulps water and tries to rid his palate of the overwhelming taste of Cheese-its.

But in the back streets of San Francisco's Mission District, in a tiny fourth floor walkup, two females, one thirty-something and the other just out of elementary school, poke each other in the ribs, making each laugh and beg for mercy.

"Calm down, Calm down," Barbara says between giggles. "You know it's too…too soon to hope for anything."

"Yeah, Mom. I know." But Lisa is optimistic. *It's been so long since Mom's been happy. This Sergeant sounds, like, really neat… but I'd wish she'd meet somebody that's not a military type.*

CHAPTER 14

A week later, Saldano sits on a bus bench outside San Pedro's Ferry Terminal. He's waited for two hours, having given himself plenty of leeway before the appointed time to meet Barbara and her daughter. Paul's dressed in a fresh khaki uniform with everything pressed and polished, something he hopes an Army woman will appreciate.

About a half block down, a smoking Subaru station wagon pulls into the taxi zone. The driver's door swings open, and a woman gets out. She's dressed in a loose white blouse, jeans and sandals, slender, with a long braid of black hair extending to rounded hips. She walks toward him slowly. Her skin is smoky, and she has dark eyes and full eyebrows...could be Latina, but the body form and the way she moves don't quite fit.

As the woman nears, Paul stands, his heart thudding against his chest. *Damn, I'm never good at this.*

"Sergeant Saldano...ah, Paul, so good to meet you." Barbara extends an almost-frail hand. Her forearms are slender with dark hair. She stares into Paul's face, and he fights the urge to harden off and become all business.

"Barbara, thanks for coming. Could you find this place without trouble?" Paul takes her slender hand and gives it a gentle squeeze.

"Your directions were perfect, and Lisa only got carsick once while we passed through Santa Maria. We stayed in Ventura last night and drove down this morning." She smiles, her voice thick with an accent that still puzzles him.

Saldano retrieves his briefcase from the bench, feeling self-conscious now that this woman is casually dressed and he's all spit and polish. They walk toward the Subaru. As they near, the passenger side door pops open, and a stick-of-a-girl gets out.

Barbara grins, "Lisa, this is my partner in crime, Sergeant Paul Saldano."

The girl looks up at him and offers her hand for a formal shake. "We're…I mean, I'm glad to meet you."

"I'm happy to meet both of you, too," he says.

Lisa bounces into the back seat while Barbara hands Paul the car keys. "I thought San Francisco's streets were crazy, but these freeways are bloody insane."

Paul smiles at this often-made comment of true non-Angelinos. He cranks up the engine, and they merge into the flow of traffic on the Harbor Freeway. As they drive, Lisa keeps up a steady barrage of questions from the back seat: Where are you from? How long have you been a cop? Are there palm trees and sandy beaches on Catalina? Have you ever been married? Why did you break up? Do you have kids? What are their names? What was your toughest case to solve? Have you ever met a movie star? Have you ever killed anybody?

"Lisa, give the man a break," Barbara yells over her shoulder and smiles at Paul. He's dutifully answered each question, trying to be personable while remembering the disdain his own daughters must feel for him. They'd taken the brunt of his drunken anger when he and Julie broke up. In some ways, dealing with Lisa is more nerve-racking than being with this strange woman.

"No, it's all right. It's good to ask strangers questions, that way, they don't stay strangers for long. And yes, I…I have killed someone…in Iraq during the war, uh, you know, the first one, *Desert Storm*."

Barbara turns in her seat to stare at Paul. Wind from the cracked side window whips strands of hair around her oval face.

"I am Saudi, from Ad Damman. Do you know my city?" Her smile has vanished.

"It's on the East Coast or close to it, right? We did training in the desert near there before moving north across the border. Barbara, I've been struggling to figure out your accent these past weeks. I knew I'd heard it somewhere before…but it's been twenty years, and we're both a long way from the Peninsula."

She asks in a cool voice, "So you don't have a problem with me being Arab and Muslim?"

"No, of course not. The Middle East is one mixed-up place. But the people I met there were genuine, although I never saw any Saudi women that looked quite as…well, as beautiful as you."

He extends his right hand and rests it atop Barbara's. The sound of stifled giggles from the back seat fills the car. Barbara flashes a frown over her shoulder, then, without prompting, tells her story.

"My father and uncles are wealthy merchants and could afford to send me out of the country to be educated. I attended the University of London, studied at the marine biology station with a minor in comparative literature and English. Normally, Saudi women are only allowed to study medicine or teaching, but things are changing, and I had a chance.

"Those four years away from Ad Damman made returning home nearly intolerable. I would sometimes refuse to wear the headscarves required by the Salafi, and they made it hard on my family. But then we are Shia, and the Salafi always treat us as second class citizens…not quite Muslim.

"I worked for the government, teaching English to Saudi oil executives' wives."

"Their wives?" Saldano interrupts.

"Yes. Unrelated or unmarried men and women can't work together in Saudi society. I taught the wives, who in turn taught their husbands. I gave them tests to take home, and the men would ring me up when they had questions. But religious law prohibited face-to-face instruction."

As Barbara speaks, she stares through the windshield, dark eyes focused far down the freeway, her breathing slow and steady. *She smells of cinnamon and mint. God, she's so hot. I know what I'd be thinking if she were my teacher.*

"Then a friend of my father told him that an American soldier, who somehow had seen me at one of the Saudi installations, wanted to propose marriage. Bob was a supply sergeant, well respected in our city, and part of the early buildup force for *Desert Shield*. When his tour of duty ended, we drove to Riyadh and located a Christian minister in a compound for westerners.

"Anyway, we got married, and I followed him to Fort Lewis, Washington. I became a U.S. citizen, had Lisa, the joy of my life, and we settled down in the married NCO quarters."

"I can't picture you living in base housing," Saldano says.

Barbara frowned. "It was one of the many things that changed me."

"Sorry, didn't mean to interrupt."

"I hated the Northwest's rain squalls and fog. I became depressed, and my relations with Bob were…were not good. We divorced before he shipped out to Korea. I joined the Army, thinking that my knowledge of Arabic and English might be useful. But so far, I've been stuck doing records management."

She grimaces, and they both laugh, apparently, each having their own reasons for detesting paperwork.

"About a year ago, I was lucky to be stationed in San Francisco. That city is more to my liking. It's on the ocean, still too cold to comfortably scuba dive but a much better place to raise Lisa. Most people think I'm Latina or maybe Thai."

"Yeah, you could pass," Paul says and chuckles. "Have you been back home since emigrating?"

She laughs. "I've grown accustomed to California's cool climate. I'd probably die of heat exhaustion the first week back."

Paul makes a weaving motion to avoid a stalled car that's pulled onto the inside fringe. He instinctively reaches for his radio to call it into the Highway Patrol but finds only the knobs of an AM radio. Barbara watches him and smiles, relaxing in her seat.

Paul expertly navigates the maze of freeways and a latticework of on and off ramps until they arrive in Pico Rivera and stop at a McDonalds for early lunch. He warns them, "We're gonna have to work fast because we have to be back in San Pedro by six o'clock to catch the jet boat."

"A jet boat!" Lisa squeals. "Does it have wings?"

"No, but it's the fastest thing on the water."

At the Station House, the desk Sergeant raises his eyebrows when Saldano introduces Barbara and Lisa as his assistants and requests that they have access to Catalina's old police force files. The Sergeant hands Paul a key and walks them out to the parking lot, where he points at a metal barn-like building.

"The old stuff's packed in banker's boxes and goes back to the late 19th century. It's consolidated by year, so you can get close without too much of a hassle. But all types of files are jumbled together, and a lot of the stuff from the 1950s and before was handwritten. I hope your eyesight is good."

Paul unlocks the storage building and flicks on the lights. Racks of shelves extend upward toward the dark ceiling and along both sides of a half dozen aisles, with a platform ladder on wheels stationed at the end of each corridor.

"Okay, guys, we're looking for records from 1943 to 1946. Fan out, and the first one who finds them gets a special prize."

They split up and cruise the aisles. While the files are consolidated by year, they are not arranged in any obvious order. It's a half-hour before Barbara calls out, and they join her at the back of the building, where they find fifteen boxes of stuff.

"Here's what we must do," Barbara says with authority. "Let's each take a box and go through it quickly. Look for documents that contain the words Avalon or Catalina, and set them aside. If you read the material, we'll be here all bloody night. We can sort through what we've collected afterwards."

Paul climbs the ladder and brings down a box for each of them. They quickly page through the jumble of reports, ledgers, handwritten pages, and perfect-bound notebooks, occasionally pulling out a particular sheet or ledger and setting it in a wire basket that Barbara has found on one of the shelves. In two hours, they've gone through the boxes and have a modest stack of files and folders to study further.

"Paul, you and I should do the first screening, and Lisa should take a second look just in case. What we're looking for is anything to do about missing persons, homicides, or any event or incident that has to do with the military."

The three of them set to it. At the end of another hour, there are maybe a dozen documents left in the wire basket.

"Let's take them to the office and get them copied," Paul says. "None of the ones I found provided any new leads, but a closer look might turn up something."

Like moviegoers from an afternoon matinee they emerge with squinting eyes into the afternoon sunlight. The desk Sergeant makes Paul sign for a copy of each document, some of which are faded pencil notes on lined binder paper. But by 3 pm, they're back on the freeway for the half-hour jaunt to Bel Air and UCLA's main library.

"I want to look up the family names of those eight GIs stationed in Avalon, including DeVaul's. Barbara, maybe you and Lisa can check out the "Who's Who" and make copies of anything you find. I'll check the special collections to see if any of those families left their papers to the University. It's a long shot, but we could get lucky."

Barbara grins. "I've already Googled all of the names and didn't find a bloody thing. Hopefully, this place will have useful hard copy material."

They enter the five-story library, and Paul leaves them in the lobby, agreeing to meet up in two hours.

He has no trouble with the graduate student at the special collections counter. His uniform and official I.D. get instant cooperation. The student directs Paul to a nearby computer terminal, where he's instructed on how to sort through the listing of special collections. After a half-hour of querying the nine names, he succeeds in finding one family that matches. He requests the hard copy files for "Spangler," and the grad student gives him two folders.

From what Paul can discern, the Spanglers invested heavily in oil development around Huntington Beach during the first half of the 20th century and made their money in Southland industries. They owned an estate somewhere in the Santa Monica Mountains. He finds a birth certificate for a son, Robert Jeffrey Spangler. It matches the name of the GI on the Camp Ord photograph, which gets Paul excited. But that discovery is nothing compared to the grainy sepia photograph of a group of white men posing in tuxedos at a formal function. The photograph's caption reads: "Laurel Canyon Gentlemen's Club," and the names of listed members include the eight names of the GIs in the Camp Ord graduating picture, including a Stanley DeVaul Sr.

After copying the photograph, Paul finds a hand-written note tucked in between other papers of no consequence.

20 November 1942

Mr. Michael Spangler
P.O. Box 432
Topanga, California

Dear Mr. Spangler:
I am in receipt of your letter dated November 3rd and have carefully considered your request. I am well aware of the Spangler family's contributions since I, too, am originally from the Los Angeles area. I'm also well aware of your organization's good work and high community standing. I hope you find my response to your request satisfactory and that after my pending separation from the Armed Services I might contact you and Mr. DeVaul and discuss possible business ventures. Do not hesitate to contact me if you have further concerns.

Sincerely,
Brigadier General Patrick O'Neal, Commander
Fourth Army Training Center
Camp Ord, California

Paul copies this letter and then hurries to meet Barbara and Lisa in the lobby. He's ten minutes late, and they scramble to get back on the freeway and avoid the rush hour traffic to San Pedro. They make the ferry landing with twenty minutes to spare. Paul helps Barbara and Lisa with their luggage and buys them passage.

"I think I've found something for you to research," Paul tells Barbara. They settle in and await the firing of the jet boat's engines. "We'll talk about it over dinner.... I have a great place picked out."

Barbara smiles, leans back in the reclining seat and pulls Lisa toward her. The girl yawns and before the boat has cleared the harbor's outer jetty, she's snoring. The ship glides over the waves toward the dark horizon and the twinkling lights of Avalon.

CHAPTER 15

The SS Avalon rumbled to a stop at the Wilmington dock, then reversed engines to cinch the hawsers around their cleats. Jose and the dozen or more bored civilians gathered their belongings and waited at the rail for the gangplank to be rolled into place. A cluster of cars parked in a gravel lot included the Lincoln belonging to Señor DeVaul. Jose climbed into its front seat, and without a word, the driver gunned the engine and headed toward the green coastal hills and the estate.

Jose had been gone four days, having spent the last afternoon on Catalina buying a huge order of groceries for Rosalia, including fresh meat from the gringo market. They'd drunk a lot of red wine the night before. The next morning, Rosalia and his cousins were up and gone before he departed. A throbbing headache reminded Jose of the cost of losing control.

The limousine bounced up the steep driveway and through the outer gates. Señora DeVaul raised her head from her kneeling spot in a newly dug flowerbed and waved, unusual for her to be out so early. Jose smiled and waved back. The white driver continued to stare straight ahead without expression and stopped the Lincoln in front of the main entrance.

Jose got out, and the heavy door swung open. Juanita motioned him inside, her eyes hard as onyx. He dipped his head and followed.

"Put your luggage against the wall and wait here," Juanita said and slipped inside the study. When she reappeared, Jose stood hat in hand with eyes lowered.

"He is waiting for you," she said, her voice harsh,

unforgiving.

"Thank you...and I am sorry, Juanita," he whispered and left, a puzzled look on the woman's face.

Inside the study, DeVaul Senior called from his reading table at the far end. Jose hurried across the immense Persian rug and stood waiting while the old man completed paperwork and pushed his chair back.

"Tell me everything you know about Junior," he barked without preamble.

Jose paused and tried to decide what he should say and how to say it.

"Come on, come on, I don't have all day."

For a moment, Jose's anger boiled up but did not break free. "Your son is doing very well. I visited his room at the St. Catherine Hotel and delivered the art supplies. He has been making many drawings. But I never talked to him."

"Why the hell not?" DeVaul shouted, and Jose took a step back.

"Another soldier in the room nearby told me that Stanley spends his time roaming the island and *Ciudad* Avalon, only comes back to the hotel late at night."

"Christ, the place is tiny. You didn't see him the entire time you were there?"

"Once, but only briefly."

"Where was he? What was he doing? Who was he with? Come on, man, give me details." DeVaul glared at his outside man.

"He rested on the other side of the island with a woman, and they were...it looked like they were good friends."

DeVaul bounded out of the chair and started pacing the rug in front of the fireplace, a blackened cavern large enough to roast a steer in. "Tell me about this woman. What does she look like? Do you know her name? Does her family live on the island?"

"I don't know her family name, but she is *muy bonita* and a Mexican. I wish she was *my* friend."

DeVaul eyed him carefully but kept pacing.

Jose continued, "I described her to people in the marketplace where the families gather. They said she's called Flavia and is the daughter of the *Patron* of one of Avalon's barrios. They wouldn't say more."

"So how good a friend did she seem to be to my son?" DeVaul demanded.

Jose hesitated. "The best," he said, remembering their brown and white bodies locked together and undulating on the open seaside terrace. He'd be damned if he'd give this old man any more information.

"All right, you can go…but tell Juanita to telephone George and have him come out from the City right away." DeVaul slumped back into his chair and stared at the paperwork in front of him. The early afternoon fog drifted into the canyon, and the room darkened.

In the hallway, Jose retrieved his kit and looked for Juanita. At a side table near the far end of the passage, she arranged cut flowers in Señora DeVaul's favorite vase.

Jose approached quietly. "Juanita, Señor DeVaul wants you to call *Jorge* and have him come out from the City immediately."

Juanita nodded and turned away. He felt the full weight of his emptiness. Jose left the main house and climbed the trail through orange and avocado trees to the cluster of outbuildings and the bungalow where his aging mother awaited his return. It took Jose the rest of the afternoon to pack their belongings, all the while arguing with his mother.

"Mister DeVaul has been good to us," she complained. "Why must we leave?"

"We are prisoners here…can't you feel that?"

"But we know so few people in the City…"

"I'll have a chance there to be married like you and Poppa."

"I am too old to make a new home."

"Don't worry, I will take care of you…and so will Ernesto and his family…. I am sure."

Pulling a single trunk, the unlikely duo hobbled down the fog-shrouded canyon, reaching the Coast Highway after many stops and much pain. Jose and his mother were bound for Los Angeles and Olivera Street, an unannounced visit to a cousin that neither had seen in years, to a new city and a new neighborhood, almost to a new country. He could get a job as a gardener working for rich people. His mother would have family around her when the cough finally took her. His chances of finding a wife should be much improved.

They sat on a bench, facing inland. A brightly-lit Venice Short Line trolley clattered to a stop, sparks popping from its electric wires in the fog. Jose helped his mother up the steps, and they disappeared inland, leaving the DeVauls to fend for themselves during the upcoming pick of oranges.

At four o'clock, after the foghorn at Point Malibu began its monotonous song, George DeVaul arrived in his blue Lincoln, the straight-eight engine thumping softly below its ported hood. These *required visits* to his father's estate were not unusual, although Juanita normally could provide reasons for the summons. But not this time, and to add to the mystery, George thought he'd seen his father's outside man with his old mother, sitting on a bench along the coast road, apparently waiting for a trolley into the City. He never liked Jose. *The man's too damn sullen,* George thought. *And the way he stares at me is rude.*

George climbed out of his car, buffed his Florsheim wingtips on the pant legs of his blue serge suit, and entered the house. He was a small, compact man, already balding in his late twenties, with thick eyebrows and a prominent nose, a feature that his wife Sarah said made him look Roman. The president of the bank's board of directors liked George's slow, methodical style of unscrambling the most complex problems…so different from the old man who'd storm in every few days and upset everyone.

George had plenty of practice absorbing his father's wrath, and he expected more tonight. It didn't matter why. Juanita took his hat and he moved to the study where he found his father slumped in a wing-backed chair pulled close to a blazing fire. A half-empty carafe of wine and glasses sat on the sideboard. DeVaul Senior motioned to it. George collected a chair from against the wall.

"God damn that kid. All he had to do was sit tight," DeVaul Sr. muttered.

George poured himself ink-black Zinfandel and patiently waited for the thundering invectives to begin. After an eternity of quiet moments, they did.

"Do you know what that son of a bitch has done now?" the old man shouted, slurring his words.

George took a deep gulp of the spicy wine and shook his head.

"That little peckerwood has gone and got himself a Mexican girlfriend. You know how those families are…"

George stayed silent, waiting for more.

"There'll be no brown bastards crawling around this house, I can tell you that." The old man picked up a silver bell off the side table and rang for Juanita, ordering her to refill the carafe.

"I thought his screwing Betty was bad…you know I never told him I knew about that…but this could be real trouble. All I need is for those wetbacks to find out who Stanley is and about our family."

"Father, don't get all worked up. It's wartime, and

Stanley's probably just lonely."

George slid a cigar from an inside coat pocket, used a silver pocket knife to cut off its tip, and lit it with a match from a golden case.

DeVaul glared impatiently and tossed off his wine, a dark trickle running down his chin. He wiped it with a meaty hand.

"Figure something out, George. The war's gonna be over soon, and I want Stanley back here where I can introduce him to the Laurel Canyon Club, get him properly connected…like I did with you. Christ, I'd even send him to see Betty if I thought he'd go."

George nodded, drained his wineglass, and poured another. "Give me a couple of days, and don't worry. Stan's on an island and isn't going anywhere. By the way, I saw your outside man and his mother waiting for the trolley down at the highway. What happened? Did you fire him?"

George smiled to himself while the old man's lips tightened. He knew that one day, his father's anger would make him do something stupid, and George would be ready to take over the estate when that day came. He must be patient, watch and wait.

"I didn't know that bastard had left," DeVaul muttered. "I'd sent him to Catalina to find out about Stanley. But all he did was spend my money and come back with no more information than what I've told you. Now I have an orange pick and no foreman."

"Relax, Father, I'll contact some of your club families. I'm sure they'll know somebody to recommend. And if that doesn't work, I'll ask at the bank."

He stood to go, and the old man made an attempt at rising but slumped back in his chair and stared at the fire.

George left quietly without visiting his mother. He carefully negotiated the twisting turns of the canyon highway until it merged with an inland boulevard leading into Culver City and his modest three-bedroom house west of the studio district. Sarah waited for him with a martini, the evening newspaper, and supper. Not being hungry, George apologized, took the drink and retired to his study to stare into the night through Spanish casement windows and plan his next move.

Sarah peeked in around nine and found him snoring in his chair. On his desk, a scrap of paper flashed a cryptic message scrawled in George's schoolboy handwriting: *Stanley has a girlfriend – <u>FIX IT</u>!*

CHAPTER 16

Laura collected the dirty dishes and scraped the leavings into the metal tub that sat on top of the bus cart. She pocketed the thirty-five cent tip tucked under the edge of the shielded candleholder. The seamen had been generous and the past two dinner shifts had been great, what with her covering for Flavia and Mr. Burke over town. There'd been talk among the cooks that the owner might close the Grotto until after the war or maybe sell out.

Laura welcomed the extra money. *If I get canned,* she thought, *I'll need it for my own passage.* Factories in Santa Monica still hired line workers, and wages would be enough to tide them over until pre-war prosperity returned to Catalina, if it ever did.

Jimmy came out of the kitchen and told her to go home, that he'd lock up. Laura pulled on a cardigan, retrieved her purse from the storage room, and passed out of the dark restaurant into the blustery night. She refused to think about her empty apartment, cold bed, and her crippled husband fishing the frigid sea three miles off San Clemente. But at least he wasn't fighting the Japs on some desolate Pacific atoll. His bad hip had earned him a 4-F deferment and a lifetime of pain that he bore with patience.

Laura turned toward town and the moonlit outline of the Casino. A late picture show started soon in the Casino's huge dome-topped theater crowded with bored seamen. At least she wouldn't be alone, although she'd seen the film twice already. Laura approached the pier. A dark figure stepped from behind a palm tree. She crossed to the other side of Crescent Avenue and walked faster. But the man angled to intercept her. She clutched her purse to her chest and prepared to run.

"Wait, *Señora,* I must speak with you," the man said slowly, his English clear and unbroken.

"Who are you…you scared me," Laura hissed.

The man fell in beside her, and they strode past dark shops with boarded windows.

"I am Flavia's father. You work with her, *si*?"

"Yeah, sure."

"My daughter says she had to work for the past two days, but she comes home so late, and I've checked the restaurant, and it's long closed." The desperation builds in his voice. "Do you know where she is? Her mother and I are *muy* worried. Surely you must know something?"

"She asked me to cover her last couple of hours. I don't know where she is," Laura lied and continued to move toward the Casino.

"Please, I need to know if she is…is with a friend."

Laura forced her voice to remain unwavering. "Flavia left the restaurant alone."

In truth, Flavia had been gone since the beginning of the dinner shift, escaping with her GI boyfriend, who had set up camp at the corner table. Laura had watched them talk and stare into each other's eyes, their trembling hands lightly clasping then releasing. And this GI was no regular Joe. He spoke too politely, held his artist's charcoal like a magic wand, and pestered the help to let him sketch them while they worked: Jimmy sweating over the steam tables, Leonardo flipping fish and steaks on the grill, or Laura with her slender hands resting on hips, giving unruly mariners the what-for.

"But you must know something," he repeated, clutching her arm with strong fingers. "I'm her father…you know what this island is like."

"I'm sorry. Flavia and I are not that close. I wish I could

help." She pulled away, turned uphill at the El Encanto Café, and pushed onward toward her apartment and its solid lockable door.

After a few minutes of climbing the steep slope, her heart racing from fear and effort, she turned and found the street empty. Laura shivered and stood motionless for a few minutes to make sure. She continued upward, turned onto Vieudelou Street, and climbed steadily until reaching a narrow passage between two boarding houses. She stopped to check the street again, then entered the passage and felt her way along the rough plaster walls. The alley opened onto a fieldstone courtyard in front of a tiny tile-roofed apartment.

Before the war, every square foot of building in Avalon not used for business had been converted to housing for the white island workers. The Mexicans lived mostly in their own barrios. But then the tourist trade disappeared, and property values plummeted. Bungalows and small houses could be rented for the week or month at reasonable rates. *I never shoulda done it for 'em,* Laura thought. *Her trigger-happy father could get us all killed.*

The apartment bathed in moonlight, windows covered with thick blackout curtains. Laura knocked softly on the plank door. In a few minutes, its hinges creaked open, revealing a tall man wearing pale pajamas.

"Yes, what do you want?" he asked sleepily, rubbing his eyes.

"It's me, Laura. I…I'm sorry to bother you, but…but I need to talk to Flavia."

"Who is it? What do they want?" a woman called from inside.

"It's me, Laura, we gotta talk, it's important." Laura's voice echoed in the cold courtyard.

Stanley stepped aside, and Laura entered. The door thudded shut. A light clicked on. Flavia sat on the bed, pulling on clothes and trying to control her long hair.

"Do you realize how late it is?" Laura hissed.

Flavia laughed quietly. "If you don't want me to stay out so late, you shouldn't have got us this place."

"Look, I ran into your father. He's out looking for you. You'd better get your excuses in order and get home. I've already told him you left two hours before shift's end and that you were alone. But the rest is up to you; I can't get in the middle of this."

"Gracias, Gracias, Laura, we'll figure something out."

Laura glanced at a wide-awake and unsmiling Stanley. She felt awkward standing in the low light, watching Flavia dress and watching Stanley watch her. She excused herself and passed into the night.

She remembered her own clandestine meetings with Carl before they got married and the flames of their passion doused by her mother's inquisition, always critical of Laura's choice of a crippled seaman, as if her own pick had been so much better. Laura continued her homeward trek, imagining her husband waiting in their warm bed to fan the flames.

Inside the converted carriage shed, Flavia finished her hasty toilette.

"So what can you say to him?" Stanley asked. "Or should I tell your father we're in love? I'm sure he suspects anyway."

Hearing those words spoken so boldly sent a chill down Flavia's spine. "No, not yet…but soon. For tonight, I'll tell Poppa that I went to the late show at the Casino. Laura has told me all about it, so I know the story. It normally lets out about *once y media*, so if I hurry, I can make it home at the right time. But we can't do this much longer."

"You're right about that." Stanley sighs. "Briggs has been riding me for missing midnight bed check. They've cut me a lot of slack, but I don't want to push it. Everybody thinks that the war is winding down, and the brass is starting to run this place all spit and polish. If it weren't for you…"

Flavia came into his arms for a long goodnight kiss. With a giggle, she pulled away to let him adjust his pajamas.

"I'll see you at the restaurant tomorrow," she said. Wrapping herself in a shawl, she slipped outside.

Stan relived the warmth and fullness of Flavia. Their love was exciting and full, nothing like the quick indiscretion with Betty or any of his arranged liaisons with pretentious debutantes. He could talk with Flavia, could share his feelings, and she knew more about art and its importance than most of his school classmates. "Ah, my brown Flavia," he murmured, then thought, *If* my *father had any idea I've been with a beautiful señorita, he'd be roaming the streets trying to stop us.*

Stan pulled on his wrinkled khakis and the Army-issue woolen overcoat, clicked off the light, and left the apartment, his leather shoes ringing hard on the fieldstones and the sidewalk beyond. With a half-hour to make it back for bed check, he ambled along the harbor's edge. From his coat, he retrieved a half-pint of whiskey, leaned against the railing, and tilted the bottle back. Liquid fire poured down his throat. He hoped the booze would let him fall asleep quickly, would dissolve the vision of Flavia's soft brown body and flowing hair lying on the bed beneath him.

As Stan turned toward the St. Catherine Hotel and passed along the palm-lined promenade, a dark shape pulled itself up the sea wall and over the railing. Eduardo shivered in the night wind, making sure to stay silent and not lose sight of the young woman in the distance.

CHAPTER 17

The whine of the jet boat's engines drops in pitch as it enters Avalon Harbor and burbles toward the Ferry landing. Several dozen sleepy passengers rouse themselves and line up to retrieve their luggage from storage lockers on the fore deck. Lisa seems cranky after her short nap. But she comes around quickly when Catalina's night air hits her. Saldano offers Barbara his jacket while they wait.

Lisa points overboard into the clear water: "What are those things? They sort of, like, ya know, glow!"

"A variety of goldfish called Garibaldi," Paul tells her. "They're supposedly good to eat…but it's illegal to catch 'em."

At the base of the dock where it joins Pebbly Beach Road a bevy of noisy golf carts wait to pick up returning residents. The few winter tourists are spirited away in taxicabs to island hotels. Within a few minutes, Paul, Lisa, and Barbara are alone. The jet boat's crewmembers call to each other as they secure the ship for the night.

"Meet you at The Landing…your turn to buy…the Chi Chi Club is better…you guys go ahead, I'm gonna see if Nichole's at Antonio's." Their voices float over the gentle lapping waves.

The Pavilion Lodge's lights glow softly a block away. The trio strolls toward it along the harbor's edge. Paul helps Barbara check-in, then waits awkwardly in the lobby as the two disappear to their room. When they finally return, Barbara still wears jeans and a simple blouse, but she's combed out her full mane of thick hair. It cascades down her back. Lisa wears a pretty dress with a golden necklace and matching earrings. Paul escorts the one-

and-a-half women to Armstrong's Restaurant near the base of the pier. He's eaten there plenty of times and noticed that it's a favorite place for Avalon residents to take guests.

"Good evening, Sergeant Saldano. A table for, ah, three?" The waitress smiles at Paul, then eyeballs Barbara and Lisa.

"Yes, next to the window if we can."

"Sure, no problem tonight. This wind keeps most mainlanders away…except for a few pretty ones." She motions to Barbara and Lisa.

Paul grins. "Great, then we should get excellent service, right?"

The waitress rolls her eyes. "I'll getcha some menus, but what do ya want to drink? I know you're on the wagon, but maybe your lady might like something?"

As the waitress and Paul talk, Barbara and Lisa stare openmouthed.

"We'll wait on drinks until we've had a chance to look at the menu. Thanks."

"Who the bloody hell is that?" Barbara whispers after the waitress leaves.

"Oh, her?" Saldano says innocently. "That's Sally…what a character, huh?"

They gaze at the middle-aged woman who wears a dress that exposes a perfect surfer girl's figure and young-looking legs and who balances a miniature nativity scene outlined in twinkling lights on her head.

"I think she's dated every unmarried guy in Avalon…ah, except me."

"Aye, sure," Barbara cracks, a smirk curling the corners of her mouth. "So what's wrong with *you*?"

Paul feels his face burn. "You'll…you'll find out soon enough," he stammers and hurries on. "I hope this restaurant is all right. I never thought to ask what type of food you guys like."

"If it's hot, we'll eat it." Barbara laughs. "Since Bob and I split up, I haven't cooked much of anything, been eating *Lean Cuisine.* Lately, I've tried teaching Lisa to cook Saudi. But it's hard to find good chickpeas."

"They're called Garbanzos in California, and I'll be happy to show you how to fix Tex-Mex anytime you want."

Sally returns and Barbara orders a glass of white wine and a Shirley Temple for Lisa while Paul orders a diet Coke.

Barbara raises an eyebrow. "The waitress mentioned something about..."

"Yeah. I knew you'd pick up on that. I stopped drinking alcohol about five months ago. It nearly ruined my life...so I had to..."

"Do you go to meetings?"

"No, but I probably should. I depend on the islanders to help me stay straight. Sally wouldn't have served me booze even if I'd ordered it."

Barbara smiles. "I'm glad you're trying. I've known more than my share of alcoholics...can appreciate a sober man. Being Muslim, I didn't drink at all until entering London University, and then only bad French wine."

They talk about the boat trip across the channel, about their full day digging through musty records. Lisa crows about finding hand-written notes that describe a missing *señorita.*

"Tomorrow, I want you guys to come see me at the Station. We'll go over what we collected," Paul says. "Come after nine, so you'll miss the Station Commander. But before I forget, what do you think of this?" Paul shows them the photocopy of General O'Neal's letter that he's kept folded in his shirt pocket.

Barbara scans it; her thick eyebrows knit together. "Never heard of General O'Neal, but then there were one star generals scattered everywhere during World War II. A lot were recruited from industry. Maybe O'Neal knew Spangler and DeVaul Senior from before the war? I can check central records to see what they have on him and maybe take another trip down to Fort Ord, although you'll have to forgive me if the museum curator insists on a date this time."

"Well, there is definitely something going on here," Paul says, ignoring the comment about the curator. "Since when do Brigadier Generals do favors for civilians? To really know what's happening, we'll need to find Spangler's November 3rd letter, if it still exists."

Barbara smiles, liking the idea that Paul still considers her a partner in this escapade. The longer it continues, the more she's impressed. *Praise to Allah,* she thinks, *how many men would invite a woman to bring her daughter along on a first date to a romantic island?* And she had caught the way Sally eyed Paul while seating them and sensed that others have noticed his finer qualities, *although he covers them well with his sergeant persona.* But being an Army woman, Barbara's used to that.

"Maybe if General O'Neal connected with Spangler after the war, there's something about him locally. Another trip to UCLA?" Barbara asks.

Paul sighs. "I've shot my one chance. The Station Commander won't let me off island again any time soon. I can e-mail the University and see if O'Neal is listed. If there's something there, maybe you could check for us on your way back north? I can draw you a map."

"Let's talk about that later," Barbara says, not wanting to think about departing the island. Dinner finished, Paul leaves Sally a huge tip. *Maybe he's guilty about bringing his girlfriend here?* Barbara wonders and laughs to herself. *I'm on this island two hours and already getting territorial. I'm not his girlfriend yet. But the night is young.*

Paul walks Barbara and Lisa back to the Pavilion Lodge.

"Mom, I...I can't keep my eyes open," Lisa complains.

Barbara turns to Paul at the hotel room door. "Why don't you go change out of your uniform and come back and show me Avalon."

"Sounds great...but are you sure it's okay if Lisa stays by herself?"

"Come on, you guys, I'm not a little kid. I can keep the door locked."

Barbara nods and covers a smile with her hand.

"Well, okay then. I'll be back in half an hour, and Lisa, I'm really happy to meet you." Saldano extends a hand toward the girl, but she turns shy and disappears inside the hotel room.

Paul reaches his hillside apartment, breathing hard from his fast-paced jog. He tries to remember what clean civvies he can wear to go clubbing. This will be his first time in the cabarets as a patron. *I hope the bartenders don't give me a hard time about being out on a date. And then there's the "on the wagon" thing.*

Paul slips into dress slacks, a new cambric shirt right out of its cellophane wrapper, and a sports jacket. He stares into the mirror. *Jesus, I look like some rube Tejano.* Discarding the cowboy hat, he combs his black hair back to cover the thin spot before leaving the apartment to rejoin Barbara. Lisa's snores fill the hotel room like a cat's contented purring. Barbara has put on a warm shawl and finely tooled silver jewelry. She looks Mid-eastern for the first time, impressive, elegant.

They work their way down Crescent Avenue, gazing into brightly lit shop windows, and momentarily pause outside Luau Larry's open door. The music from a solo guitarist reaches out to them, along with the drunken howls from the backroom crowd. They turn up Catalina Avenue and duck into the Marlin Club. On weekends, the club really rocks. But tonight, only a few hard-core alkies sit at the bar watching a colored TV with its sound turned low. The jukebox is unplugged. Paul deposits Barbara in a back corner and goes to the bar to order soda water, wine, and something to nibble on.

"Out on the town tonight, Sergeant?" Luis Venezuela grins. Paul can't help himself and grins back. "She looks too refined for wetbacks like us, don't you think?" Luis says.

"Well, maybe for you...but I've been improving my manners. You should try it sometime." Paul chuckles and attempts to carry their drinks and snacks back to the table without spilling anything. He's only partially successful.

Barbara asks, "So what does the bartender think of the Sergeant's Arab girlfriend?"

Paul sets the drinks down. For a moment, he's afraid she's heard their entire exchange.

"He thinks you're too beautiful to be with a common Chicano like me."

"Yes, well, what do *you* think?"

"I agree. I think you're *muy bonita*...that means beautiful."

Barbara laughs. "I'm glad the time Lisa and I spent selecting this outfit paid off. But I feel a tad uneasy drinking wine when you're not. I hope it doesn't make you uncomfortable?"

"That's okay. Most people think us *Tejanos* are raised on Tequila with beer chasers. I feel so much better being off the sauce...but it's still hard."

"You'd have to work hard to get me drunk, mister. I'm only a sipper." Her eyes grow large. "Hold still a moment." She leans forward and pulls a straight pin sticking through the collar of Paul's new shirt. "Looks like we both tried hard to dress up. If you don't get 'em all, one wayward pin can hurt you."

"Story of my life," Paul says. "I'm used to getting stuck."

They talk. By the second bowl of pretzels, they're past discussing the case and start in on abridged versions of their life histories. By the third, they're gossiping about past friends, recent lovers, and their distant families and crazy relatives. Barbara speaks animatedly about an Uncle who lives near the Jordanian border and deals arms to anybody who can pay for them…Iranians, the Iraqis, Palestinians, it doesn't matter. Even the Jewish settlers are his clients. Paul counters with a story about his Great Uncle Domingo, who claimed that he'd fought with Pancho Villa and had met their Great Aunt on a raid of a border village, carrying her away into the north Mexican desert where they became lovers.

In a rare pause in the conversation, Paul glances at Luis. The bartender reads a Penthouse and eyes them anxiously. They're the only ones left in the Marlin Club.

"I think it's time," Paul says and he helps Barbara on with her shawl.

They push out through the padded door into the dark street. Barbara stops and looks up at the clear night sky filled with stars and sways for a minute before heeding Paul's call. She follows him back to Crescent Avenue and Seven Moons Bay. Only the streetlights still glow. They pass slowly along the harbor's edge until Barbara leans against the railing. They stare across the channel at the twinkling lights of San Pedro and Long Beach. Paul places his hand over Barbara's on the railing. He turns to look at her. The silver jewelry twinkles like stars against her black hair.

"To answer your question, you are beautiful and just right for me," Paul says, trying to keep his voice from catching in his throat.

Barbara stares at him, then, without a word comes into his arms. She smells of sandalwood and spicy flowers he can't quite place. They embrace and stay locked together for a long time, the steady beating of their hearts keeping a syncopated rhythm. Finally, Barbara pulls back.

"Sergeant Saldano," she whispers, "you'd better be what

you seem. I'm not yet ready to suffer more pain over a man." Her eyes fill and start to spill.

Paul kisses her on the mouth and then caresses her hair. "Don't worry, I'm too simple to be complicated. What you know is what I am."

Barbara manages a smile and ducks her head to wipe at her eyes with the edge of her shawl. Paul glances at his watch.

"Christ, it'll be dawn in less than four hours. I've kept you out all night…and on the first date, no less." Paul laughs. Barbara kisses him with more passion than the last time. In a daze, he escorts her to the Pavilion Lodge, then wanders uphill to his garage apartment. He craves the whiskey bottle he used to keep next to the bed back on the mainland. *Christ, it'll be tough finding sleep tonight.*

Inside Room 211, Barbara stretches out fully clothed on top of the bed, listens to Lisa's deep night breaths, and tries not to dream too much before drifting off to sleep.

CHAPTER 18

Deputy Beverley Hanson knocks and then enters Saldano's office. "There's a Barbara Spencer and a young girl here to see you. They say they have an appointment."

The Sergeant looks up from his desktop cluttered with paperwork. He's been trying to catch up with his watch commander duties. But the events of the previous night have distracted him.

"Show them in and have Elsa screen all my calls for a couple hours. I'll be working on the China Wall homicide."

The Deputy nods and retreats into the hallway, smiling to herself, glad that the Sergeant's getting some action. The office staff has gossiped about Saldano ever since he arrived on the island, how he never goes out, never travels and seems content to hole up in his cave of an apartment. The Station's two female deputies have brought their unattached girlfriends by to try and fix him up. But Paul has shown little interest, and they suspect he doesn't like women. The arrival of this slender beauty adds energy to their gossip, and they've already heard through Avalon's grapevine about his date at the Marlin Club.

Barbara enters Paul's office with Lisa trailing and he motions them into chairs. He avoids looking into her eyes for fear that the electric connection might be gone, that last night's episode is only an example of Catalina's "island madness." He reaches into a drawer and pulls out a folder containing all the file material that they've collected from the Pico Rivera Station. One by one, the trio reviews each item. Most of the materials are hand-written logs and notes penned by a Deputy White, Catalina's only civilian law enforcement officer during World War II.

After a slow hour, they're done. "So what have we got?" Saldano asks.

"Not much," Barbara says and sighs. "White's notes don't include anything about the military...not surprising, since the Shore Patrol handled anyone in a uniform. Only the notes that Lisa found have any connection."

"Yes, but how? White tells us a Mexican named Eduardo reported his daughter missing, says she hadn't been seen for six weeks...which seems weird. Why wait so long to report a missing daughter?"

Lisa interrupts. "Yeah, if *I* ever got, ya know, lost, Mom'd be phoning the cops before I got to the end of the block."

"Count yourself lucky," Barbara says soberly. "If we were with a Saudi harem, you couldn't go anywhere without a family member."

Paul shakes his head and continues. "I know that the island's Latinos didn't like to deal with the Police, but why would Eduardo say anything at all after so much time?"

"You will have to question them, Paul."

"Who? What do you mean?" He rolls his chair back from his desk.

"I know you feel like an outsider here...believe me, I know about being alien. But you'll have to find a way to get inside this community."

"I've already talked with the La Mesa Club and got squat," Saldano says and frowns.

"What about that old guy Felipe that you told me about? Would it help if I came with you? You know, I look Latina."

Paul laughs, and their eyes meet. He fights back the urge to grab Barbara and cover her with kisses. She must realize his intentions because she dips her head to stare at the paperwork, her pale cheeks turning a darker shade of beige.

"Yes, you might help break the ice," Paul says. "Maybe tomorrow we could ride out. But this afternoon, I need to go across the island for my weekly check-in at Two Harbors. Maybe you'd, ah, you'd like to come with me?"

Barbara raises her eyebrows and nods toward Lisa.

"Mom, you know, after lunch, I like to take a nap or watch TV. You go ahead. When you come back, we can, ya know, play miniature golf at that place next to the plaza."

Paul smiles to himself, impressed by how easily Lisa established her quid pro quo. "Meet me at the Explorer at one o'clock," he says and escorts them out of his office and through the reception area, acting businesslike and professional. But from the look on Hansen's face, he's sure the rumor mill has kicked into high gear.

At one o'clock, Saldano leaves the station and unlocks the Explorer for Barbara. He senses at least three sets of eyes staring at them from inside the Sheriff's Department. *What the hell,* he thinks. *It feels great to show off a beautiful girlfriend.* Barbara's dressed in her jeans and peasant blouse outfit. The women deputies gossiped about her when they thought Paul couldn't hear: "God, I wish I could get my hair to grow that long without split ends." But mostly, they talked about where Barbara's from and what nationality she is. They decide that she's either Middle-eastern, Eurasian, or from South America, maybe Brazil.

The whine from the Explorer straining in second gear up Stagecoach Road makes conversation impossible. But once on top, Saldano muscles the heavy SUV along the ridge road, stops on the shoulder, and cuts the engine.

"Be careful getting out," he tells Barbara, "and watch your footing."

"You're not kidding about this place," Barbara murmurs

and edges out the passenger side door.

He points out the clear patch downslope where he'd spotted the skeletal remains of the human arm and then the location where he'd recovered the dog tag. Strips of crime scene tape still tethered to the brush flutter in the wind.

"The female was shot in the back?" Barbara asks.

Paul nods and studies the hillside below as if answers might magically appear out of the chaparral.

Barbara folds her arms across her chest and mutters just loud enough for Paul to hear. "She must have had her back to the sea, and somebody on a boat took her out. They would need a scoped rifle and squeeze off a remarkable shot. Or she faced the sea, and the shooter crouched behind her on the hill…a clear shot but still tricky with the wind.

"Jesus, how do you know so much about shooting? I'll have to pay you as a consultant pretty soon," Paul jokes.

"My ex was a gun freak…used to take me shooting in the back woods with his high-powered rifles. But when Lisa was born, I told him I didn't want any guns in the house." Her voice turns hard. "I couldn't have him cleaning the bloody things in our living room with a baby sleeping nearby."

Saldano frowns. "My ex-wife wouldn't let me bring my service pistol into the house. I had a locker in the garage where I stored it."

"She sounds like a sensible woman," Barbara says, and grins.

"Yeah, she was...about some things," Paul mutters. "I'll check that hill and ridgeline with a metal detector. Maybe our shooter got sloppy and forgot to police his brass. But in seventy years…I'm not holding my breath."

They talk more about possible sites for a shooter to hide and agree that the grove of stunted live oak trees near the crest of the mountain would be the best place, although it's more than two hundred yards from the road.

Back in the Explorer, they bounce along the barely paved road to the airport, then turn south across Catalina's seaward slopes and snake their way along a ridgeline before dropping into Little Harbor. The sheltered cove with its rocky shoreline, picturesque emerald water, and palm-thatched lean-tos is deserted, odd for Paul, who remembers many cell phone calls during the summer months, begging for the cops to come out and break up a beach party gone sour.

Traveling west and inland again, Saldano rockets along Little Harbor Road until yanking the wheel to the right and turning onto a barely discernable track that cuts upslope across sage-covered hills and climbs to the crest of a high knoll. From on top, they can see the ocean on both sides of Catalina. Paul pulls the Explorer over and shuts off the engine.

"So this is what you do with your women," Barbara says, chuckling, "bring them out in the middle of nowhere and have your way with them."

Paul laughs and takes her hand. "Catalina's women are safe from me, not necessarily my choosing."

They sit quietly for a few minutes, enjoying the grandeur of white-capped seas. The insistent onshore wind buffets the car, rocking it on its springs. Barbara unclips her seatbelt and slides next to Paul, kissing him on the mouth, softly at first but with growing passion. Paul fumbles with his seatbelt and gets his left arm ensnared in the shoulder strap.

"Never did do well in cars," he says, chuckling.

"Especially not this one." Barbara eyes the rear of the Explorer with the back seat filled with emergency gear and the far back area caged with heavy wire mesh. "And it's too cold outside. It's like bloody Scotland out there." She kisses Paul lightly before sliding back into her seat. "We'd better go, or those people at Two Harbors will send out a search party for you. And besides, some things aren't meant to be done quickly."

Ah, man, this is as bad as a hot date in high school, Paul thinks…*ready for action with no place to go.* He twists the keys, the engine races before he lets in the clutch. They slowly descend the ridgeline overlooking Empire Landing and motor toward the Isthmus or Two Harbors, as the *west enders* call it. The village is a disorganized collection of cabins, small cottages, and a restaurant and bar bordering a rocky beach lined with palms.

They drive along red clay streets while Paul points out the two harbors, one on each side of the island, separated by a narrow neck of land less than a quarter mile wide. "The bigger boats tie up in Catalina Harbor on the seaward side, but most pleasure crafters moor in Isthmus Cove and camp on the beach or onboard. This place really rock-and-rolls during the summer."

They pass by a deserted cluster of bungalows and pull up outside the Harbor Reef Saloon.

"I'll check in with Al and be right back."

"Like hell," Barbara says. "I didn't ride all this way to wait in the car." She bounds from the SUV and strides onto the building's long veranda before Paul can say anything. He hurries to catch up.

The two o'clock boat from San Pedro clears Ship Rock, noses into the cove, and sounds its horn. A few cottage doors pop open and sleepy occupants venture out into the afternoon sunlight, heading toward the pier to check on mainland deliveries or to gossip with the boat's crew. The ferry's arrival reminds Saldano of the Wild West, how folks must have felt when a dust-encrusted stagecoach rolled into town, connecting them somehow to a larger world.

Paul and Barbara pause to watch the ferry dock before turning inside and passing through an empty dining room to the saloon tucked away in the back. In the narrow train car-shaped room, a bar with stools extends along one wall while tables and chairs crowd the opposite. A huge painting of a Polynesian beauty, naked, with her hands coyly arranged to cover important details, hangs behind the bar. Barbara laughs when she sees it, but only for a moment. She digs Saldano in the ribs and motions to the bartender hunched over the counter, reading a thick dog-eared book and smoking a cigarillo.

"So this is Al?" Barbara asks Paul, smirking.

"Yes…er, Barbara, I'd like you to meet Alice Carter, proud owner of the Harbor Reef Saloon."

Alice looks up from her book and extends a man-sized hand to engulf Barbara's. "Any friend of Paul's…glad to meet you."

"Please to meet you," Barbara murmurs.

"So the Sergeant has finally found himself a lady. But go easy on the poor bastard, Barb. Livin' on this island can shrink your sense of self-worth, warp your core values, and drive you into a state of psychiatric entropy."

Barbara's smooth forehead wrinkles.

"You'd better explain yourself," Paul says.

"Oh, yeah. Sorry about the psychobabble. I own this joint, but I'm studying psychology at Long Beach State. I'd be coming in on that boat right now if I hadn't racked up my knee.

Barbara peeks over the counter to check out the complicated-looking knee brace that Alice has wrapped around her right leg. "Looks nasty. How did it happen?"

"I was kicking some drunk's ass when his friend thought he'd try helpin'. It wasn't nothin' I couldn't handle."

Barbara eyes the towering Nordic blond woman and grins. "You sound like a woman I should know."

"How long you gonna be on island?"

"I go back on the eight o'clock express tomorrow night."

"Well, before you go, at least get the good Sergeant to buy you one of my Buffalo Milks. It'll calm your stomach for the trip across island."

She sets bottles of kahlua, vodka, crème de cacao and crème de banana on the counter. Paul laughs. "Hold on, Alice. I'd like Barbara to stay conscious for the rest of the trip."

"I'll bet you do."

"Yeah, yeah, just tell me what's been going on around here. Anything I should know about that Deputy Randolph hasn't bored me with?" Paul tries to shift the conversation to a safer topic.

Alice sighs. "On Tuesday, a new crop of grad students came out on the noon boat. They're interning at the Science Center and more or less behaving themselves...although the frat boys think they're God's gift to women. Last night, I had to remind a couple that they're not ...nothing rough, but let's just say I practiced being assertive.

"There's a work crew at Cherry Cove fixing up the campgrounds. I'm not sure what's the rush since the season doesn't start for months. The Coast Guard hauled a ninety-foot trawler into Cat Harbor with a broken steering gear. The crew hung around for a couple of days until the parts came in. But other than the daily boats, not much traffic.

"I keep checking on Angela. She's pretty good about taking her meds, but I'm not sure for how much longer. I'm gonna set her up here at night to keep my eye on her...it'll be quiet enough until New Year's, and she likes the big screen TV. And my final divorce papers came through, so I'm a free and available woman." Alice stares at Paul and grins.

Paul and Alice talk more about the meager village life, and Paul asks about any suspicious boats or off-season campers. The year before, some Asians had moored a powerboat west of Fourth of July Cove and rendezvoused mid-channel with inbound tramp freighters. They'd scored enough black tar heroin and hashish to supply the Southland for at least a day or two and had only been caught after a long chase by the Coast Guard. Ever since then, Frank insists that the Department send its watch commander to Two Harbors at least twice a week during the off-season.

"Yeah, Frank tells me people would slip on and off this island without anybody noticing," Paul continues. "There are stories about the original West Coast mob bosses from Sicily, coming ashore at Little Harbor and taking the ferry to the mainland. Nobody checked for papers back then."

Leaving the saloon, Barbara slips an arm through Paul's, and they walk through a grove of palms to the pier. Paul talks with the ferry's first mate about who came across the channel and who's going up island…mostly Avalon residents and a few winter tourists taking the slow boat to the east end. A blast from the boat's air horn signals its departure.

"If you want, you can take the ferry back to Avalon…it's a beautiful trip by sea," Paul offers.

Barbara laughs and squeezes his arm. "That's the second time you've tried to ditch me. I'm starting to think you have more girlfriends hidden out here somewhere."

The mate grins and heaves a three-inch thick hawser at Paul as the boat backs out into the cove. They watch it disappear around Blue Cavern Point before returning to the Explorer and heading east.

"So what's this about a marine science center at Two Harbors?" Barbara asks, her voice calm and casual.

"Oh yeah. The University of Southern California maintains quite a laboratory setup: classrooms, research stations, the works…mostly graduate study stuff, but they also bring undergrads out here to spend a week diving the Isthmus."

Paul glances sideways at Barbara as they bounce along Little Harbor Road. She seems content to stare out across the landscape, admiring the jagged peaks along the island's central spine. They remain quiet all the way back to Avalon.

CHAPTER 19

A black book lay at the bottom of George DeVaul's desk drawer. It looked something like a pocket-sized Bible but was much too dog-eared to be one unless George sidelined as an ordained minister, which he didn't. In fact, George hadn't been to church for years. He spent most Sunday mornings at the Bank going over accounts.

He sat at his desk with coat off, tie loosened, shirtsleeves rolled up to expose dark-haired arms and boyhood tattoos. He yanked open the drawer and retrieved the book, a bottle of twenty-year-old bourbon, and a square-cut glass. Pouring himself two fingers worth, he leaned back and thumbed through the pages, jotting down names and numbers. Five telephone calls yielded three names he could work with. By the eighth call he'd made an appointment to meet with a Jorge Valenzuela at the DeVaul estate on the following Tuesday afternoon. *The old man should be happy that I found a replacement for Jose,* George thought, *not that he'd ever thank me.*

George took a gulp from his glass and studied the book before copying two more names and telephone numbers. He leaned back in his oak chair to think. His eyes scanned a framed photograph on the wall of George and his father and brother on safari two years previous. They stood over a downed bull Wildebeest somewhere on the Serengeti with the guides, gun bearers, and porters crowded around. George returned to the book and found one more number. On the seventh ring, a deep-voiced man answered.

"Yeah?"

"Hello, this is George DeVaul. Do you remember me?"

"Yeah, I remember," the man said flatly. "What da ya need."

"I don't want to talk about it over the phone. Can we meet somewhere in, say, an hour? How about the Santa Monica Pier?"

"I'll find you there," the man said and hung up. George poured himself another drink and tossed it off with a twist of his fleshy face. Scooping the Lincoln's keys off the desk, he slipped on his suit coat and exited a side door into the rear alley. As a boy, his father had instructed him to back the car into the alley with its nose pointing outward, in case a quick getaway was necessary. During the early 1930s, East Coast bootleggers had invaded Southern California and tried to muscle in on the banking business as fronts for their booze and prostitution operations. All that was now an imperfect memory. But George hadn't lost the habit of planning for the unexpected.

Sliding onto the leather seat of his '41 Darien Blue Lincoln coupe, George reached across and unlocked the glove compartment. He grabbed a chrome pistol with a pearl handle, its cold metal heavy in his hands. He chambered a round, slid the gun into an inside coat pocket, turned the ignition key, and stabbed at the starter button. The car roared to life. He motored out of the city, picking up Venice Boulevard that took him to the coast, then drove north along the shoreline to the pier. The warm winter morning brought out beach goers and heavy traffic. George maneuvered the Lincoln into a stall north of the pier and climbed out slowly. Schools of families with children flowed around him on the sidewalk, dressed for the water. They made him feel out of place in his double-breasted jacket. George unbuttoned his coat and let it hang open. The hard winter sun burned his face, and he pulled his hat brim down. He moved toward the pier ramp and walked across its rough planks with the shimmering sea flowing beneath him.

Mexican fisherman occupied sections of the pier's railing, their lines dropped into the green water. They sat on campstools next to pewter-colored buckets full of mackerel, lingcod, and occasional sea bass, talking amongst themselves in Spanish. George found a clear spot near the pier's end and stared south along the crescent of white sand to the string of tiny beach towns and the Palos Verdes Peninsula. His father had brought them here on Sunday outings, back before his mother started drinking. The old man would talk to George about how the Southern California coast would be one great city someday, with millions to be made in real estate. He was right, of course. But George couldn't help feeling jealous of his kid brother, allowed to run free on the sand below and dodge the incoming surf while the father instructed George on how his future would unfold. The old man had been right about that, too, although George's elopement and marriage to Sarah, a former nightclub hostess at the Hotel Hunt, had brought him down a notch, creating a detour in his plans for George's ascendance to the banking throne.

As he gazed southward, a brown pelican folded its wings tight against its body, extended its beak, and plummeted into the Pacific. The bird bobbed to the surface with a full gullet. George felt a slight pressure at his left elbow. Startled, he reached for his pistol but relaxed when he saw who it was.

The man seemed too short to have such a deep voice, dressed in a rumpled brown suit and dirty white shirt without cuff links. Watery blue eyes stared out from beneath a battered Fedora. The two men gazed southward without acknowledging each other, hands clasped, elbows leaning on the pier railing. After a few minutes, the newcomer broke the silence.

"So, what's your problem this time?"

"It's my brother. I need some information."

"If you want information, go to the library," the man said, his voice unhurried. "What do you really want?"

"Stanley's in the Army on Catalina, and he's got a Mexican girlfriend."

"So he's banging some broad, what's the problem? She after the family jewels? Has our boy got her knocked up?" Mr. Brown Suit chuckled.

George looked sideways at him with contempt. "Not yet, but we need to make sure that doesn't happen."

"So, how permanent a fix do you want?"

"Make it go away. I don't want to know the details."

"Money talks. Three thousand, and it'll be fixed."

"Fifteen hundred, and you'll have our family's undying gratitude," George said.

"Two thousand, and I'll stop by the bank on Wednesday. Have the money in small bills, nothing new, and no sequential serial numbers."

"Are you crazy? I'll meet you back here on Wednesday night at eight. One thousand up front, the second when our problem is solved."

Mr. Brown Suit nodded and moved off without another word. George's hands trembled. He wiped his face with a handkerchief. Seagulls circled overhead and shadowed the pelicans, waiting for their chance to steal their catch. George studied them intently until his heart stopped racing, and he felt calm enough to walk back to the car.

Driving home, George meditated on the money end of the deal. It would take him a day or two to assemble the cash from one or more of the Bank's contingency accounts. But he also daydreamed about his skinny, anemic brother lying naked on top of a sleek brown girl with pouting lips, a pushed-out chest, her legs spread wide, and hips pumping. A surge of lustful jealousy washed over him and he narrowly missed hitting a hulking oak at a bend in the canyon road.

He pulled into their Culver City driveway. Sarah looked up from her seat on the veranda, surprised to see him home so soon from his Sunday accountings. His hands fumbled with the car door handle. He slipped from the Lincoln and carefully walked toward the house, staring at her in a way that she hadn't seen for years, from that long ago time before the miscarriage and news from Dr. Bertram. When he approached, Sarah closed her book and advanced to meet him, adjusting her simple housedress to show more of her still-graceful body. They went inside, closing the door tightly, and without speaking, moved to the bedroom. She couldn't decide whether George's lust was born of anger or of love. But as they collapsed into the rumpled bedclothes afterwards and lay quietly side-by-side, Sarah didn't care, knowing that it could be a long time before she felt him again.

She smiled at his snoring, slipped quietly out of bed, and moved toward the bathroom. On her way, she gathered up his clothes from the floor. The suit coat's heaviness surprised her. She explored its pockets and found the silver pistol. A frown creased her forehead, and she thought about waking her husband and demanding an explanation. But the tingling in her loins told her that now was not the time to be critical or inquisitive. By the time she finished her bath and toilette, the pistol's existence had slipped to the back of her memory.

She returned to reading on the veranda and was there when the neighbors arrived from a late morning church service, dressed in their Sunday best. Sarah felt deliciously sinful.

CHAPTER 20

Rick DeBlough's body was a faded portrait of all his faults, though few people had ever taken an inventory. His low-life friends saw his yellow nicotine-stained fingers, blue-purple patches of folded skin under each eye, a pockmarked face, and a developing paunch. Rick kept everything else hidden under cheap Brooks Brothers suits. But on those rare occasions when he lay with a woman, and only after making the requisite payment, the pink lips of scars under his rib cage and violet-rimmed punctures above his collarbone bore testament to his less than genteel life growing up in Baton Rouge.

At eighteen, Rick left Louisiana and came west. After years of working the rackets, he'd gotten handy with a jackknife and preferred it to guns. He kept it in a front trouser pocket, his soft, fleshy hand resting comfortably on it. But as the depression worsened, he'd bought a .38 Smith and Wesson and wore a shoulder holster under his trademark brown suits.

In the late 1930s, DeVaul Senior hired Rick to deal with the Scarlotti brothers, two wop punks trying to extort the bank for protection money. Rick shot them, stuffed their bodies in the trunk of his LaSalle, and dumped them in the hills east of Ojai, where the coyotes had them for lunch. After that, Rick became an occasional well-paid employee of the DeVaul family.

But this new assignment from George would be tricky. *I hate workin' with anybody on a job,* Rick thought...*could lose money on the deal...and those bastards could swindle me. But two grand is not bad.*

Before dawn on a blustery Monday morning, Rick parked

his car at the San Pedro docks, retrieved a slender leather case from the trunk, and walked down the ramp to a row of fishing boats and skiffs. The boat owners and crews huddled in clumps along the bucking gangway, sipped steaming coffee from mugs, and stared at the white-capped sea.

"Any of you fellas goin' anywhere near Catalina?" Rick announced.

A smooth-faced kid dressed in a P-coat and denims motioned him over. "My pop's boat is goin' out if this wind lets up. But the Coast Guard won' let us put in there, not since the war."

"I have a hankering to hunt those island wild boar and thought maybe…maybe you could drop me someplace." Rick shivered, his scratchy woolen Mackinaw barely keeping out the cold.

"Have to talk to the skipper if ya wanna go anywhere with us." The kid motioned to a stocky man with a salt-and-pepper beard in the wheelhouse of the *Sailor's Dream,* a seventy-footer rigged for yellowtail and albacore.

Rick climbed over the gunwale, picked his way across the cluttered deck, and banged on the cabin window. The boat owner turned and slid the door open.

"I was telling your kid that I'd like to get onto Catalina somehow," Rick said, slinging the carrying case strap over his shoulder.

"Too damn windy…and the Coast Guard will stop us if we try putting in at Avalon or the Isthmus." The old guy started to close the door.

"What about someplace where nobody's watchin'?"

The skipper grinned. "You'd have to go in through the surf."

"What about a raft or a dinghy?"

"Yeah, I suppose we could fix you up, but that's gonna

cost extra, and it's already a hundred for going out." The old man's smile broadened.

"Jesus, and I thought *I* was a crook." Rick glared at the skipper, mentally calculating his reduction in pay.

"Look, mister, if we get boarded and they catch you with that pea shooter, it'll be the hoosegow for you, and I'll lose my license."

"Yeah, yeah, just tell me how much."

"Two hundred, and we'll drop you at Moonstone Beach."

"Where the hell is that?"

"It's about five miles up coast from Avalon, far enough away that the patrols are easy to dodge. But if Avalon's where you want to go, you'll have one hell of a hike up canyon to the ridge road...and you don't look like the outdoor type." The old man chuckled.

"Don't worry about that. What about picking me up?"

"I could swing by in three days, say a couple hours after dawn. If you're there, we'll take you. If not, you're on your own... and the return will cost an extra hundred." The skipper held out his callused hand, palm up.

Rick counted out a stack of faded 20s, using his body to shield the transaction from the nosy crew who'd been mumbling into their coffee during this entire exchange.

As if by magic, the storm flags at the end of the dock went limp, filled again for a few brief flutters, then went limp again. The fishermen boarded their boats for the morning channel run, and the old man told Rick to wait in the boathouse while he went outside to instruct his crew. They eyed Rick suspiciously but went about their chores, casting off and working the nets.

The *Sailor's Dream* and a flotilla of others steered toward the harbor mouth and the gray shadow of Catalina on the horizon. Their boat moved against the incoming swells, smacked into each green roller, and took on white water over her bow.

The crew scarcely noticed the water running across the aft deck. They tended the nets and the rigging. The skipper kept the boat pointed at a particular notch in the side of the island with the throttle wide open. Catalina grew larger gradually and gained detail as they approached its chaparral-carpeted hillsides.

In two hours, the *Dream* stood off a small rocky beach at the back of a deep-cut cove. Toyon grew right down to the waterline. Six-foot swells rolled onshore, a distant thunder as they dragged bottom and pounded the black gravel beach. What looked like a goat trail extended up a near-vertical mountain face and disappeared toward the fog-shrouded ridgeline.

"Now it's your turn to play sailor." The skipper smiled.

"Don't worry about me. Have your damn boat back here on time." Rick shouldered his case and went on deck. The shaded cove made him shiver.

The crew unlashed a cork and canvas raft from the side of the wheelhouse and tossed it overboard. They tethered its rope to the rail. Rick gingerly lowered himself over the side into the bobbing raft, trying to keep it steady with his feet. The captain handed down a wooden paddle and set him loose.

"In three days, be here," he yelled to Rick, then disappeared.

The *Dream's* engine roared, and the boat swung toward the mainland, creating a huge wake that pushed the raft toward the beach. Rick scrambled to sit down and paddle. He'd never learned to steer a boat or to swim.

He saw how steep the black beach slanted away from the surf line. *I'll let the waves take me in,* he thought, *step off this raft without getting' ma feet wet.* A swell raised the raft up and took it to the edge of the shore break, then dropped it into a trough that exposed the sea bottom. Rick didn't notice the next wave cresting early. A shadow fell across the raft. He turned to face the descending curl. It turned his world upside down and filled it with frothy foam and brown, stinging saltwater. Like a rag inside a churning washing machine, Rick struggled to free himself. He grasped the talisman jackknife in his trouser pocket as the thundering undertow compressed what little air was left from his three-packs-a-day lungs.

CHAPTER 21

Driving Highway 101 through Ventura, Barbara calls to Lisa, "How'd you like your island holiday?"

She gets no response. The clogged Southern California freeways and traffic jams near the airport have worn her daughter out. She's asleep in the back seat. *I'll let her rest until we reach San Luis Obispo,* Barbara thinks, *break for lunch, and fill this wheezing beast with oil. This is probably the Subaru's last long trip.* Barbara frets about making it home, about money to buy a replacement, and about a hundred other things doing laps in her brain.

During the hours of noisy freeway driving, she relives the long weekend, memories that both excite and depress her. She forces herself not to think about reporting to Major Selser in the morning, dressed in a pressed green uniform. Paul's kisses, his strong embrace, the scent of bay rum, and the moving things he's told her all steer Barbara toward the edge of heartache. She forces herself to think about the China Wall case and the progress they've made.

The afternoon following their trip to the Isthmus, Paul and Barbara had driven out to Pebbly Beach in search of Felipe. They stashed the Sheriff Department's golf cart in the parking lot of the Buffalo Nickel Café, walked along Pebbly Beach Road, then turned into the box canyon that houses the aging Mexican barrio. Mongrel dogs howl from the porches of cabins and Quonset huts bordering the dead-end street. Old brown people work in their gardens and pause to watch the two approach…Paul in his squeaky-clean uniform and Barbara lithe as ever in a knee-length dress.

"Excuse me, señora. Can you tell me where Felipe lives?" Paul asks in Spanish. The old woman weeds a lush vegetable garden. She pushes back her straw hat and swipes at the stray gray hairs with a gloved hand. Snapping black eyes peer up at him.

"Allá, allá," she says and points to a Quonset hut, its curved metal roof supporting a dozen or more cats, each guarding a patch of filtered sunlight. Across a decaying porch, a screen door hangs open on one hinge next to the gaping black entry. Paul tests his weight on the rotting floorboards and raps on the door jam. A mumbling television's light casts ever-changing shadows on the hut's interior. Clothing, old newspapers, and destroyed furniture litter the front room. Paul edges inside with Barbara behind him, moving in a synchronized step.

"This place smells like the produce section of my uncle's grocery," Saldano mutters, then sneezes loudly. There's a sharp click as the bolt of a rifle slams a round into its chamber. Paul yanks the pistol from his waist holster and drops to one knee. Barbara is silhouetted in the doorway.

"Get back," Paul orders, and she vanishes.

"What do you *pendejos* want?" comes out of the darkness, the voice in garbled Spanish.

"It's me, Sergeant Saldano. You remember…from the La Mesa Club meeting?"

"No. I don't know you…and who was that witch at my door?"

"That was no witch. That was *mi amiga,*" Paul says and laughs. He stands, clicks on the safety, and slides his 9-mm into its holster, affixing the strap.

A round-shouldered figure emerges from the gloom and pushes past Paul to the doorway. *"Lo siento, señorita.* I didn't mean to scare you."

Barbara stands in the front yard with hands on hips. She looks ready to kick the old man's ass around the block. Felipe ejects a round from the rifle's chamber and leans it against the outside porch wall. Motioning both of them to follow, he leads them down a narrow side yard to the rear of the hut that shields a neatly swept patio, outdoor bar-be-que, and a whining black Labrador pup with dangling pink tongue and wagging tail. The dog guards a pride of kittens that hide behind its haunches and stare uncertainly at the intruders.

"Sit, please sit," Felipe says, motioning to newly-painted deck chairs. He disappears into a tool shed and returns, holding three long-necked bottles of cold Pacifica beer. He pulls his chair close to Barbara's, then pushes a beer bottle toward each of them.

"*Lo Siento, señor*. I no longer drink," Paul says. "And *mi amiga* only sips wine."

"*No importa*." Felipe grins. "And it is I who should apologize. I really don't remember meeting you, but I drink too much at those meetings." Felipe takes a long draw off his beer, making Barbara smile for the first time.

"It's okay, but go easy with that rifle. Don't give me a reason to lock you up." Paul settles back into the patio's cool shadows and listens to the eucalyptus trees tossing overhead in the afternoon wind.

"That rifle…it's an old one," Barbara says, "a Mark III Enfield made by the British before World War I."

Felipe stares at her in amazement. "Yes, yes, you are right, señorita. It hasn't been fired for many years. In its day, a good shooter could hit a target at a thousand yards with open sights if the wind was down."

"Are you a good shooter, Felipe?" Paul asks quietly.

The old man takes a deep swallow of beer and stares at the sergeant, fingering his salt-and-pepper goatee. "No, señor, not me. I never had the chance to practice, and by the time that rifle became mine, I had no interest in it. During the war, enough things got shot up, including half the sons that never returned to this barrio. I keep it to shoot snakes and rats…to keep doctors away with their damn needles."

"Do you remember who owned the gun before you?" Barbara asks.

The old man pretends that he doesn't hear the question. He struggles out of his chair and moves toward the tool shed to dispose of his empty bottle. When Felipe opens the shed's door, they get a good look inside. A drawing of a young woman hangs from a top shelf in the shadow of the roof. She lays across a couch with the sheen from her long hair perfectly captured in what looks like charcoal or some type of pencil. Barbara moves close and inspects the artwork, its paper badly yellowed with cracked edges. But the figure looks alive. The faint initials "S.H.D." are printed along its bottom fringe.

"Who is this woman?" Barbara asks. "She is so beautiful."

Felipe fumbles with the lid of a garbage can half full of empty beer bottles. "She…she was someone I knew *muchos años* ago. I was young, and she didn't know I existed."

Felipe slams the shed door and returns to his chair. They sit without speaking and listen to the trees clatter in the freshening breeze.

Paul tries the direct approach. "I'm trying to identify a girl from the barrio that disappeared in 1945. We think she was a friend of a rich gringo GI. Do you remember anything about that time?"

Felipe empties half of his second beer before answering. "No, señor, I can't remember anything special. I was a young man, and girls disappeared all the time. The families wouldn't talk about it, and it was impolite to ask."

Saldano nods. "Are you sure? Conrad Gomez says you've been around the longest and are the most knowledgeable."

"That fool Gomez doesn't know his ass from a…."

The old man finishes the second beer and opens the third.

"*Muchas gracias* for your time, Señor," Paul says, "and keep that rifle unloaded if you want to keep it."

He and Barbara stand and walk slowly down the entry road, leaving Felipe drowsing in the afternoon wind.

"Did you notice the initials on that drawing?" Barbara asks as they climb into the golf cart. Paul shakes his head, stomps on the starter, and motors up Mount Ada Road.

"The artist initialed it 'S.H.D.' Barbara grins as Paul brings the golf cart to a screeching halt at a turnout overlooking Pebbly Beach.

"Too much of a coincidence…but could our man Stanley have been an artist?"

"If he was, he was a well-trained one. That's a professional-quality sketch, definitely executed in an Anglo style. Mexican art is less realistic and more romantic."

Paul laughs. "Now you're going to tell me you're an art history buff, too. But that may be a link. If we can find out if Stanley attended a West Coast art school, we could get lucky. I'd have a reason to lean on Felipe for more information."

Barbara's eyes sparkle with excitement. Paul cranks up the golf cart and continues uphill. She reaches over and places a hand on his thigh. He jumps, stomping on the accelerator in the process. She laughs but doesn't remove her hand. They near the top of the ridgeline.

Barbara leans over and speaks into Paul's ear. "Where does that go?" She points to a dirt track that cuts off to the left.

"Back to an old silver mine, abandoned in the early '50s."

"Let's take a look."

Paul yanks the tiny steering wheel hard to the left, and they bounce uphill around the shoulder of a ridgeline into a deep box canyon. They don't travel far before coming to a locked gate installed by the Island Conservancy to keep tourists out of the backcountry. Paul jumps out, uses his master key to unlock the gate, and they push forward. The brow of the hill protects the canyon from onshore winds. Barbara removes her cardigan, showing off the upper part of the low-cut dress. Her breasts are smoky tan. Paul struggles to steer the cart around major washouts and ruts in the dirt tract.

They reach the end of the road at the gaping entrance to an old mineshaft. Paul kills the engine, its final mutterings echo into the filtered darkness. The back canyon swelters and smells of sage and coyote brush.

"They mined silver here when the Bannings owned the island," Paul explains. "It's supposed to be boarded up. But kids use it as their tunnel of love, and the barriers never stay up long."

Barbara steps down from the cart and walks slowly into the mine's mouth. Paul follows nervously. She continues into the blackness to a point where sunlight barely illuminates her skin. Turning, she reaches for him, and they kiss. He can feel the fluttering of her body in his arms. They gaze into each other's eyes.

"Please," she says.

She reaches behind her neck, unclasps the dress, and slides it over her head, tossing it onto a pile of serpentine boulders. Her underclothes are plain and barely cover her ample figure. Paul reaches forward and unclasps her bra, and Barbara struggles out of it and casts it aside. Her large breasts sway gently, and Paul grasps them in both hands, fingering the nipples that are already taut and extended. Barbara groans as he squeezes them, and their lips lock again in a more frantic kiss.

Paul backs away and undresses, struggling with the shorts to stretch them over his erection. Barbara stares at its size and wonders if she will be right for him. She slides her panties down her legs and deposits them with the rest of her clothes. They stand nude, facing each other in the mineshaft's cool draft. It reminds her of how naughty she felt as a young girl, wandering naked into a desolate section of the Ad Dahna desert, far from anyone's eyes, feeling free for the first time.

They embrace. Slowly Paul's kisses leave her lips and take a descending route. Barbara struggles to stay upright, gasping. His lips suck her nipples. Her groans echo down the mineshaft like some forlorn ghost of lovers past. His descent crosses her quivering, flat belly until he reaches the clitoral entrance. She squeals when Paul's hot tongue enters her, and Barbara feels close to climax. Warm, smooth fingers slide inside her and move rhythmically in and out until her moans are a constant harmonic resonance in the cool air.

She pulls Paul upward and drops to her knees, takes his penis into her mouth, and encircles it with her tongue. Paul sounds off in a high-pitched call like the dancing Arab women in her father's village. But he pushes her back. They stand breathing hard and staring. Barbara moves to one of the mineshaft's support posts and bending over, her back to Paul, grasps it, legs spread, her long mane of untied hair covering her back like a shawl. Nothing happens, and she looks over her shoulder to find Paul admiring her body. Then he enters her, and with each slow rotating thrust, her body sings with love's electricity. The climax comes quickly for both, leaving them laughing at their excesses. But they manage to recover enough to explore the few love positions that don't involve lying down.

When they emerge from the mineshaft, spent and barely able to walk, the sun has dipped below the ridgeline. Avalon Bay is dark and moody, and the town's lights along the harbor glow in the dusk. Traveling downhill and through the gate, they encounter a pickup full of teenagers that's turned off the main road. Paul waves them over.

"You kids, this road and the mine are off limits," he says

in a stern policeman's voice. "Just turn around here."

Barbara covers her mouth and laughs at the hypocrisy of it all.

"Mom, why are you smiling like that?" Lisa calls from the back seat of the buzzing Subaru.

They've reached San Luis Obispo. Barbara's glad that she can ignore her daughter's question and focus on more mundane things, like finding lunch, gassing and oiling the car, and on more delicious daydreams on the long drive home.

CHAPTER 22

They sat together in the empty officers' mess hall at the Saint Catherine Hotel, contemplating their breakfast of powdered eggs, toast, and stiff blobs of oatmeal.

"Did yah hear what happened last night?" PFC Briggs yawns.

Stanley DeVaul smiled, "Nope, had other things on my mind." He took a long gulp from his mug.

"The Coast Guard found a body floating in the surf off Moonstone Beach." Briggs stabbed at a sugarcoated mound of oatmeal with a large spoon.

"Was he a mariner?" Stan asked, still not awake enough to feign interest easily.

"I don' know. The boson's mate said the body was dressed in civilian clothes, and they picked up a rifle and raft on the beach. Could be some kind of spy. Just thought you'd like to see this guy. You artists like to draw people, right?"

"Well, yes, but we'd prefer them to be alive."

"You might like this stiff. He's got more tattoos on his ugly body than bare skin. They've got him laid out in the cooler waiting for the County Coroner."

"All this excitement, and I slept right through it." Stan attempted a smile and resumed reading a week-old edition of the Los Angeles Times.

"So you've been getting a lot of sleep lately?" Briggs grinned at Stanley and got up to leave, having abandoned any further attempt at excavating the oatmeal.

"Ah, to sleep, perchance to dream – Aye, there's the rub,"

Stan called after Briggs in his best Shakespearean voice. The private disappeared upstairs for another hard day of boredom.

The empty mess hall popped and wheezed in the cool morning air. The kitchen crew had already cleared away the steam tables and stowed the leftovers. Finishing his coffee with a grimace, Stan bussed his tray and moved toward the main entrance of what had been the hotel's grand dining room.

A decade before, he'd visited the Saint Catherine on a family outing and remembered its former grandeur. Red satin curtains still framed windows that overlooked the emerald blue bay. But the chandeliers hadn't been cleaned in years, grease smudges decorated the walls, and gone were the potted palms, the delicate crystal and china settings on snow-white tablecloths, and the checkered quarry tile floors, all casualties of the military occupation.

Remembering the great fun he and his fellow art students used to have drawing the cadavers at the San Francisco Morgue, Stanley retraced his steps and explored the hotel's rear kitchen with its meat lockers and cold rooms. The third heavy plated door he unlatched revealed the sought-after treasure…a short naked guy lying face up on a metal table, eyes open and body still in pretty good condition. Stanley noted the scars and body art. *This poor fellow must have spent a lot of time in bad tattoo parlors,* Stan thought. He mentally rearranged the crude drawings to improve their clarity and composition.

As Stanley gazed at the dead man's parted purple lips and open eyes, the hair on the back of his neck stood on end. He knew this man from somewhere and tried to place that pockmarked mug…finally connecting it to a stubby figure hunched over a campfire somewhere in eastern Africa. This guy had been one of his father's paid associates, brought along on the safari for no apparent reason but always close at hand, wearing badly-fitting khakis and a shoulder holster filled with a dull black revolver.

Stanley's father had never told him anything about the man, but he appeared to know George, and they often had whispered conversations.

Hurrying upstairs to his room, Stan selected a clean linen sheet and a freshly sharpened box of pencils, yanked on a woolen jacket, and returned to the cooler. Concentrating so hard that his back teeth hurt from grinding, Stanley took only a few minutes to capture the dead man's facial likeness, its rugged topography, and, of course, the scars. But he stayed on, working hard to be accurate, noting the stippled purple under the man's eyes and the misalignment of the nose. Back in his room, he carefully folded the drawing, stuffed it into an envelope, and sat down to pen a short note.

14 October 1944

Dearest George:
It's been a long time since we corresponded. Hope you and Sarah are doing well and that Father isn't too demanding of your life.

Speaking of life or rather the opposite of it, yesterday, the Coast Guard fished a body out of Moonstone Bay, and the dead man looks familiar to me. I think he's that strange man that Father brought along on our last African safari years ago. I've enclosed a drawing. Is this the man I remember, and do you have any idea why he'd be trying to come ashore on Catalina? They say they found his rifle and raft washed up on the beach. Such a mystery, and it gives me the willies. Maybe you could let me know what you know.

I haven't told anybody here that I know anything because they think he might have been a spy of some sort. But the fellow I remember wasn't smart enough for that.

Anyway, sorry about the melodrama. Hope the banking business is keeping you out of trouble. Hope this damn war is over soon.

Your Brother,
Stanley

Stan signed the note, slipped it into the mail drop, then walked out into the rain-spattered morning with the wind making the island feel fresh and new. He wandered aimlessly as usual, but today preoccupied by thoughts of the dead guy. *Was there a connection between that creep and my father?* he thought. *Would George know anything? And why would anybody try to sneak onto Catalina during high winter seas, especially that guy?*

CHAPTER 23

Three weeks later, Stanley sat on a tile-covered bench outside of Bird Park, listening to the macaws, pink flamingos, and cockatiels cavort in their huge wire cage. The Wrigley family had constructed the aviary from the iron framework of an old hexagonal dancehall that graced Casino Point before the depression. Stanley spent afternoons in its soft shade, sketching the birds, whiling away the hours until Flavia got out of school.

The lovers limited their time together, especially since Laura refused to cover more of Flavia's night shifts for fear that Eduardo would accost her in the dark streets. So, while Flavia supposedly studied after school in the town's tiny library, she lay in Stanley's arms at their love nest, all the while watching the clock so she wouldn't be late for the evening shift. Her father had relaxed now that she came home when expected, and the few times he'd checked up on her, she'd been at the restaurant, serving the mariners in her friendly way, with that tall gringo artist nowhere in sight.

Stanley left Bird Park and hurried to their apartment. Barely inside the door, Flavia pounced, unbuckled his belt, and pulled his trousers down. She peeled off her blouse and skirt and sat naked on a hard wooden chair in the sunlit kitchenette with legs spread, inviting Stanley to kiss her love spot. For Stan, all thoughts of the dead man, Flavia's father, or anything else disappeared. He concentrated on pleasing her, and then she him as he sat on the chair with Flavia astride, rocking slowly and moaning in his ear.

They'd been making love for weeks, and Stanley wouldn't

let himself think it would ever end.

"I should wear something," Stan had once told Flavia, his face reddening.

She had looked at him strangely, then giggled. "I know a woman who will take care of everything if I get in trouble. Don't worry, my sweet. Besides, I want to feel all of you."

After making love, they talked about the town's happenings and how their lives would change after the war, which everybody thought would be over soon. Ramón had been promoted out of the back kitchen to assistant cook, replacing Leonardo, who'd been drafted. He worked alongside Jimmy, staring out at Flavia through the ordering window with his sad brown eyes. And Señor Burke had announced that he'd sold the restaurant to a mainland cousin and that everybody would keep their jobs. But the couples' conversation always returned to how they would disclose their love and marriage plans to their parents.

"My father will have none of it," Stanley said with great bravado. "I'm sure he'll disown me."

Flavia's face darkened. "Can you accept that if it happens?"

"Yes. I've never been a part of their world anyway. Although, God knows what I'll do to support us."

Stan kissed her deeply, which led to another tumble in the sheets that left them weak and sleepy. He felt their lovemaking somehow insulated him from the cold truth that lived across the channel in the Santa Monica Mountains.

Later at the restaurant, Flavia relaxed into the pace of work, flirted with the kitchen staff, and thought about tomorrow and making love with Stanley. They had both agreed that he'd stay clear of the Grotto to ease suspicions.

On a smoke break out back by the garbage cans, Laura begged Flavia to recount the details of the couple's plans...to disappear to Mexico so Stanley could study the revolutionary muralist Diego Rivera. But mostly Laura pestered Flavia about how Stanley treated his mistress, personal stuff that left Laura wishing her own husband wasn't a sailor and away from port so long.

"When we make love," Flavia said, "he can be so gentle or like a stallion taking a mare. Either way, my mind and body just…just shine. I feel excited and…."

"Yes, but you'd best be careful, Flavia," Laura warned. "I know you love Stanley, but he's rich and educated. Who knows what his family will do."

"I know, I know. But he's smart and will find a way to make his parents accept us. His mother sounds kind. But both of our fathers must have come from the same village…they'll like each other if they live through their first meeting."

"It's not just them, Flavia. What about the rest of the people here? You and I were not born to his…his class…and you are Mexican. Do you think any of your friends or kin will accept him?"

"Probably not. But in Mexico, we can live well, and the people in our village will accept him. Other American artists have done the same…and after a while, when the war is a far memory and the hard feelings have softened, we can return, and everything will be *muy simpatico*."

"Ah, Flavia, I know you're in love 'cause you make it sound so simple. Tell me more about how Stan…"

Their conversation continued, punctuated by bursts of bawdy laughter. The two young women returned to the restaurant, waited on the few remaining customers and helped Pepe clear the dining room and set up for the following day's breakfast.

On weekends, Flavia managed to meet Stanley between the lunch and dinner shifts for a quick hour of touching.

"You know things must change," Flavia warned.

"Yeah, I know…and pretty damn soon."

"I'll be graduating from school. My mother wants me to work at the Tremont Street tamale factory."

"Why there? Will you make more money?"

"No. But her friend Rosalia helps manage the place. She thinks I can learn the business and meet respectable Mexican men. She still distrusts the gringos at the restaurant…and… and you. They never say anything, but I know they're glad you haven't been seen around me."

"We must set a date for telling our parents."

"Ah, Stanley, can't we run away? It would be so much simpler."

"Yeah, but the Army will come after me, not to mention my father. The war's gonna end soon. If we can just hold out until then."

On a clear blue Monday morning, Stanley checked his mail slot and retrieved a single pastel envelope. His brother's perfect handwriting covered its face. He ripped it open and read:

October 25,1944

Dearest Stanley:

Your letter was a very strange surprise indeed. I don't hear from you for years and then I receive a perfect portrait of a dead man in the morning post. Sarah opened the letter before I returned home from the bank, and it upset her terribly. We both remember the man from that African safari we all were on – I think it was the summer between your freshman and sophomore year at Berkeley. Father had hired him on as a bodyguard. But I haven't seen him since, and to be honest, I'm surprised that he lived as long as he did – quite the character. I've mentioned the incident to Father who knows no more than I.

But enough about dead men. Father tells me that you've been painting up a storm on the island. I'd love to see some of your recent work – from what I hear about Catalina, there's a lot more color there than in Mother's rose garden.

I happen to know the Provost Marshal at Wilmington, an old banking customer, and he says he can bring me over as a banking consultant. I've already made the arrangements and should arrive on the SS Avalon on Thursday, November 2nd. Hope you don't mind my intrusion, but you're my only brother, and it's time we became closer. Be looking for you.

Regards,
George

George would arrive in three days. Stanley re-read the letter and tried to decipher its coded meaning. *He never cared one tinker's damn about my art,* Stan thought. *He got jealous when Sarah said she liked my floral pieces. Yeah, I can see him taking the steamer out here, heaving his guts out the entire trip. The pieces don't fit. I know Father sent George to spy on me. But why? And Flavia…*his heart turned cold. *Christ, maybe they already know.* Stanley returned to his room to devise a plan for George's welcome and to make sure Flavia stayed out of sight.

CHAPTER 24

Sergeant Saldano has it bad. Barbara's been gone two weeks, and every night after work, he phones her to discuss the case…that's the pretext. Afterwards, he lies in bed and studies the pattern of water stains on his apartment's ceiling. He feels her supple body softly collide with his and wakes to find himself hugging a pillow, aroused beyond belief. Paul knows that he's got to make the next move. He wrestles with ideas for how they can be together. Across the channel, in Los Angeles's galaxy of twinkling lights, thousands face the same desires. For the first time, Paul regrets that he lives on an island with so much water in the way.

Four hundred miles north, in a fourth-floor walkup perched over San Francisco's Mission District, Barbara and Lisa lounge on a ratty sofa, read magazines, and make fun of the fashion models in their underwear ads. Barbara announces the time and hustles her daughter off to bed. Afterwards, she pours a glass of Zinfandel, sips the purple elixir, and waits for Paul's call. She's tried filling her days with data entry work, focusing on the names, numbers, and military hieroglyphics, anything to keep from remembering Saldano and his touch. But they are running out of things to talk about, having purposefully steered clear of their lovemaking on Catalina.

When the telephone buzzes, Barbara jerks upward, snatches a sheaf of papers, and picks up the receiver.

"Hello."

"This is Paul. Is Lisa in bed?" Can you talk?" he asks quietly, as if the energy in his voice will wake the child over the airways.

"I'm already craving a second glass of Zin. What do you think?" Barbara chuckles and then launches into what she's found out before the awkward silences begin.

"I've run all of the names and service numbers of the seven GIs stationed in Avalon with our boy Stanley. The VA's database had some stuff, and it's pretty easy to hack. I got a hit that I think you'll be interested in. A PFC Roger Briggs was stationed in Avalon from July 1942 until the war's end…and he's still alive."

"Hopefully, it's someplace I can get to," Paul says, and sighs. "Frank isn't gonna approve of any cross-country flights to visit some aging geezer."

"You're in luck. It seems PFC Briggs has been at the VA Hospital in Long Beach for the past four months."

"Jeez, he's got to be in his early 90s by now. Have you ever visited old guys in a vets' hospital?" Saldano asks with disdain.

There's a long pause before Barbara answers. "No, I've only seen mangled Iraqis on the wards in evacuation hospitals during Desert Storm, mostly from Republican Guard tank divisions."

"I'm sorry, I forget how…how traumatic the war must have been for you. I was too young and gung-ho to pay much attention. But it's different now."

"Well, maybe you can steel yourself and talk Frank into a quick mainland visit. The VA Hospital is close to the ferry landing. A half-hour with Briggs could break something open."

"Good idea. I'll work on it. So what else have ya found out?"

"I'm still checking the records for General O'Neal but only have a few sketchy details. He left his Army post at Fort Ord well before VE Day, received no special commendations, and had a home address in Culver City. It's a long shot, but maybe his name might turn up in the town's records. A lot of World War II brass became local business leaders and politicians after the war."

"You're correct, as usual. Maybe I should come to San Francisco and do your job while you come here and do mine." Saldano laughs but gets no response. The silence builds.

"Paul, we need to see each other again, don't you think?" Barbara says, her voice shaky.

Paul swallows hard and his words come in a rush. "Good God, yes. I've been trying to figure out a way of seeing you, but I'm stuck here at least until March and I know you don't have any leave coming for a while. But we've got to figure it out. I can't be away from you for that long."

"I feel the same. Maybe we could meet somewhere in between and at least have a few hours," Barbara says. "You know, Morro Bay's a halfway point down the coast and a four-hour drive for both of us,"

"I could find a half day and a night somehow…and if I could fly there, maybe extend our time together. But what about Lisa?"

"She has school friends that she can overnight with for a day or two…and I have half Sundays and all day Mondays off. It just might work."

The two lovers talk more about plans for their rendezvous, each getting more animated as their scheme starts to jell. In the end, possible dates are identified, and Paul promises to call every night to fill in the details.

"You know," Paul says, "while I can't see you face to face, I have a wonderful imagination and memory. Our evening calls don't have to be all business."

"If you think I'm into phone sex, you're crazy," Barbara says and laughs.

"No, no, that's not what I meant and…"

"But listen," Barbara continues, "a neighbor of mine has a digital camcorder, and I can e-mail you short home movies if you'd like?"

"That would be great," Paul says. "But keep them "G" rated. I don't have a home computer. The office staff already suspects I spend lunch hours surfing porn sites. It's tough being single on an island."

"It's not any easier on the mainland," Barbara says, and they ring off.

Paul stares at the patterns in the apartment's ceiling. His mind races, identifying and discarding options, strategies, clever deceptions, and outright prefabrications. He finally drops off to sleep long after the up canyon chimes clang their off-key one A.M. call.

During the next few days, Saldano evaluates legitimate angles to get away while covertly stealing time to view the daily videos from Barbara...mostly of her and Lisa eating dinner in their tiny bohemian apartment with its mid-eastern features, working on school projects together or night shots of the San Francisco skyline from their window. But Barbara also sends one clip of a steamy bathroom with herself bathing behind a frosted glass shower door. That night, she laughs when Paul complains about being teased. It makes him feel all that more desperate.

The solution falls into their laps without much planning, and it comes from Frank. "Saldano, I want you to take Charley Folsom over to the County lockup tomorrow morning. He beat up his wife pretty bad, and she's pressing charges this time."

"So, how should I get him there?"

"Waldenburg will fly you across to John Wayne, where a car will meet you. I want you to stay with Folsom until he's processed. That son of a bitch can get mean, and you're the only beefy guy I've got, so be careful."

"Is Waldenburg bringing me back," he asks, "or do I wait and take the late boat?" His mind is already spinning.

"Naw, he's got some other mainland business. You'll have

to take the boat. But you're off the next day, so it's no rush."

That night Paul and Barbara talk excitedly about their long-awaited rendezvous and set up a time to meet at the Breakers Restaurant overlooking Morro Bay the following evening. Paul had been there years before and had gotten drunk in Happy Jack's Bar while Julie stomped back to their motel room in a huff with their girls. *Christ, I hope this visit will erase the memories of the last,* he thinks.

The flight across the channel goes without a hitch, although takeoffs from Catalina's airport still scare the crap out of him... the ground suddenly disappears below the plane, replaced by the cold crumpled sea far below. Folsom had cooled his heels in the Island's lockup overnight. He's too hungover to put up any resistance. At the end of a fifteen-minute flight, the tiny plane bounces to a stop at John Wayne Airport, where two deputies and a squad car greet them.

"You think you two could process this guy without me?" Paul asks smoothly. "I've got a case to investigate and need to be done before the afternoon boat."

"Yeah, sure," the heavyset deputy says. "But next time we come to Avalon, we'll look you up."

Saldano grins and hands over the paperwork. He moves toward the Avis rent-a-car desk, where his contract and keys await. He's driving north on the 405 freeway toward Long Beach fifteen minutes after climbing out of the Cessna's cramped rear compartment.

CHAPTER 25

The ten-story Veterans Hospital rests in the center of an office complex. Vehicles crowd its parking lot. Saldano wheels the rented Accord into a "doctors only" space, places his business card on the dash, and enters the building.

"I'm here to see Mr. Roger Briggs," he tells the smiling candy stripper at the central information desk.

"Can you spell Roger's last name, please?"

"B-r-i-g-g-s."

She keys the name and stares at the computer screen. "Mr. Briggs is in the Geriatric Care Unit, fifth floor." She points to the elevator. "Are...are you a friend?" She eyes his uniform.

"No. I'm here on police business."

"Oh." She frowns and returns to reading some type of textbook.

The elevator slides upward and grinds to a halt. Its door jerks open onto a hallway half-lit by flickering fluorescent tubes. Near one end, a warm pool of light surrounds the nurses' station. Saldano walks toward it, leather shoes slapping against green linoleum, past quiet occupied rooms. At the nurses' station, he finds a large man in whites leaning back in a chair, reading a mystery novel. A tired-looking blond sorts through charts.

"I'm here to speak with Roger Briggs," Saldano announces in his best law enforcement voice. The reader glances up momentarily but lets the blond respond.

"Are you a relative or friend," she asks, "or are you here on official business?" Her voice is cool, efficient.

"Business. Can you direct me to his room, please?"

The woman sets her charts aside and joins Saldano in the hallway. She leads him toward its dark end and a red emergency exit sign. The Pine-Sol odor barely masks the stench of urine. Saldano takes shallow breaths. They stop in front of a half-open door.

The nurse speaks quietly, "Mr. Briggs has been here over four months. You're his first visitor." Her voice warms a few degrees. "He won't be with us much longer...kidneys failing, with a tacky heart. Go easy on him if you can."

"I'm only here for information, Miss...and besides, I've left my rubber hoses back in the car." Paul smiles.

The nurse manages a quick grin. "For most of these men, any contact is welcome. Stay as long as you want and hit the call button next to his bed if you need me." She walks away, her soft white shoes barely making a sound.

Inside the dim room, a maladjusted color TV flickers with the volume turned off. With half-opened eyes, Rodger Briggs stares at a soundless football game. He's the room's only occupant. A mountain of pillows helps support his tall, withered body. He notices Saldano and motions for Paul to come near.

"My name is Sergeant Paul Saldano with the Los Angeles County Sheriff's Department. Are you Roger Briggs?"

Black eyes track his approach. Bruised and age-spotted arms try feebly to smooth over the covers. "Yes, and I can see by your nametag and shoulder patches who you are." His voice booms in the empty room.

Jesus, this guy looks almost dead, Paul thinks, *but he can still bark like a drill instructor.*

Briggs pulls himself up in bed and scratches at the dialysis shunt near his collarbone, almost hidden by the hospital gown.

"I don't mean to disturb your game. Who's winning?" Saldano asks and motions toward the TV.

"Don't really know. I like watching. My son was a halfback and got me interested. Used to go to his Friday night games. But he's gone…Vietnam, you know."

"I'm sorry. My father was stationed there also." Saldano tries to figure an angle on how to start his questions.

"You didn't come here to talk with me about any of that," Briggs snorts. "What's on your mind, Sergeant?"

"I work out of the Avalon Station on Catalina Island. I'm investigating a case. I understand that you were stationed there during the war."

"Yeah, the most boring years of my life, sitting on my ass waiting for the war to end. Jesus, by the time the Army discharged me, I was ready to volunteer for the front lines just to get off that damn mountain. But at least it kept me alive. I guess I should be grateful."

"Do you know why you were stationed there? The Army's records are a bit sketchy."

"I've asked myself the same question for years. I even asked my father after I got back home to Malibu. But nobody knew anything. Besides, things were really busting loose, and I got caught up in all the craziness…mostly helping with my Pop's investments and then starting up for myself."

"So what was it like back then?" Paul asks.

Briggs sucks in a deep breath. "Southern California was ripe for the picking for those who had what they now call 'venture capital.' They sunk oil wells near Long Beach as quick as they could stick straws in the ground. Signal Hill was the richest field anywhere. And all those discharged GIs, sailors, and men imported to work the West Coast factories didn't want to go home to Philly or Selma or Bum Fuck, Arkansas. They had the GI bill and VA loans, and the housing market really cooked. That was my line, apartments, subdivisions, and later condo projects."

"So you worked as a realtor?"

"No, not really. I was the guy who put the deals together, found the money, and linked it up with the developers. Sometimes, all I did was arrange for raw land sales. I had made a lot of connections while working for my Pop...you know, bankers, architects, politicians. By the mid-50s, I'd branched out on my own. By then, Dad wanted to enjoy his senior years and get the hell out of the rat race. He sure did a better job of it than I have."

Briggs leans his head back onto the pillows and closes his eyes, drawing in deep, noisy breaths. Saldano waits for the breathing to normalize before continuing. "So tell me some more about your tour of duty on Catalina. Do you ever hear from any of the other men stationed there? Anything unusual happen during your hitch?"

"I'm not sure what to say, Sergeant. Eight of us GIs lived on the top floor of the St. Catherine's Hotel. I didn't get to know those guys very well. But since I had the highest rank, I kept track of them while we were on Island. I remember they came from families in the same social club that my father belonged to. We'd sometimes go into Avalon and get plastered but mostly kept to ourselves. The last time I remember seeing any of them was on the steamer to Wilmington after we got our discharge orders."

"What about Stanley DeVaul? Do you remember anything about him?"

Briggs hesitates a minute before answering. "Yeah, I remember Stan. He was a blue-blood-looking kid, skinny, always carried around his art materials and drew things. He did a sketch of me that I gave to Shirley as an engagement present. She's been gone ten years now; cancer took her."

"Do you remember Stan coming back to Wilmington with the rest of you?" Saldano prompts.

"You know, now that you mention it, he wasn't with us. I think in December '44 or maybe early '45, I reported him AWOL. He hadn't been around for days and failed to pick up his pay. They ordered all of us to search the island since there was no record of him taking the steamer to the mainland. I figured he'd swiped a sailboat and disappeared with his honey. We never did find anything, although we searched for a couple weeks."

"What else can you tell me about DeVaul? I know it's a long time ago, but anything would help." Paul adjusts the vertical hold on the ancient television that's been rolling for minutes.

"Well, he was the most hoity-toity guy in our group. But because he could do artwork, he was luckier with the ladies than the rest of us...not that we had much contact with women. The few unattached girls on the island would sometimes come to the Casino to watch Friday night boxing matches or visit the Chi Chi Club run by the USO. But Stanley had this Mexican cutie that was a real knockout. She worked at one of the restaurants. The two of them had their own hideaway somewhere, and he wouldn't make it back for bed check until after midnight. But Stan was tight-lipped about his affairs. I only saw her once...man, she was really built." Briggs smiles weakly and leans back on his pillows, breathing deeply with eyes closed.

"Anything else about DeVaul that you can remember? Any detail is important."

Briggs answers in a tired voice. "Years after the war, I met his brother...I think his name was George, a manager for Security Bank in Culver City. He and I got involved in a land deal. I asked him about Stan and never could get a straight answer... something about Stan being killed in Belgium, which was a load of bunk. But now it's my turn." Briggs' voice is slurred. "Why... why all of this interest in DeVaul? Christ, that was....was more than seventy years ago."

Saldano stares at the gaunt figure with outstretched arms

and hooded eyes. He decides that this guy can keep a secret.

"We found his dog tag on a hillside off Stagecoach Road. We also found skeletal remains nearby. We think it might be Stanley." Saldano watches Briggs for a response.

"Sorry to hear that. Stan was all right, and I could see he had talent. But then starving artists are a dime a dozen and only make money after they're dead…as if I should talk."

"Mr. Briggs, if I can ask, why are you here in *this* hospital?"

The old man's eyes open far enough for one more story. "After Steven was killed, Shirley and I started gambling a lot, mostly the horses, but we liked greyhounds too. Then they built I-15 out to Vegas, and that about finished us off. By the '80s, we lost it as fast as I brought it in, and then I had a couple of huge deals go sour, and they wiped us out, including the inheritance. What was left went to pay for Shirley's cancer treatments. When she died, I tried selling real estate, but I was way too old and had lost my connections. I've been living at the Cabrillo Hotel in Long Beach. It's not far from here, a nice place, cheap."

"Thanks for your time, Private Briggs. While the Saint Catherine Hotel is gone, Avalon's still a beautiful place." Paul stands to go. "Maybe when you're stronger, you can come and visit your old island haunts. It's only an hour boat ride away."

Briggs manages a quivering smile. Paul imagines the old man dreaming of himself as a young PFC dressed in summer khakis, strong, with his life in front of him, itching to get off an island that had stolen two years time, time that he longs to steal back.

Saldano finds the television remote and clicks it off. Briggs snores softly in the dim light.

"Please, come back again," the blond nurse calls after Saldano.

"Thanks for your help," he answers and hustles down the dark hallway toward the elevator. He tries to convince himself that Barbara will be worried if he's late getting to Morro Bay. But he knows that he must escape this warehouse of quietly dying soldiers before thoughts of his own mortality make him crave a bottle of something bad.

CHAPTER 26

"Why couldn't that son-of-a-bitch DeBlough have taken care of this," George muttered.

He clutched the aft rail of the SS Avalon as it lurched toward Catalina Island, his collar unbuttoned, ascot askew, and vomit splattered over the tops of his two-toned Florsheims. A cold northwest wind buffeted the coast and turned the gray Pacific into fields of white-capped waves. Even Avalon's protected anchorage churned, with heaving fishing boats and military craft tethered precariously to their moorings. The rolling steamer approached the pier slowly. The shore crew stood ready to secure the hawsers. After considerable maneuvering, the ship calmed. George steadied himself, wiped his mouth with a silk handkerchief, and joined the first stream of passengers that staggered down the gangway. Most of them wore chalk-white faces and moved with the reeling gait of drunken sailors.

George focused on each step while clutching his leather suitcase. On the pier, he scanned the faces of the milling crowd, but no one fit his memory of Stanley. George stumbled toward the shore and the promise of solid ground. He paused to dry heave over the railing. Finally, he straightened and spat into the choppy surf below. A tall soldier approached and extended a hand.

"I see that you and ships still aren't on friendly terms," Stan said with a sardonic smile.

George nodded, as his stomach lurched once again.

"Come on, let's get you off this pier and onto terra firma. Maybe some hot tea with brandy will help."

Stan grabbed George's suitcase and led his brother by

the arm toward Crescent Avenue. George stopped several more times to heave over the railing and made it to the head of the pier, where he plopped down on a wooden bench. The Shore Patrol checked his papers, asked a few questions, and then let the brothers pass. George studied the fronts of shuttered shops. Only a couple of restaurants and the Island Pharmacy showed any sign of activity.

He smiled weakly at Stan. "I think I'm ready for that brandy. Don't know about the tea."

Stan laughed. "You must really want to see me bad. You look like living hell."

"Well, I can tell you one damn thing…I'm not leaving this rock until the sea calms. Two hours of vomiting into the wind is enough misery for a lifetime. Why couldn't you be stationed in Long Beach?"

"Don't ask me," Stan said. "I still don't know what I'm doing here on Catalina."

After more deep breaths, George struggled to his feet, and they moved westward toward the Busy Bee Café's welcoming portal. Stan thought they resembled the comedy team of Laurel and Hardy, cutting a crooked path, although George hadn't yet reached Hardy's rotund shape. After a few rest stops, they stumbled into John's Café, deciding against the Busy Bee because it was crowded with mariners. They took a table against the rear wall, away from any view of the ocean. Stan ordered hot tea. When the waitress served it, he extracted a flask from an inside pocket and topped off each of their cups.

They sat quietly. George nibbled soda crackers from a green Spanish bowl. The color returned to his cheeks, and he straightened up and inhaled deeply. He retrieved a cigarette case, lit a Chesterfield with a flick from a gold lighter, and blew a long stream of smoke toward the ceiling. "Jesus, how can you stand being surrounded by the sea? It would make me sick looking at it every time a storm blows in."

"You forget, I don't have much say about where I'm stationed. At least there's nobody around here shooting at us… although a local skipper claims his fishing boat almost rammed a Jap submarine off San Clemente. Our boys got away before the nips could fire their deck gun.

George smiles. "There have been similar incidents near San Pedro and up the coast. But the Navy and Coast Guard's got it under control."

"Maybe so, but the folks around here got scared after the sub incident, figuring anything near the water could be an invasion site. And they're serious about the blackout, so no outdoor cigarettes after sunset."

The brothers sipped their tea. Outside, the gray clouds opened, and a rain squall enveloped Avalon, chasing pedestrians inside the cafes to wait it out. John's filled with chattering mariners, making quiet conversation difficult. The brothers watched the crowd. The lone waitress danced between tables, delivering late lunches and trays of coffee.

"So ya want something to eat?" Stan offered.

George grimaced. "Maybe by suppertime, I'll be ready for food. Why don't we go to the hotel, then set a time for dinner."

"Well, I didn't rent you a hotel room, but a little bungalow that's even better. It's just up the hill from here. I'll get you settled, then come by about seven. I've already picked out a great place, the Hurricane Cove, where we can get a light dinner, and the drinks aren't bad."

"Sounds fine. I'll need a couple of hours rest to recover from that damnable crossing. Show me the way."

The rain slacked off. The brothers trudged uphill and passed down the narrow passageway between boarding houses to the small cottage off the fieldstone courtyard. After Stanley departed, George opened his suitcase and removed the shirts, ties, and dinner jackets, and hung them in the open armoire. He stored his underclothes in the dresser against the wall. In the kitchenette, he found a crockery bowl to use as an ashtray, lit another Chesterfield, and peered outside at the stepped foundations of surrounding houses that clung to Avalon's hillsides. *You'd have to be a damn mountain goat to build something on these slopes.* George stretched out on the bed and thought of how to trick Stanley into telling him about his girlfriend and their intentions. *Maybe with enough booze, Stan would spill the beans.* In a few moments, the world disappeared. He awoke to a loud pounding on the door.

"Just a minute, just a God damned minute," he yelled and sat up in bed.

In the black room, he fumbled to find the light chain for the corner lamp, stumbling over his shoes in the process. But he finally got it lit and yanked open the door.

"Close the damn curtains," Stanley barked, rushed past George and slammed the door.

The blast of night air made George retreat. Stan moved to the windows and yanked the heavy drapes shut.

"Jesus, George, you've got to be careful with the light. The marshals will kick you off the island if you're cited for a blackout violation."

"Sorry, I forgot," George muttered. "No need to get your nose out of joint." He doused his face in the bathroom sink, struggled with the laces of his shoes, and selected his warmest dinner jacket for the evening's outing.

A half moon lit the cold courtyard and the storm clouds had disappeared. Stanley took George's arm and led him through the black passageway and downhill to Crescent Avenue. George felt stronger with the intake of each cold breath.

"I just realized I'm starving," he said jokingly.

Stan grinned at him. "Great. I always skip lunch at the

mess hall, so I'm ready to consume a large stallion myself."

They moved along the harbor's edge, then turned up canyon at the second side street and approached a particular clump of palm trees that marked the entrance to the Hurricane Cove. George struggled to keep up with Stan's long strides.

"The Cove has wonderful seafood and a full bar," Stan said cheerfully. "You should like it."

But as they approached the building and Stan tugged on the front door, the bare outlines of a sign became visible in the moonlight: "Closed until after Christmas."

"Christ, I checked them at lunch and assumed…." Stan apologized to George and stared down the black street.

"This berg's gotta have more than one place open, right?" George asked.

"Ah, yeah, sure," Stan mumbled. "The Grotto is one cove over and has good food."

"Great, let's go…and hurry before they decide to pack it in for the holidays."

Stan hesitated, "Yeah, ah, sure."

They walked back to Crescent Avenue and continued eastward along the harbor's edge and around Pelican Point. As they climbed the stairs and entered the Grotto's dining room, a slender blond waitress warmly greeted the brothers and showed them to a table against the window.

"Thank you, Laura. Before you hurry off, I'd like to introduce my brother, George. He's here on business."

"Pleased to meet you, George. Stanley is one of our best customers." Laura grinned and hurried off toward the kitchen, disappearing behind the heavy blackout curtains.

In a few minutes, a Mexican girl approached and smiled casually at Stan and George. "Gentlemen, can I get you something to drink?" she asked professionally.

"Thank you," Stan said. "We'll have a bottle of your finest

cabernet, maybe…ah, two.

"Very good. I'll bring that right away." The girl spun and headed for the wine rack, a smirk curling the corners of her mouth.

"I say, do they all look like that?" George said and snickered.

"Like…like what? I hadn't noticed."

"You know exactly what I mean…built like brick outhouses, long hair and those eyes."

"There are a few beauties on the island…but most are kept under wraps since this place is overrun with servicemen. We don't exactly have honorable reputations."

"I wouldn't think the Mexicans would mind that much… some Chiquita might snatch herself a rich gringo in the bargain." George stared at Stanley.

The brown waitress delivered the wine, and Stan busied himself, pouring the black liquid into their glasses without spilling a drop.

George sniffed, took a sip, and smiled. "Tastes like they've squirreled away some stock from before the war. On the mainland, this quality would cost you."

"Yes, evidently, Avalon was deluged with tourists before Pearl Harbor. They still have a few cases left…although I've been doing my best to reduce their inventory."

Stan grinned and leaned backward to drain his glass. George quickly refilled it.

"So what's this about you going crazy over your art? Father says you mysteriously ask for supplies and Jose delivered them. But you never talked to Jose or wrote Father back."

"Well, I *am* an artist, George," Stan said curtly, "and artists need their tools." He gulped more wine.

"Yes, yes, I know that. But before the Army, you hated your work, and now you've found something to paint. This place isn't close to being a tropical paradise, Stan. What could be so inspiring? Can't be the sagebrush…and if you've seen one seascape, you've seen 'em all. Is it the people or the buildings or what? I'm curious."

"George, I wouldn't expect a banker to understand the beauty in this place. But it's really here…in the Spanish buildings, in the people. Catalina's an island, isolated by the sea and remote from all that craziness you and father call progress and industry. There is something beautiful about its isolation, about how Avalon clings to the slopes of a mountain above a thrashing sea, resolute, determined." Stanley took a deep breath.

"Yes, I've been meaning to talk to you about the people here. Jose told Father that he saw you with a Mexican girl. What's that about? You know you need to be careful…"

Stan pushed back from the table and drained his wineglass. "So, Father now has Jose spying on me? I finally contact that son of a bitch, and all he can do is go crazy that I might have met a girl. I suppose that's why you're here too…all that malarkey about being interested in my art."

"Your right about Father, Stan. He doesn't want the DeVaul name mixed up with—"

"With what, somebody with brown skin? Doesn't want any brown bastards? Well, you can sail your landlubber ass back to the estate and tell him to stay out of my life, and I'll stay out of his."

The two brothers go silent. Stan fills his glass and gulps wine. He stares at the ghostly outlines of albacore boats bouncing into the dark harbor.

On her rounds of the dining room, Flavia caught most of the brother's sometimes loud conversation and noticed that the two have gone quiet. She fought back the urge to step forward and introduce herself as Stanley's lover. George didn't look all that disagreeable, although these two men barely looked like brothers. But somehow, they belonged to the same class. She imagined Stanley dressed in an outfit like George's, drinking iced cocktails at the Tuna Club and boasting to other rich gringos about the day's catch. She frowned and returned to the waitress station.

The silence between the two men had grown. Neither could restart the conversation, and, to make matters worse, they'd finished the wine. Stanley waved at Laura, who came over and took his order for another bottle. But the more wine Stan drank, the more determined he seemed to shut his brother out.

"You know George, I really don't feel like eating," Stan said and stood up and stared down at him. "Give my apologies to the waitress and I'll come by the bungalow tomorrow morning, say around nine. The steamer leaves at 11, so you can make the return passage. You can tell Father I'll write him a long letter. I've been meaning to for some time."

Stanley turned and deftly slipped between the tables and out the restaurant door before George could protest. He contemplated his failure, all the while lowering the level of the second wine bottle. Finally, the Mexican waitress approached.

"Will the other señor be returning for dinner, or should I take your order now?" she asked quietly.

George looked up into her dark eyes, stabbed at something on the menu in front of him, and then returned to staring across the channel, with only the eerie searchlights from Fort MacArthur illuminating the mainland.

When the waitress delivered his meal, George greedily devoured it, the morning's seasickness already a fading memory. He left her a large tip, although her smile had faded, and her long Mayan nose made her face look older and sadder than when George first admired her. He passed out into the blustery night, hoping he could remember the way.

At least now Stan knows what the family thinks about him having a Mexican girlfriend, George thought. But he knew it wouldn't be enough to keep his brother in line, and with Rick pushing up daisies, the options for resolving this situation grew limited. George shuddered at what he knew would be the old man's reaction to his failure. He climbed the black hill and felt his way along the dark alley to the bungalow. Maybe by the morrow, he'd have more ideas.

The next morning, Stan pounded on the bungalow door at nine. He smiled, as if nothing had happened the previous night. George grabbed his packed suitcase, and they walked downslope and onto the steamer pier. Stanley babbled about how San Pedro's hillside homes glittered in the morning, about harbor seals pulling themselves up on the Casino Point jetty to bask in the sun.

With no wind, the sea had flattened. The SS Avalon smoked in her berth. The few lucky mariners with shore leave milled about, waiting impatiently for the call to board.

"You know, you and Father don't need to worry about me," Stan said quietly and grasped his brother's arm to gently steer him toward the ticket agent standing at the steamer's gangway. "I'm not a child anymore."

"Well, you still need to grow up a bit," George snapped, his frustration showing. "Anybody who deals with you deals with our family, and there are plenty of gold diggers out there waiting to take advantage."

Stan lets go of George's arm. "Oh, and I suppose that you and your banking buddies and Father aren't taking advantage of this whole war? Or is that just good business?"

"Yes, it's business, all right. The same business that paid for your fancy art school. It's about time you realize how the world works, Stan. This war will make us millions. You can try and ignore it or join Father and I in shaping the future. The whole

West Coast will be opening up. Go ahead and paint your stupid flowers and peasant girls while the rest of us mold it. Just don't blame us for taking charge."

George stepped onto the gangway and briskly climbed, not looking back. Reaching the second deck, he stared down at the pier. Stanley had vanished. The dock crew moved forward to retrieve the gangplank. Blasts from the ship's air horns bounced off the hills that framed the harbor and echoed up Avalon Canyon. George grabbed his suitcase and reached the main exit before the crew removed the ramp. The ticket agent scowled but quickly retrieved his ticket from the wad in his hand.

George wandered inland along quiet side streets. *Christ, why am I still here?* he thought. *What the hell can* I *do?* But he knew that he'd better have damn good answers for the old man before he set foot again on the mainland.

CHAPTER 27

Driving north, Saldano maneuvers the Accord through heavy Sunday traffic. San Fernando Valley towns and a few remaining citrus groves flash past on the freeway. But the disturbing images of the VA hospital and of Private Briggs don't leave him until he reaches Santa Barbara. At Santa Maria, the traffic thins. Paul considers stopping for lunch but decides against it. The vision of Barbara waiting for him at a restaurant bar, surrounded by tourists and hit on by a cadre of lonely guys, drives him on.

At a gas station in San Luis Obispo, he changes into civilian clothes and hopes the slacks and sports shirt will make him look less dorky. As a kid, his buddies chided him for being an uptight *bobo,* especially when he refused to get a gang tattoo from the old witch in Cuero. *Christ, I'd better get there early, take a walk on the beach, loosen the hell up,* he thinks. *I'm 'bout ready to pop.*

In Morro Bay, strong winds push huge rolls of the Pacific over the breakwater, spilling white foam into the protected harbor. Paul parks the car outside the Breakers Café and slips inside its tiny barroom. He finds an empty stool at the end of the counter and orders a soda water. Saldano sips his drink and instinctively takes inventory of the room's occupants and the comings and goings of the Sunday afternoon crowd. A football game flashes across a huge TV. Paul stares at it unseeing, his mind and heart racing.

A sudden gust of wind flexes the Café's windows. The side door opens, and Barbara steps in, clasping her flying hair. Paul watches from his corner. She moves smoothly, with confidence, wearing the simple dress he likes so much. Her long black hair looks washed and combed, held back by a single silver barrette. The heads of men hunched over their cocktails at the bar turn ever so slightly to check her out. Paul slides off his stool. Barbara removes her sunglasses and smiles. She comes toward him. The heads at the bar swing ever so slightly toward Paul and then resume their straight-ahead meditation. Paul can almost hear the incredulity racing through their brains.

"Well, Sergeant, you certainly look quite the tourist," Barbara says, and they lightly embrace, but not so lightly that he can't feel the thudding of her heart.

"And you look, well…ah," Paul stammers. The old guy next to him shakes his head and continues sipping bourbon.

"I'll take that as a compliment. Why don't we get a table?" Barbara deftly slips between the clutter of chairs until they are seated against the window overlooking the harbor. A cocktail waitress arrives. Barbara orders a white wine, and after it's delivered, they stare at each other and nurse their drinks.

"I hope you got us a room without any trouble." Paul breaks the silence. "I'd forgotten how much of a tourist Mecca this place is, even during the winter."

"Well, it succeeded in getting this Muslim to show up." Barbara laughs, and Paul chokes on his soda, embarrassed by his unintended pun.

"So, how long have you been here?" he asks, wanting to say more but holding back, waiting for a better place.

"I checked in two hours ago and have already toured the Embarcadero. There are nice shops that Lisa would have liked, but she'll see it another time. How was your visit with Briggs at the hospital? Did he give you much?"

"To tell the truth, I spent the first two hours driving up here trying to forget that place. Let's leave business for later and go out and enjoy the town."

"Are you kidding?" Barbara smiles. "In case you haven't

noticed, the wind is blowing at thirty knots. My hair already looks like a banshee's. Let's go to the room so I can put it up."

Barbara leads Paul out of the bar and down the sidewalk to a bluff-top cluster of buildings with blue roofs. The frigid wind stings his bare arms as they climb to their second-floor room and hustle inside. A broad window looks out onto the harbor and white-capped Morro Bay, half full now with sailboats bending to the wind. Lines of white pelicans wheel around the up-jutting mass of Morro Rock that guards the harbor entrance. The Rock's ancient volcanic flanks burn golden in the afternoon sunlight.

"I'll go get my stuff from the car while you fix your hair," Paul says and moves toward the door.

"I don't think so." Barbara smiles and slips off her dress and sits on the bed's edge. Paul joins her and they kiss while each clumsily finishes disrobing. Unlike the mineshaft, the room's filled with light, the actinic winter sun picking out every detail of their bodies. Paul stares at tiny dark moles that adorn Barbara's thigh, resembling the distinctive zigzag line of the constellation Cassiopeia. As they sink onto the bed, he struggles to maintain control for at least a few moments longer.

"Should I wear protection?" he whispers into her ear while caressing her breasts.

"Are you bloody kidding? I've been on the pill ever since our last time. But you'll have to forgive me if I gain a couple of pounds." Barbara smiles wryly, then, without warning, rolls on top of him, where she stays until her first climax.

The sun nose-dives toward the sea. Both lovers are breathing hard from their last event when shadows cross the room and cloak their bodies. They have done things that Paul knows his ex-wife would never consider. As they lie side-by-side, he thinks how there's no telling about sexuality and different cultures, with lust and love being such an individual thing.

Barbara gets up and crosses to the window to stare at the

sunset, her figure cutting a sharp edge against the gold horizon. Paul watches the rise and fall of her rib cage, the beautiful confluence of curves that form her lower back. He comes up behind her and enters smoothly. She braces herself against the window. In a few minutes, the telltale pace of her breathing lets him know that she's close. Afterwards, they struggle to catch their breaths.

"Please let me sit down before I fall over," Barbara says, giggling.

They slump into armchairs, weak-limbed, heads tilted back.

"Did you know that in many Arab countries, women can divorce their husbands for not satisfying them in bed?" Barbara smiles and playfully digs Paul in the ribs.

"Well, at least they don't cut something off like they do with thieves," Paul cracks, and they both laugh.

"Sergeant Saldano, methinks you will be safe from the ire of Arab women…not that I'll let you get near any of them."

"Maybe so, but those yachtsmen sailing into the harbor will be jumping their wives tonight after that X-rated show we gave them." Paul stretches a leg to touch Barbara.

"Quit worrying. They can't tell who we are without our uniforms." She bounces up to take a shower while Paul retrieves his kit from the car.

The wind no longer flexes the windows, and a quiet charcoal darkness envelops the town. The loudest sounds come from squawking night herons, assuming their sentry posts at the water's edge. The couple walks along the Embarcadero holding hands and climbs the stairway to Rose's Restaurant. They hole up in the crowded saloon and nibble munchies until a table in the dining room opens. Perched on bar stools, they stare through windows into darkness. Paul catches Barbara steeling sideway glances at him, causing the color to rise in her cheeks. He imagines she, too, relives the afternoon. After an hour's wait, they're seated and order liquids and entrees.

"So…so how did it go with Briggs at the Vets hospital?" Barbara asks and tongues her wine. "You've been so quiet about it."

"I won't go into detail about the hospital. It's not a place I'd want to end up. But from what Briggs told me, I'm convinced that Private DeVaul never got off Catalina Island."

"Why? What did he say?"

"Briggs said DeVaul went AWOL in late 1944 or early '45 and never returned. That contradicts the Army's account that he died in Europe. I believe it's his skeleton that we found."

"But you can't be sure without a DNA match, right?"

Paul mutters, "Yeah, or unless an eyewitness steps forward…not likely after almost seventy years."

"My investigation of General O'Neal didn't go that much better," Barbara says. "O'Neal commanded Fort Ord from August '41 to March of '44 and returned to his home in Culver City after resigning his commission. One interesting thing I've found out, though, is that Stanley had a brother who also lived in Culver City. It seems that O'Neal also sent a letter to a George M. DeVaul. I found it in some old files at the Fort Ord Museum. But it reveals less than the Spangler letter, although it does provide a street address for the brother. I've brought along a copy for you to look at. There was definitely something going on."

"So you've been visiting your boyfriend at the museum," Paul says in an accusing tone.

"Yes, and he won't be divorced by any Arab women either," Barbara says with mock indignation. But she can't pretend to be mad for long and lets out a loud guffaw that turns the heads of a family sitting at an adjoining table.

Saldano ignores her outburst. "Briggs told me about meeting Stanley's brother after the war, a banker of some sort. That

Culver City address will help, although those old neighborhoods around the studio district have since been replaced with commercial crap. But I've also got an idea from something you said. If we could find the remains of the DeVaul estate, if we can find something that definitely belonged to Stanley, we might be able to match it with the DNA from our skeleton…if the lab can pull cellular material after all these years."

"That's a lot of ifs, Paul, and you'd have an incredible job tracking down the family, especially if you're doing it solo from your island hideout. Why don't we follow up on the Culver City thing? Maybe the brother has left some trace, and as a retired general, the municipal records should have something on O'Neal."

"Yeah, I know you're right. Frank isn't going to let me do anything more than the minimum. I'd better leave early tomorrow morning so I can spend time in Culver City and still make the six o'clock boat."

The mention of Paul's departure throws ice water on their conversation, and the couple plays with the remains of their dinners. They gaze across the harbor at the barely visible sandbar speckled with flocks of white gulls bedded down for the night. Finally, they return to the motel, undress, and slide under cold sheets. A full moon casts blue light across their room. They lie next to each other, not touching, and finally drop off to sleep.

Sometime during the early hours, Barbara shakes Paul's shoulder and he startles awake. The moon is down, and their room is pitch black. Paul reaches for her, and she comes into his arms. He feels her trembling, his chest wet from her tears.

"What are we going to do, Paul?" Barbara cries softly. "I can't be away from you for weeks and months."

Paul holds her tight, knowing that he has few answers. "Christ, I feel the same. We'll have to work something out, somehow."

"We have to. I have so many things I want to share and... and Lisa needs a man around during her teenage years. I know it's way too soon to say it, and I don't want to scare you off, but that's how I feel."

"She's a good kid, and I'd love to be there for both of you. But I already have two daughters who hate me for being a drunk. I'm scared that I won't measure up. If I were you, I'd be scared too."

"I'm afraid, Paul, but not of that. Please hold me." They lie together, rocking gently. The night winds pick up and buffet the motel. Both are a long time awake before sleep returns.

In the morning, Barbara rises early, showers, and dresses, her long hair sleekly combed back and fastened with a golden barrette. Paul's self-conscious about how he must look to this beautiful woman, rumpled and unshaven. He hurries off to the sanctuary of the bathroom. When he emerges fully scrubbed, scraped, and dressed, Barbara sits in the armchair near the window, watching the outgoing fishing boats approach the huge ocean swell that defines the harbor's mouth.

Paul sits in the neighboring chair and extends a hand. She takes it and laces her fingers through his.

"I'm sorry about last night. I...I didn't mean to make it worse," she says, smiling.

Paul squeezes her hand. "You didn't, but I know this. If we can figure out this DeVaul thing, we surely can figure out a way of being together. I'm convinced of it. It'll just take time."

"I know, I know. Speaking of which, we'd better eat breakfast and get you on the road. But not before I leave you with one last thing."

Barbara stands, kicks off her sandals, and playfully raises the front of the dress to reveal her soft, smooth nakedness. Paul has barely enough time to adjust his trousers before she climbs on top of him. Their bodies shiver from the cool air and the delicious first touch of early day.

CHAPTER 28

Banana trees and mustard-colored bungalows bordered the red concrete stairway that climbed the hillside. George could barely read the faded "For Rent" sign posted in the far cottage's window. He left the sidewalk to inspect the sign that instructed prospective renters to inquire at Apartment A. George thumped softly on the solid door. A large, round man that looked Hawaiian swung the door open and peered out. After brief negotiations, the man disappeared inside and returned with a key. George lay twenty dollars onto the man's broad palm and hustled up the stairs. Struggling with the tricky lock, he pushed inside Apartment H and closed the door quickly.

Decorated in a 1920s Art Deco style, the room's stuffy air smelled of old newspapers and shoes. George opened a rear kitchen window, then slumped onto an overstuffed chair. *This is God damned crazy,* he thought. *What the hell am I doing? But I gotta do something before leaving this island.*

He stared through Venetian blinds at the banana trees flapping in the late morning wind. *At least I've made it farther than that idiot DeBlough…and I'm still breathing.* He dragged the metal ashtray stand next to the chair and sat chain-smoking Chesterfields. Outside, legions of merchant marine trainees dressed in their white sailor suits marched down Sumner Avenue. As the afternoon shadows grew longer, the trainees stopped their parade.

George changed into casual clothes, pulled his broad-brimmed hat down, and left the bungalow. He walked at an unhurried pace but altered direction every block or so. In two hours, he'd scouted the town, understood its layout, where the servicemen gathered, and had located opportune places to observe them without being obvious. *Following Stanley shouldn't be tough since his Army uniform makes him easy to spot. The trick will be to spot him without getting caught.*

George checked over his shoulder constantly and took cover whenever a tall man came in sight. The Shore Patrol stopped him on Crescent Avenue and demanded to see his papers. But they let him go after only cursory questioning.

At a side street grocery with stained wooden floors, George spent all but five of his red and blue ration coupons to purchase supplies, not wanting to risk being seen in the cafés or restaurants. He returned to the bungalow. All night, the winter wind smacked the banana leaves together as if applauding his meager accomplishments.

In the morning, he showered and shaved and stared out at the Merchant Marines marching up canyon to the training grounds. Dust motes drift in and out of sharp bands of sunlight cast by the Venetian blinds. George thought about his brother, tried to imagine where a lovesick artist might wander. But art and maybe love were unfamiliar territory, and he resigned himself to days of prowling before anything might come of it.

As he peered out the window, his gaze fixed on the gold and tortoiseshell barrette lying on a nearby dresser. He'd found it in the bungalow that Stan had rented for him and figured that giving it to Sarah might curtail her ire over his extended absence. He reached for the barrette and turned it over in his hands. It reminded him of the flashy hair ornaments worn by his father's Mexican servants. It gave him an idea, a far-fetched one, but worth pursuing.

The day passed slowly. For lunch George snacked on bread and cheese washed down with cheap red wine. It soured his stomach and forced him out of hiding to purchase Bromo Seltzer at the Island Pharmacy. In the quiet afternoon, he wandered slowly down Crescent Avenue and turned uphill toward where he had slept the previous night. He climbed with purpose and energy. Perspiration stained his shirt. George arrived at the alley blowing hard, his face burning. Stepping into the passageway, he moved forward and paused at its far end, enjoying the cool, deep shade. The courtyard before him was empty. George took a step toward the bungalow but retreated quickly into the shadows. A movement at the window had caught his eye. Someone had pulled the blackout curtains closed in the back of a casement window propped open with a precariously balanced black leather shoe. George crouched and tried to calm his breathing. Wind gusts swirled in the courtyard. But between gusts, he could hear what sounded like low conversation.

George sat on the cool stones and removed his leather Florsheims. He tied their laces together and slipped them over his shoulder. Moving forward on black argyle stockings he approached the partially open window and knelt to listen, toes and knees pressed hard onto the paving stones. From inside, he heard rustling and low moans coming from the bed, one sound being higher-pitched than the other.

A strong gust of wind momentarily sucked the curtains out through the window. He caught a quick flash of two naked bodies, one upright and brown and one lying down and white. The wind calmed, and the curtains fell back inside. In the stillness, the sounds became more distinct and frantic. George's breathing increased as he listened. The sounds stopped, followed by the creak of bedsprings and footsteps on the wooden floor.

George rose and beat a hasty retreat across the courtyard to the alley's shadows. He rubbed his sore knees but kept moving until reaching the street. The deserted neighborhood offered few hiding places. George settled on a row of garbage cans surrounding a dragon tree on the far side of the lane. A space behind the cans in deep shadows and against the house could conceal him. He settled in and put on his shoes. In a few minutes, hard footfalls sounded in the alley.

Stanley and a brown Mexican girl stepped into the golden afternoon sunlight. They checked the street for people, then kissed. George immediately recognized her from the restaurant. He wondered how she had remained so aloof while the half-drunk brothers had argued over Stanley's affair. The girl stayed behind when Stan disappeared downhill. George held his breath for fear that she would cross the street and discover him. In a few minutes, she, too, departed. A dog barked, and he bolted from his lair and wandered uphill through a maze of narrow streets and lanes in a direction opposite that taken by the lovers.

In the late afternoon, George returned to his banana tree bungalow. He knew the identity of his brother's slutty girlfriend and where she worked. *Now, what the hell am I supposed to do? I usually hire somebody to take care of this kinda crap...but here on this island? Who am I gonna get to make it go away?*

Before sunset, George ventured forth and bought wine and cans of deviled ham from the grocery. He sat at the bungalow's window with the lights out, chain-smoked, gulped wine from the bottle, and shoved spoonfuls of spiced meat into his mouth, chewing slowly. In his head, he laid out the options; they all had significant risks of discovery or failure.

The following day, with acid eating his stomach, George slipped into the Busy Bee Café for a huge breakfast. Feeling revived, he walked eastward along the waterfront to the Grotto Restaurant. A tall Mexican boy slumped at a picnic table out back, the stub of a cigarette dangling from his full, dark lips.

"Excuse me, *hijo*, but maybe you can help me," George said in his best business voice. The kid's hooded eyes blinked a few times. He expertly flicked his cigarette butt into a nearby trashcan but said nothing.

"I ate dinner here a couple of nights ago, and I think I might have left my fountain pen on the table. Do you know anything about it?"

The kid slowly lit another cigarette and inhaled deeply before answering. "No, señor, I work in the kitchen, but I don't remember hearing anything about it."

"Well, what about the waitress? Maybe she would know. I didn't catch her name but she was a Mexican girl and *muy bonita*."

"You must mean Flavia. She's not working today, but she'll be here *por mañana* lunch. Come back then."

"I'm afraid that won't do. I have a ticket for the morning boat to San Pedro and have to board at *diez y media.*"

"Well, she could be anywhere with her gringo boyfriend since school is on holiday." The kid frowned, and George sensed something that he could use to his advantage.

"Is she a friend of yours?" George asked softly.

The boy's eyes blazed for a moment before returning to their dull stare. "No, nothing like that. If you want to find her, she's up on the China Wall with Señor Wonderful. They like to go there and think that nobody knows. It's unfair what gringos get away with."

George ignored the last statement. "Well, she is very pretty," he said in a consoling voice, "and any man would be lucky to have her."

The kid nodded and sucked hard on his cigarette until the ash dropped off.

"Maybe you can still help me. I have a free afternoon and I've heard that there is great wild boar hunting on Catalina. Do you know how someone might get fixed up?" *Maybe DeBlaugh's plan will work this time…or get me killed.*

"I wish I could help you, señor. But the military banned hunting. I know people who used to be guides that now collect garbage. They don't even go out."

"Well, I could make it worth your time if you'd set it up." George pulled his billfold from an inside jacket pocket and extracted a half-inch thick wad of twenty-dollar notes.

The kid's face cracked into a smile.

"How about two hundred now and two hundred if we're successful, *comprende*?

The kid nodded, quickly grabbed the crisp twenties, and stuffed them into a jeans pocket. "I will meet you back here in two hours, señor. The javelina like to feed in the late afternoon. Excuse me for asking, but have you ever hunted before? You don't look…"

"I was in Africa tracking wildebeest on the Serengeti, but that was years back. I'm still pretty good with a rifle, though." George smiled broadly, and the two shook hands.

The banker quickly calculated that he'd still save money on this deal over what DeBlough would have charged, although the odds of failure were greater. But then George liked to create his own odds.

CHAPTER 29

Driving southward through Ventura, Sergeant Saldano thinks about Culver City and his pending research. He pushes nagging black hairs out of his eyes. His hand smells of Barbara. The scent jerks him back to their lovemaking in Morro Bay. He fights hard to concentrate. Their tearful departure reminds Paul how exasperated he gets when faced with a crying woman. They promised each other that they'd work something out. So far it's been Barbara who's arranged their rendezvous. *I'd better step up,* he thinks. *No macho heroics, just a way forward that works!*

In bumper-to-bumper traffic, he passes through the gap in the Santa Monica Hills and crawls into the Los Angeles basin. Tall Italian cypresses stick up through a mustard-yellow ground fog. He misses the ocean. Near the airport, everything stops. Paul turns the motor off and listens to the radio while the Highway Patrol and a Caltrans crew clear away an overturned big rig loaded with lettuce. It's an hour before traffic moves. He takes the Venice Boulevard off-ramp and pulls into the Culver City Hall parking lot before noon. With a badge clipped to his belt, Paul moves inside the glass-fronted building and follows the signs down a hallway to a counter where a pretty woman wearing a telephone headset works on a crossword puzzle.

"I'm Sergeant Paul Saldano with the County Sheriff's Department. I'm looking for information. Can you help me?"

The woman looks up and arches an eyebrow but says nothing.

"I'm looking for information on a Patrick O'Neal. He was a General during World War II and a Culver City resident."

"Wouldn't he be dead by now?" the woman says in a high valley-girl voice. Paul tries not to show impatience. "Yes, I'm sure he is. But I'd like to know if the City has any of his records, anything about his history. Maybe he was a Council Member after the war. I'd be happy with anything you've got."

"Just a minute, please." The woman sighs, grasps the computer mouse, and clicks her way through dozens of directories and file folders until stopping at one.

"You're almost right, Sergeant. He wasn't an elected official. But in 1946, Culver City hired an Administrator named Patrick O'Neal. He worked here until 1952. But that's all I can tell you."

"Don't you folks keep personnel files on employees?" Paul asks. "Surely there's a home address listed in there."

The woman stares blankly back. "Sergeant, we're talking more than seventy years ago. We didn't even have a personnel office until the '80s."

"What about other City records?"

"All of our old stuff was shipped to the Historical Society to archive."

"Can you direct me to their offices and give me a contact person to speak with?"

The woman smiles unexpectedly and stifles a laugh. "I sure can. You'll need to talk with Miss Clayton March…and boy, she's gonna really enjoy your visit."

Paul's forehead wrinkles. The clerk continues. "Miss March has never married and is pushing 90. She runs the archives as if they are her own personal papers. Her record keeping is, how can I put this kindly, not exactly state of the art. I once spent three days down there digging through cardboard boxes, only to have her find what I needed in an unlabeled folder on her desk."

"Sounds like the Sheriff's Department's system. I'll feel right at home."

"Better not tell Miss March that, 'cause she'll never let you outta there without reciting her life story."

"I'm kind of a history buff."

"Well, good luck then," the clerk says and grins. "Her office is down the block in the only brick building on the left side."

Saldano has no trouble finding the Historical Society, an East Coast style edifice with a steeply pitched slate roof and a portico supported by granite columns. Paul pulls hard on the heavy bronze door and enters a room filled with glass display cases and bookshelves. Portraits of men in double-breasted suits, some riding in open cars with spoked wheels, stare down at him. A huge chandelier draped in cobwebs provides light. The place feels like a bank lobby from the 1930s. Paul's the only one there.

"Can I help you, sir?" a strong, mannish voice calls out.

Paul glances to his left and discovers a tall woman seated in a carved mahogany chair. She reaches for a silver-handled cane and pushes up. Her unsteady movements cause dangling glass earrings to dance wildly and accentuate her precarious battle with gravity and age. She pulls a shawl over liver-spotted forearms and slowly strides forward to meet Saldano under the chandelier, extending a bony hand for him to grasp. They barely touch. Saldano realizes, *this old gal may be ninety, but she can still manage men.*

"You must be Miss March. I was told you could help me. I'm Paul Saldano with the County Sheriff's Department. I'm looking for information about a Culver City man."

The heron-framed woman extracts a pair of silver glasses from a pocket hidden under the shawl and puts them on. She studies his face as if trying to understand his history and character. Feeling embarrassed, Paul moves to a nearby table and pulls out a chair for Miss March to not-so-gracefully slump into.

"Actually there are two Culver City residents that I'm

interested in. Both lived here during World War II."

"Sergeant, you have come to the right person. I was a young woman working in the steno pool for the Selznick Studios back then. This town was full of movie people and those who wanted to be around them. You know, they used to call Culver City the *Heart of Screenland*, but the war changed all that. Who is it you wish to know about?"

"Well, first, do you have anything on a George DeVaul? I have a letter written to him that includes his address." Paul gives her a photocopy of General O'Neal's letter.

Miss March adjusts her glasses and stares down her nose at the looping handwriting. "Well, I can't tell you much about the recipient, except that this home address is now part of a Wal-Mart parking lot over on Palms Street. That old Washington Boulevard area was a comfortable neighborhood back then but was taken over by Sony Studios when they gobbled up MGM in the '80s. There are directories that I can look in, but I can't remember any prominent citizen by that name. But the author of this letter is another story."

"So you know something about Patrick O'Neal?"

"Most certainly. During the war, the Hal Roach studio was commandeered by the Army and produced nothing but training films. They used to call it Fort Roach. They hired General O'Neal as a part-time advisor near the end of the European conflict."

"So you met him doing steno work on a project?"

"No, silly. Remember I worked for Selznick, not for Roach, and besides, Roach himself was off in Europe somewhere getting shot at by the Krauts. But all us peons from the various studios, including people like Patrick, would meet after work at the nightclubs on Venice Boulevard. I was young once, you know, and cut a fine line in my day. Patrick was married to a dreadful woman and had a family, so we never could be legitimate. We'd just meet for drinks and talk." Miss March sighs, the color comes up in her cheeks and her eyes glaze ever so slightly.

"He had gotten a job with the studio right after coming out of the Army. Some local hotshots must have recommended him because those jobs were scarce. But he worked out well for Roach and got dozens of screen credits, although most were training films. I've got a few in the basement if you want to preview them." Miss March pauses, and Paul quickly shakes his head.

"Patrick did all right for the studio, and they recommended him for a job with the City."

"Yes, I've been to City Hall, and the woman in the Clerk's Office said that he'd worked there long ago."

A grimace crosses the old woman's face. "You probably talked with that ditzy dame, Kerrie. She couldn't file anything unless somebody recited the alphabet to her first."

"Well, she did have a few things to say about you, too."

Miss Marsh tries to look indignant but can't quite control the smirk that curls her wide, creased lips. "All the men looked so handsome in their uniforms back then. I had my eye on the best of them, but it never took. Patrick was spoken for and didn't come to the clubs after quitting the studio. A few years later, he had a stroke, and the family sent him to a rest home out in the valley. He died in 1956.

"The man was barely in his 50s and already gone, just like most of the studios. The town council used to complain that they never credited Culver City for being the production site of all those great films. The companies knew that Hollywood sounded sexier. But now that they do credit this morass of urban sprawl, most of the studios are gone, replaced with this new commercial junk they call shopping malls and big box stores." Miss March scowls, her bitter voice echoing in the musty room.

"I know what you mean," Saldano says gently. "I've been working on Catalina Island, and it's hard getting used to this mainland clutter again. But tell me, did General O'Neal leave any of his papers or records with the City? I'm trying to determine his relationship to this George DeVaul and maybe others."

"I have several file folders downstairs that you can go through. It's been four decades since I've looked at them. Nobody cares about the war years in Culver City, except for us few survivors. Follow me, and I'll set you up at a table."

Miss March hobbles to a stairway that leads downward. She fingers an old push button style switch, and a bare light bulb glows over a wooden table. Disappearing into darkness, she returns carrying two accordion files with Patrick O'Neal's name written on their jackets. She hovers over Saldano. He unclasps the files and quickly pages through yellowed papers, journals, sepia photographs, and official-looking documents: Army orders, children's birth certificates, old bank books, and a few unredeemed war bonds.

"Thank you, Miss March. This is wonderful," Saldano says. "I'll take an hour or so to go through it. If I have any questions..." The old woman's sad eyes make him stop. "Tell you what, why don't you sit here with me and I can ask questions as I go along. We can hear if anybody comes in upstairs."

"Don't worry about that, Sergeant. This is Monday, and I'm lucky if I get a couple school kids doing a history report or some such foolishness."

They sit quietly in their spot of brightness. Paul extracts each document reverently, studies it, and occasionally asks her about references. The afternoon drags on. The curator leans back in her chair, eyes half closed. Paul unties the binding around one last bundle of envelopes. Near the middle of the stack, he finds a letter that wakes him up.

November 3, 1942

Brigadier General Patrick O'Neal, Commander

Fourth Army Training Center, Headquarters Battalion
Camp Ord, California

Dear General O'Neal:

I am sure that you will keep the contents of this letter in the greatest of confidence. I am writing you about a matter that is extremely important to myself and other prominent members of the Laurel Canyon Gentlemen's Club. Since you are from our part of California, you undoubtedly comprehend the standing of our organization in civic and political circles. Therefore, you can imagine our great shock and dismay when we discovered that many of our sons received their induction notices at the same time and are now undergoing training at your camp.

While all of our families support this Country's efforts to rid the world of such tyranny that threatens both our shores, we are afraid that tomorrow's community leaders may not survive this conflict. To avoid this waste, we humbly request that you consider our plight when making duty assignments for our boys. Surely, there must be some benign West Coast installation where they can contribute to the war effort. I have attached a list of their names, service numbers, and training units to ease the need for any research on your part.

Please do not hesitate to contact me if you have further concerns. This war will be over someday, and on behalf of the Laurel Canyon Gentlemen's Club, we would welcome you back into our community's society and commerce with open arms. Thank you for your consideration of this request.

Respectfully,

Mr. Michael Spangler, President
Stanley H. DeVaul Sr., Secretary
Laurel Canyon Gentlemen's Club
P.O. Box 432
Topanga, California

Saldano scans the list of names and serial numbers of the Army trainees and confirms that they're the forgotten platoon stationed at the Saint Catherine Hotel. Paul reads the letter over three times to make sure. *Those good ole boys really did it,* he thinks, *bought their sons a pass from active duty in return for setting up O'Neal with cushy jobs after the war.*

The remaining papers in the file include short thank-you notes from other members of the Laurel Canyon Club. *O'Neal probably kept these in case he needed favors from them.*

Saldano scrapes back his chair. Miss March startles from her nap. She tries to cover her embarrassment with questions about Paul's research.

"Yes, I think I've found what I was looking for," he says. "Do you have a copy machine I can use?"

"Certainly, but let me see what you've found."

Paul hands over the linen page. Miss March stares at it and shakes her head. "There's that DeVaul name again. I don't remember ever seeing it before. But then Patrick was one of the people I tried to forget from that time. We could have been an item, but…"

The old woman leads Paul upstairs, where he burns three photocopies.

"So, do you think there might be anything on George DeVaul here?" he asks.

The curator shakes her head. "But I know something about that Laurel Canyon bunch. Patrick talked about their stylish parties that he and Edith attended. The Club families were rich snobs who owned major holdings throughout the LA basin. But that was before the war. After VJ day, every carpetbagging idiot came to town, and this place was torn apart by progress, so they called it. The Club was old money, as old as anything ever is in California. They faded away, sort of the reverse of *The Great Gatsby*, if you get my meaning."

Paul nods and collects his papers. "You've been more helpful than you know, Miss March."

The old woman smiles toothily and extends a hand to be clasped for the last time. "You've never told me the reason for your research, Sergeant. Come back when you can and give me the whole story."

"I will, Miss March, I will."

But like PFC Briggs in the VA hospital, Saldano knows these last remaining members of the swing era won't survive much longer. The grandfather clock in the corner strikes five. Paul hustles to the parking lot and drives as fast as rush hour traffic allows. He arrives at the San Pedro terminal as the ferry's air horn announces its departure. Once onboard, he orders a soda from the bored snack bar attendant. The hawsers are let go, and the ship noses into the calm backwaters of the Wilmington inlet. *I can hardly wait to call Barbara and give her the news*, he thinks, *but then I still haven't figured out....*" Saldano pushes the whole affair out of his mind and stares at the harbor lights as the ship presses outward onto the rolling seas of the San Pedro Channel.

CHAPTER 30

Barbara Spencer feels like she's been here before. Not this particular stretch of highway but in this emotional junkyard where the wrecks of past and yet-to-be relationships reside. The Salinas Valley's lettuce fields flow past her windshield unnoticed. She clicks on the radio. The upbeat Mariachi music sounds like European polkas or maybe Arabian folk dances. But even this joyful noise can't shake the blues from her heart.

Barbara was happy that Paul hadn't freaked out when she'd declared Lisa's need for a father. But that hadn't resolved anything...and Paul hadn't been convincing in his promise to make their relationship work. *Praise be to Allah, he's hanging on by a thread there in Avalon,* she thinks, *too shy to even show us his apartment...and his drinking problem...*

Barbara picks up Lisa from her friend's house in Daly City. Through the last hour of stop-and-go traffic, her daughter chatters about how Marsha can wear makeup; how Marsha has already gone out on dates to Junior High dances; how Marsha has her own training bra and cell phone; how the Reynolds never cook anything but live on fast food and pizza delivery. Barbara's glad to hear this schoolgirl prattle. It keeps their conversation away from her own weekend with Paul.

But Lisa isn't totally self-absorbed. While helping her mother unpack the suitcase, she peppers Barbara with questions: "So what does Paul look like in civilian clothes? Is he really handsome, or was it the uniform? What did you guys do anyway? Did you go shopping or maybe fishing? Are there neat things for kids there? Can I come with you next time? You *are* going again, aren't you? He didn't do something stupid, did he? Ah, jeez, Mom, you didn't give him the speech about Muslim women? Why are you crying, Mother?"

Barbara shakes her head and escapes to the bathroom, emerging a few minutes later with a pasted-on smile and red-rimmed eyes. She tugs at her tangled hair with splayed fingers and sits on the edge of the bed next to her daughter.

"I can't give you any details, Lisa. I don't know what's going to happen."

"You mean you can't tell me about the sex. I know more than you think, Mom. I *am* twelve."

Barbara hugs her and laughs. "Yes, I'm sure you do. But it's more than that. We live so far apart and it's hard to see how we can be together, to learn about each other."

"Does he want to be with us? Did he ask you?"

"I think Paul is as confused as I am right now. You can't press these things, or they can go very wrong. You will have to trust me."

"I know. It's just that you really like this guy, and he seems to like us. I can't help thinking about it. Being with the Reynolds this weekend was something else, and even if Dad's a complete idiot, I miss it, ya know?"

Barbara clutches her daughter and snorts back a sob. They rise to prepare dinner. Over the past year, Barbara taught Lisa how to cook fine mid-eastern dishes. Lisa always jokes that it's her Mother's Samboosak or Sidreyat Al Dajaj that drove serious boyfriends away. Secretly, Barbara knows that the food is a test of a man's cultural tolerance…a test that Saldano has yet to pass.

They gather the fixings to make pita stuffed with rice and lamb. The telephone buzzes. Barbara checks her watch and lifts the receiver slowly.

"Hello."

"Barbara, this is Paul. I wanted to make sure you got home

safely."

Barbara hisses at her daughter to turn off the gas range. Lisa joins her on the sofa to eavesdrop. Barbara frowns but lets her be.

"Yes, yes. The trip home was fine, although my car sounds terrible. It may never make that trip again. But Lisa had a fun weekend with her girlfriend's family…and…and so did I… actually fun doesn't quite describe it, does it?"

"No, no, it doesn't," Paul says, and hurries onward. "Let me tell you what I've learned in Culver City. At least one more piece of the puzzle came together."

Paul recounts his afternoon with Miss March and his discovery of the letter describing the circumstances that brought Stanley DeVaul to Catalina Island.

"So we know why he was there and that he didn't leave by normal military channels," Barbara says. "We also know he had a Mexican girlfriend. But how Stanley supposedly ended up getting killed in the Ardennes doesn't make sense. And none of this helps you find out who killed that island woman. There are so many missing pieces."

"I know. Believe me, I know. I have my own theories, but none of them explain how two skeletons ended up on the side of the China Wall. If General O'Neal could fix DeVaul's duty assignment, he could also fake Stanley's reassignment to Europe and his death. Proving any of it would be difficult and would take more work. But Frank has already assigned me additional duty at the West End, so I'm not sure what more I can do from here."

"What about the ballistics report on the round that killed the girl? Have you gotten anything on that?"

"Jeez, thanks for reminding me. I've got nothing, and it's been more than two months. But even if we can narrow the ordnance used, it's still a needle-in-a-haystack search."

Barbara's voice catches. "All...all I know is that I don't want us to fizzle...even if this case does."

The two of them have danced around the unspoken questions, and Barbara can't hold it in any more. Paul is quiet, and the static on the line grows louder.

"I said I'd work on it, and I will. I have an idea I want to check out before getting our hopes up. But tell me, how much time do you have left on your enlistment?"

"Well, that's just it," Barbara says and sighs, her tension finding release. "I have three months left on this hitch and must decide whether to re-up or not. But I need to know if we are going anywhere...whether you want to be with Lisa and me. I know this is a big question, but..."

"Wanting to be with you and Lisa is the easy question. I want that more than anything, and if it goes well, I want it... forever."

They laugh as their emotions surge. Lisa giggles and Barbara shushes her, trying to regain control.

"We have so much to talk about, so many questions," she says. "I'll get no Army pension if I quit now, and on your income, how...how could we live?" The silence builds again before Paul speaks.

"I could try and get another day off to meet you in Morro Bay to, you know, talk."

"We're too, ah, how should I say this, attracted to one other to talk much," Barbara replies, conscious of Lisa hanging on every word. "Maybe we can do this by phone for a while and... and Lisa and I will take a weekend during Easter break and come to Catalina. We'll both have more answers by then."

"I love you," Paul blurts.

"And I love you," Barbara says in a serious voice, the moment only marred by Lisa's continued giggling.

They shift quickly to more stable territory and begin

planning their next meeting, this time on Paul's home turf. Barbara promises to research Army records one last time to see if anything about O'Neal or DeVaul turns up.

"You know, last time when you came with me, we had good luck with the old Mexican, Felipe. It's time we shake the tree to see what falls. Are you up for another barrio adventure?" Paul asks.

"I sure am…but warn the guy ahead of time so he leaves his Enfield in the closet."

But each of them seems more focused on seeing each other than on solving the case. Paul's mind races: *How could we live on Catalina? Or should I move to San Francisco? Could I stand working a city beat again? Who can I ask for advice on this island where I'm still an outsider?* Slowly, the seed of an idea begins to grow in Paul's brain, and he shoves it aside, knowing that if he thinks about it anymore tonight, he'll never sleep.

"Barbara, tell Lisa what we've talked about. It's part of her life and her decision, too."

"Are you kidding? She's been eavesdropping the whole time. She likes you, Paul, although you've only been with us once. We'll see how it goes when we come south."

"I love you, Barbara. We'll talk tomorrow."

"I love you too," she says, and they ring off.

Paul sits clutching the edge of his bed, not wanting to put the phone down. He's reminded of the first time he'd said those words…to Juanita Vargas back in Cuero, Texas. They were fifteen, full of raging hormones and that stinging electrical current that's never forgotten. *But this time, it feels…it feels right.*

CHAPTER 31

A cool afternoon wind blew hard off the channel. George DeVaul turned up the collar of his bush jacket to fend off its battering surge. He'd been waiting at the harbor's edge for an hour and wondered if the Mexican kid had decided to keep his money and disappear back to the barrio. Two neatly trimmed Shore Patrol sailors approached and asked to see his papers. George flinched at the possibility of being taken in for questioning or worse, considered a spy like that poor bastard DeBlough. But Avalon's long afternoon sunlight had a soporific effect. The SPs moved off at a leisurely gait, leaving George to check his wristwatch and drum chunky fingers on the railing.

The sound of grinding gears and a whining motor approached. The ugliest-looking International Harvester flatbed he'd ever seen rounded Lover's Cove and jerked to a stop. Blue smoke seeped through its engine vents. The truck threatened to shake itself apart. Inside, the Mexican kid clutched the steering wheel like a racecar driver.

George laughed. "You really think this thing's gonna take us up to the ridge?"

The kid grinned and motioned him inside. George slid onto the seat and tried slamming the door, succeeding the fourth time. A bundle partially tucked under the bench crowded his feet. George didn't make a move to inspect it. *Better get the hell outta town before I check our firepower,* he thought.

On the Old Stagecoach Road leaving Avalon, the Mexican boy muscled the truck around blind corners, past sheer drops to the green Pacific. He pulled over and stopped several times to let the engine cool. But they made it to the top and halted at an unmanned gate. George jumped out, swung it open, and waved the boy through.

Ridgeline trees bent permanently toward the southeast. A strong wind buffeted the truck and forced it toward the edges of canyons wallpapered with puffy sagebrush. After a few minutes, the boy tugged hard on the steering wheel and turned the Harvester onto a dirt tract. They rolled to a stop behind a knoll hidden from the ridge road. The engine died of its own accord.

"We can walk from here," the kid said. "The javelinas use these trails."

"Are we close to the China Wall?" George asks.

"Yes, but why?"

"No reason…I've heard so much about it from the locals."

"It is a beautiful and dangerous place, Señor, not good to get too close."

George pulled the bundle from beneath the seat and climbed out. He unwrapped it and laid two rifles on the truck's flatbed. The kid set a box of 30-calibre shells next to them. The weapons looked old, of World War I military vintage. George examined them and chose a .03 Springfield with an internal magazine, leaf sights, and a huge bolt that worked smoothly. He decided that this heavy gun would be good in the wind. He remembered trying to hold his scoped Savage steady while sighting on a bull wildebeest on the Serengeti and felt satisfied with the heft of this rifle.

George flipped the leaf sights and picked a setting. He pressed five rounds into the Springfield's magazine and set the safety. The kid worked the bolt of what looked like a British or German rifle. George couldn't be sure. They each pocketed a handful of cartridges, adjusted the straps, and slipped the weapons over their shoulders. The boy led them along a barely discernable path that wound through clumps of coyote brush, dwarf oak thickets, and clattering eucalyptus. Every few minutes, he bent to inspect tracks that crossed the trail. George snuck quick glances at the ridge road off to their right, watching and hoping. But miles from town, he doubted that Stanley and his girl would walk this far just to escape prying eyes.

They took a smoke break in the shade of a rock outcropping. Circling ravens loudly announced their positions and taunted them to keep going.

"Have you brought others here?" George asked.

"No señor, not by myself. I've only been up here hunting four or five times. My neighbor, who lent us these rifles, used to be a guide before Pearl Harbor. He would sometimes take my brother, Felipe, and me with him. We would retrieve the gringo's kills. They paid us a dollar."

"Do you know if the military patrols this area? I don't want to attract any trouble that greenbacks can't get us out of."

"The Shore Patrol drives the road three times a day. But the third patrol has already passed. Camp Cactus is on the other side of the island, and the airport miles away. Nobody will hear or see us."

The two kicked dirt over their discarded cigarette butts and pushed through shoulder-high chaparral, working westward toward Blackjack Peak. The setting sun reflected off the windows of homes overlooking San Pedro Harbor, flashing random distress signals to the hunters across twenty-four miles of ocean. They trudged through soft sand, breathing hard, resting often. The sweat poured down George's back, but when they stopped, the chilling wind caused him to shiver and wish for the brandy flask he'd forgotten back at the bungalow.

They forced their way through a dense oak thicket toward the top of a knoll. A foghorn sounded from far down the island. Wisps of gray cotton poured over the ridge from the west. When they emerged from the trees, George glanced toward the road and froze. A man and woman stood along its graded fringe, maybe two hundred yards downwind, their backs to the hunters, gazing across the channel. The Mexican kid followed George's stare and shook his head.

"I knew they'd be up here," he muttered and turned to retreat along the path in the direction they'd come.

"Wait, wait," George hissed. "We can sneak past them and hunt farther down." *Damn it, I need to get closer,* he thought, *I need a clear shot.*

He reached for the kid's arm and tried to spin him around. But the boy resisted, and they lost their balance in the soft soil.

The deafening explosion quieted their surroundings. Even the foghorn sounded muffled. George pulled himself from a clump of lemonade bush. The kid crouched on the trail and brushed sand from his eyes. George still gripped the Springfield, its strap wrapped tightly around his forearm. But the kid's rifle must have gone flying. The boy looked around, panic-stricken, but found it in the brush and shook the dirt from its barrel.

Only a few seconds had passed. The hunters looked onto the ridge road. The man stood and stared out and down at the blueness before him. The woman had vanished.

CHAPTER 32

George is a pompous ass, Stanley thought. *What do any of them know about love?* He strode from the steamer pier and headed for their hideaway. At least they had only one set of family members to dodge now that his brother had sailed for the mainland. *I can almost hear George's brain grinding, cooking up some story to tell the old man. Father's not gonna like it.* Stan smiled to himself, taking pleasure in the thought of his Father's discomfort.

The low moan of the steamer's horn announced its departure for Wilmington. Stan imagined the almost-empty ship going down in mid-channel, torpedoed by a sneaky Japanese submarine, with Stan none the sadder. He tried to concentrate on Flavia's arrival and their mad lovemaking after two days of abstinence. But his anger with George washed all those feelings away. He paced the room and smoked.

She arrived late. Barely inside the door, Flavia stripped off her clothes and threw them on the bed before she noticed Stan sitting at the kitchen table.

She crooned in her best bedroom voice, "Your brother left this morning. So why such a glum face?"

Stan brushed at cigarette smoke and glowered at her. "That bastard knows about us. I can feel it. And all he can think about is Father's reaction and making money on the war. It's sad that your family suffers from the war while mine makes a fortune off it. How can you stand being with me, coming from a family like that?"

"You are not like that…and that's why I love you." Flavia rested on his lap and kissed him.

Stan still couldn't let go. "Now that they know about us, they'll be back. If I know Father and George, we'll need to make plans fast. I've been thinking. We should go to Mexico and not wait until I'm discharged."

"But my love, my parents would be heartbroken if I ran away…and yours could afford to hunt us down. And then there is the Army…."

"Yes, yes, you're right. But sitting here waiting, spending these few hours together, and hiding everything. It's got to stop."

"I have the day after tomorrow off from work, and it's a school holiday. Let's walk up to the China Wall and back. By the time we return, we will know what to do."

Stan nodded. He brushed her glossy hair away from her breasts, unhooked her bra, and nuzzled her warm womanhood. On shaking legs, he carried her to the bed. He touched her until perspiration stood out on her face. Their moans sounded in cadence to the call of the mourning doves pecking at crumbs in the courtyard.

—

Two days later, they met at the Chimes Tower above Casino Point and walked uphill steadily, the morning sun hot on their shoulders. Without tourists, few vehicles used the road to the airport. They sweated freely, savored the saltiness of their kisses, and paused to watch a Coast Guard patrol boat cut the sea far below. By mid-morning, they'd climbed the two miles to the ridge and wandered along the road's fringe, cooling in the on-shore breeze.

Finally, Stanley spoke. "I have saved some money. I know a man who will sell me a sailboat and keep quiet about it. She's not big…but looks sturdy enough to take us to Mexico."

Flavia remained quiet.

"Well, what do you think?"

"I know you are a good sailor. But can you get away from

those patrol boats?" Flavia pointed downslope to the cluster of craft moored in Toyon Bay.

"Those boats are manned by landlubbers from Kansas." Stan laughed. "Don't worry about them."

Flavia remained unsmiling. "Can you bear living where no one speaks English? Will you get tired of me after a while and want the riches your family can give you?"

"I am a solitary person, Flavia. Language is not something I prize…except with you, and besides, you can teach me Spanish. As for our love and my family…I want to paint you as you grow old. I want to paint our children and their children. If I can do that and be with you, then to hell with my family."

They kissed. The wind whipped Flavia's hair into a swirling halo above her head.

"But *mi Madre y Padre* will be so sad if I run away…and they depend on me for the money I make at the restaurant. What will they do without it?" She sighed.

Stanley encircled her with his arms. "I don't know, Flavia… but this war can't last much longer, and besides, I can write my brother and make him help out. He's always throwing his money around and it's about time he does something good with it."

"But won't your family find you…force you to return?"

"Not if we do this right. When I leave this island, I will be a deserter from the Army…and the Army shoots deserters. My family will have to leave me be in Mexico, even if they know where I am. But I'm counting on you to help hide us."

Pushing Flavia away, Stan slipped off his dog tags and, with a mighty heave, sent them tinkling down-slope to disappear into the brush carpeting the China Wall.

"So, Flavia, what do you say? Speak to me." He embraced his Mayan princess and felt the fine tremor in her soft body.

"*Si, mi amore, si, si,* yes," Flavia answered.

Stan's embrace nearly crushed her. She beat on his back,

begging for air. They stood as one for a long time. Stanley schemed about how to escape from Catalina and what they'd need on the open boat journey south. They separated and stood apart, facing the blue channel with a foggy wind at their backs.

From a distance came a soft pop, then the infinitesimal sound of a stinging wasp. Stanley glanced to his right. The front of Flavia's blouse exploded in a fountain of red. She stared into his eyes uncomprehending. Her stare became fixed. She toppled forward.

Stanley screamed into the abyss. Flavia's body dropped free for the first part, then bounced off rocks with an unforgettable sickening sound. She came to rest, a red-and-white speck in the center of a brush patch. The sugar bush seemed to part in anticipation of Flavia's landing. It closed around her and exposed barely a trace of what had been his love. Nothing moved. He knew it wouldn't.

Stanley stood frozen, looking downward, unconscious of anything but an intense desire to fling himself off the mountain and join Flavia at her final resting place. Gradually, he heard other sounds…screamed words in Spanish. He turned. Two men raced toward him. The tall, lanky one shrieked while his short, stubby partner struggled to keep up. They carried rifles. Stan recognized them. His brain numbed. Dark spots floated before his eyes. But as the men drew near, the sound of the tall one's anguish forced Stanley to remain conscious.

"*Donde esta, Flavia*? *Donde esta, Flavia*?" where is Flavia, the young Mexican pleaded in between gasps.

Stan gripped him by the shoulders and dragged him to the edge of the China Wall. He pointed downslope to the speck of white blouse. The boy let out a long animal cry and covered his head and face with his arms, letting the rifle drop.

"It was an accident, Stan, an accident, just an accident," George babbled, "nothing more, an accident. She's only a

Mexican. It'll be better in the long run."

Stanley's numbness and disbelief turned to rage. With a clenched fist, he caught his brother full in the face, smashing his nose and front teeth. George's blood splattered them both. George ducked the next punch and charged Stanley with open arms. The two struggled, like children in a schoolyard fight, grunting and cursing. They stumbled along the verge. George broke free, staggered backwards, and collided with the young Mexican.

The boy fell without a sound, tumbled end over end until smashing into a shale outcropping, sliding limply across a scree slope and coming to rest under gray-green brush. George and Stanley stared downward, the sound of their hoarse breathing mixed with a raven's cry.

The blood drained from Stanley's face, and he slumped to the ground.

George ran to retrieve the truck and began rehearsing his story. It was something he could do, something he could fix, something the family's money could help wash away. Two dead...but the DeVauls had survived.

"Fix it," George kept muttering to himself, trying to exorcise the look on his brother's face while mopping his own bloodied cheeks with a silk handkerchief. He jerked Stan's rubbery body into the flatbed's cab and propped him upright while chanting his mantra: "I'll fix it, Stan...you'll see, I'll fix it."

CHAPTER 33

Spring rains have left Catalina's hillsides green. Sergeant Saldano stares across their flanks from his Explorer, parked at a turnout high above Avalon Harbor and the glowing white Casino. He scans the island's westward curve and wonders how Barbara will react to his idea, his only idea. *I don't want to push her,* he thinks, *but if I don't do something, I'll lose her.*

The couple has talked on the phone nightly, their conversations covering the same old territory. They've tried to focus on the case. Paul followed up on the long-overdue ballistics report. But the lab boys could only tell him that the bullet that killed the girl likely came from a .30 caliber rifle, the most popular caliber since World War I.

Barbara continued her records search. She traced a Private Heber, one of the Saint Catherine Eight, to a nursing home in San Diego. But he'd stroked out two weeks before her inquiry, and the VA records hadn't been updated.

Inevitably their conversations returned to their future together. The Army denied Barbara's transfer request to a Southern California duty station. She notified her CO, Major Seltzer, that she might quit the Army, which he reacted to with indifference.

Meanwhile, Paul had surfed the Internet for job openings in the San Francisco area. But with California's less-than-golden economy, no one's hiring. Both realize that as long as Barbara stays in the Army, she could be transferred away at any time and leave Paul hanging at the end of an even longer phone connection.

After six weeks, nothing's been settled. Neither has devised a plan for how they can live together and support a family. But Paul works hard on a single idea.

From his perch high above Avalon, Saldano watches a gleaming white speck on the azure sea grow to become the 11 o'clock boat from San Pedro. As the ferry nears the harbor entrance, he fires up the Explorer and descends to the boat docks, where the crew finishes cinching the lines to the Island Queen. He watches from the railing. Arriving passengers gather their luggage and scramble down the ramp to the floating platform, then up again onto the concrete landing.

There's a large contingent of foreign families. Paul enjoys trying to distinguish northern and eastern European voices and the more difficult Asian and Far Eastern tongues. He searches for Barbara and Lisa. The last passengers disembark. His heart sinks. *Maybe they've missed the boat,* he thinks, *or…or decided not to come.*

"Well, Sergeant, what do you think of my *Abaaya*?" a voice asks from behind.

Saldano turns to find a woman and a girl. The woman's dressed in a full-length silk gown of royal purple with gold fringe. A scarf of matching color covers her head, concealing the hair. A gauze-like veil hides the face. Paul stares open-mouthed while Lisa, dressed in her own gown but without the veil, smiles from behind her mother.

"See, I told ya he wouldn't, ya know, recognize us." Lisa giggles.

Paul gathers Barbara in his arms, peels back her veil, and kisses her lips.

"In my village," Barbara says, laughing, "I'd be beaten by my father and brother for doing that. But not so fast. You haven't answered my question."

"You both look great," Paul blurts. "If I'd seen you like

this when I was in Saudi Arabia, I'd still be there." He bends and kisses Lisa on the cheek. The girl blushes and dances away. The morning breeze whips her gown and exposes tiny ballerina-type shoes.

Paul stoops to pick up their luggage, and they walk the block to the Pavilion Lodge. He stays with them while they check in. The desk clerk gives Paul and his harem the hard once-over and smirks. Paul clamps down hard on his excitement while the two females debate the day's itinerary.

"Ah, come on Mom, you promised," Lisa complains.

"I know, I know I did," Barbara says, frowning. "I said you could go shopping by yourself but…but Avalon's a strange town, and I'm afraid that—"

"Marsha's Mom lets her hang out at the mall, and all of my friends do it. I promise I'll be careful."

"She should be okay for the afternoon," Paul says gently. "We'll be back from talking with Felipe before sunset."

"Oh, sure. You just want to get me alone," Barbara cracks.

"See, even Paul thinks it's okay," Lisa persists, "and he's a cop."

"Oh, all right," Barbara mutters.

Barbara and Paul agree to meet after lunch at the Sheriff's Station, then drive to Pebbly Beach to interview the old Mexican.

"And don't worry," Barbara says, laughing, "I've brought Western clothes. I won't waltz into your office dressed like the Queen of Sheba. But it was worth seeing your face."

"Are you kidding? Please keep wearing the gown, at least until after we leave the Station. They've been whispering about us ever since the last time you showed up. It's time we give them something to gossip about."

Saldano retrieves the Explorer, gobbles lunch, and completes his patrol of the up canyon areas before returning to base. Over the last week he's thought of different ways to approach the old Mexican, how to ask the questions without Felipe clamming up. He's decided that he and Barbara should go over the questions and that she should do the asking. Her beauty and grace will disarm the old guy much better than his pressed uniform.

Paul stares at the questions he's penciled into his notebook. Deputy Hanson taps on his door and sticks her head inside the office.

"Sergeant, there's a woman…a Barbara Spencer…she says she has an appointment. Should I show her in?"

Paul looks up from his notes. "No, I'll come out and get her…she's working on the China Wall homicide with me.

"Oh really," Hansen says.

"Don't you remember her from the last time?" Paul struggles to conceal a grin.

"No…and I would definitely remember this lady. Where did you say she's from?"

"I didn't."

Paul joins Barbara in the reception area. Taking her hand, they pass slowly down the hallway to his office. Barbara has removed the veil and lowered the front of her gown to display an intricately tooled golden necklace. She also wears bracelets of similar design on each wrist. They jingle musically as she walks. The staring faces of deputies filling coffee cups, paging through files, or writing reports are flash-frozen as the couple passes. The duo ducks into Saldano's office and stifles their laughter at the reaction. They sit at his desk. He wonders what they can get away with behind the frosted glass walls and settles on a quick squeeze of her hand. "You are amazing, and I love you."

"You should have waited until later to say that," Barbara whispers and leans toward him. Paul motions to the blurred silhouettes of curious deputies passing in the hall. She sits back and sighs. He retrieves his notebook, and they talk about the afternoon's business.

"Yes, that sounds like a good plan," Barbara says. "I'll ask the questions and you translate them into Spanish if Felipe doesn't understand."

Paul smiles. "But we gotta keep it loose…the notebook stays behind. I wish I could wear civvies, but I'm on duty until six."

"Don't worry, ole Felipe will be looking at me anyway," Barbara says, chuckling.

"He won't be the only one."

Leaving Paul's office, Barbara appears to glide over the floor on a cushion of air. She slides into the Explorer. Paul notices that she carries a satchel made from the same material as her gown and raises an eyebrow.

"I didn't think Felipe would be ready for me in this attire, so I brought my street clothes. I was going to change at the station but decided against it…didn't want to ruin the illusion. Maybe you could show me your place…and I can change there."

Paul flashes to his garage apartment: dirty dishes dumped in the sink, folded clothes left on the dresser, the bed half made, the bathroom…. He mentally groans. "You sure you want to see how a bachelor cop lives? I feel like I'm taking a queen to visit the goat herder's shed."

"You forget how Lisa and I live. Believe me, it's no palace. But I really want to see your place. I can tell a lot about a person from their home. And I'm not talking about how neatly they fold their laundry.

For a moment, Paul fears that she can read his mind. He grins sheepishly and turns the Explorer uphill, then onto Middle Terrace Road, where he parks along the fringe. The three-story main house towers above them, with cantilevered decks commanding views of the harbor and the mainland. But at street level, tucked into one corner, the garage has a doorway and a small curtained window cut into its original opening. Fumbling with his keys, Saldano unlocks the apartment, clicks on a dim ceiling light, and motions Barbara inside.

A kitchenette takes up the space directly under the window. A tiny bathroom occupies one back corner, its door permanently blocked open by a full bookcase. A bed and dresser are centered along the back wall. Floor-to-ceiling bookshelves line a sidewall. Barbara inspects the shelves loaded with law journals, police manuals, works of the English and American masters, small volumes of poetry, paperback westerns, back issues of *Field and Stream* magazine, a Douay-Rheims Bible, the Koran, and dog-eared books presenting the ecology, botany, and zoology of the Santa Barbara Channel Islands, including Catalina. Barbara fingers one of these.

"I figured that if I'm stationed here, I should know what else lives on this island," Paul explains.

She continues her slow inspection. Tiny framed photographs rest on the front of one shelf: two aging Latinos, a red-haired woman with two small girls in her lap, a snapshot of a shiny black Chevy with four tattooed men leaning against its front bumper, grinning, and one of Paul clutching a girl on a dance floor with a background banner saluting the Class of '87. Old penknives, stones with multi-colored streaks of quartz, and broken bits of colorful seashells complete the collection.

"Well, Sergeant Saldano, you have definitely lied to me," Barbara says in a stern voice.

Paul feels his blood run cold.

"Remember you told me once that you are a simple person? Your home tells me otherwise. Poetry and science books are not the keepsakes of a simpleton. There is definitely more to you than meets the eye." She dips her head, her face concealed behind the headscarf.

"Well…well, I've always thought I was honest," Paul

counters. "I'm simple, but I love diverse things. I'm sorry if I disappointed you."

Barbara raises her head. Shaking with laughter, she slides into his arms. "Relax, Sergeant, this is not a visit by the Inspector General. I want to know more about you, and your home tells me there is more to know. I plan on having fun finding out."

Their lips meet, their kiss soft. When they part, Barbara removes her jewelry, slips out of her gown, and busily smoothes the bed covers. Paul clicks off the light. The hot and humid apartment reminds Barbara of cool nights on the Arabian Peninsula when the women and girls of her father's house disrobe behind thick curtains and lie awake, chattering in the dusk.

The two of them lie side-by-side, quietly touching each other until Paul gently enters. Barbara gasps as her wet flesh envelops him. They move in a rhythm of their own discovery but soon stop, their bodies shaking in a final tight clasp.

They remain quiet for a time until Barbara pushes him away. "We have work to do, Sergeant," she whispers in his ear. "I don't want you falling asleep while I'm interviewing Felipe."

But he reaches for her again, strokes her until she gives in, and they take one more lovers' dance. Paul rises and flicks on the light. He looks lovingly at Barbara's soft contours and remembers lonely nights lying on this same bed, dreaming of her in his arms…and now she's here. He feels like a school kid who's finally touched his first love. Paul reaches for Barbara, but she escapes to the bathroom, only to discover that she can't close its door without moving the heavy bookcase.

"I know we're lovers, but I'm still shy about some things." Her giggles sound girlish. "Turn your back until I say you can look."

Paul moves to the window, parts the curtains, and studies the horizon. The afternoon boat cuts the water near the far buoy. With averted eyes, he hastily retrieves his clothes from the floor where a wild force of nature has scattered them. Barbara's snicker startles him. Looking up, he finds her staring at his nakedness. She is fully dressed and combed. He ducks around her into the bathroom with its unshutable door.

"Don't worry, I won't peek." Barbara laughs, and he hurries to wash and dress.

As the mid-afternoon ferry blows its arrival horn, the couple drives downhill and around Lovers Cove to Pebbly Beach, hoping to discover the last piece of the puzzle.

The aromatic smell of eucalyptus and sage permeates the barrio. They find Felipe on his front veranda, sipping a long-necked beer and sorting through junk mail. The kittens are stretched out in the porch's spotted sunlight. They hardly raise their heads when Barbara and Saldano approach. The old man looks ready for *siesta*. But the Labrador pup lying at his feet won't let that happen. It springs up, tilts its snout skyward, and howls. The neighborhood dogs join in the fun. But the pup's wagging tail belays the impression of ill intent, and it retreats to the side yard to stake out its own sun patch.

"Hello, Felipe, how are you today?" Saldano greets him in Spanish.

"I am very fine." Felipe grins and attempts to rise from his cane-backed chair.

"Please, *señor*, we only want to talk with you some more," Barbara says. "You remember the last time we spoke?"

The old man laughs. "Yes, I had you in my sights. Have you come to make me an offer on my old rifle?"

"No," Saldano says. "But I'm glad you have left it inside."

The old man motions for them to sit, Paul on the edge of the porch and Barbara in the chair next to Felipe. He looks at her shyly, admiring her like a young hombre would. Barbara smiles back, and Felipe quickly finishes his beer and sits back in the chair.

"I am way too old to be flirting with you, señorita. But I can't help myself...you are so beautiful."

"Thank you." Barbara's face darkens. "But you have to know other beautiful women. Remember that drawing you have in your shed. Was she your...your girlfriend?" Barbara uses her smooth, sexy voice to charm the old guy. Paul watches in admiration.

"I haven't talked about her for many years. We all loved Flavia...especially my brother, Ramón."

"What was her story? Will you tell us?" Barbara asks quietly "We don't mean any disrespect."

Saldano notices that Felipe's eyes have taken on a thousand-yard stare. The eucalyptus trees rustle in the afternoon breeze. The Labrador pup returns to the porch. It lies at its master's feet, nose resting across a battered sandal. Barbara smiles at the old man, and after a few moments, he begins.

"It was during the last Great War when they moved our families from town into this barrio. None of us liked it...but that is how it was. Flavia lived with her parents and a brother. Her father was *patron*." Felipe pauses and stares at Barbara for a moment, then seems to decide something and continues.

"Flavia was more beautiful than that picture shows...and she was smart, went to school, and could speak English well. She worked as a waitress at a restaurant that burned in the '60s. My brother Ramón worked there too as a cook. He was crazy in love with Flavia but too shy to tell her...and there were so many others, including the gringo."

"Where is your brother now? Barbara asks. "May we speak with him?"

"No señorita, *mi hermano* is dead sixty-eight years."

"I'm sorry. Was he killed in the war?" Barbara's voice drops low. The old man seems close to tears. After a few moments, Felipe continues.

"Flavia loved this tall gringo, and they planned to run away. Many people knew about them, but the lovers thought they could hide it. It was hard for Ramón to watch.

"I was here, alone, when the two gringos returned with the truck. Ramón had borrowed it from Flavia's father to take the short one hunting. He had paid Ramón a lot of money. Flavia's lover was crying. The short one bled from the face and yelled at the other to be silent.

"I asked where my brother was. The tall one could barely speak. He told me Ramón was dead. Then the short one said there had been a hunting accident. Ramón had killed Flavia and then thrown himself off the China Wall when he realized what he'd done.

"I didn't believe those *bastardos* and wanted to shoot them both. But they had my rifle in the truck. The short one handed me the keys but took all the bullets. He pulled the tall one out, and they stumbled away. I never saw them again. They left me behind to tell Flavia's parents their only daughter was dead, to tell my own Mother and Father my brother was dead. I…I wanted to kill those cowards.

"But I, too, was a coward. I made up a story…said Ramón and Flavia had run off to Mexico. At least both families would not feel so much pain and could keep the memories of their children alive in their hearts.

"I went looking for them on the China Wall, but the coyotes and foxes must have carried them off. I still looked whenever I went up top…but now I never go.

"Did the families continue to believe your story?" Barbara asks.

"Si. Every few years, word from Mexico would come around that Flavia and Ramón had been seen in Mazatlán or maybe Guadalajara, and our parents still had hope. No one ever knew the truth. You are the first."

"Are any of Flavia's family still on this island?" Barbara asks. "They may want to know."

The old man looks at her as if for the first time and realizes where he is. "No...ah no, *señorita.* Flavia's older brother was killed in the Pacific...I think Tarawa. After the War, her parents moved back to their house in town, but they both died not so long after. It is bad to lose your children when you are not yet old. The police gave me that picture of Flavia when they divided up their belongings. I am the last one left of our two families. I can tell you everything now that it does not matter."

The old man reaches for his beer but finds it empty. He sits twisting the bottle in his misshapen hands, head bent, not speaking. Paul motions that they should leave.

Barbara rests a hand on the old man's arm. "Felipe, you did a good thing, both now and before, with the families. You gave them dreams...which are sometimes better than truth." Barbara wipes her eyes with the sleeve of her blouse.

"*Gracias, señorita.* I am glad it was you I told."

The couple walk quietly down the street, past rusting Quonset huts and amazing vegetable gardens, to the incessant hum of the power plant's turbines, spooling up to meet the evening's power drain. Neither says anything until they arrive back in town.

"I've been gone all afternoon," Barbara worries. "I wonder where Lisa is?"

"Avalon's tiny...she can't be far," Saldano says and puts an arm around Barbara. "She's probably back at the hotel watching TV."

"Yes, you're right. I'm a bit overprotective. But Lisa's all I've got."

"Well, not all...." Saldano grins, and Barbara gives him a quick kiss but remains serious.

They make plans for dinner, and Paul heads back to the

station to work his last hour. Before diving into the paperwork, he briefs the Station Commander on the case.

"See, I told you it was the Mexicans," Frank gloats. "They won't say anything to us unless they think we can help. In a way, I don't blame them. Glad you didn't waste a lot of time screwing with it."

"No sir, wouldn't want to tear myself away from the island's crime scene."

Frank fails to catch Paul's sarcasm.

That night, they meet at the Villa Portofino restaurant for excellent Italian food. Barbara remains quiet as Lisa reports on her afternoon's wise purchases from the harbor-front shops: a T-shirt with fish on it and the words "Catalina, the Island of Romance," postcards to send to her girlfriends, although she'll be back in San Francisco before they receive them, and a gold barrette for her Mother. *For a kid, she's so considerate,* Saldano thinks. His thoughts drift to his own daughters. *I wonder if they'll think about me when they're Lisa's age.*

"Well, what now, Inspector?" Barbara says, finishing dessert and a second glass of wine. "Have we solved the case, or do we look for corroborating evidence to prove your hillside skeleton is Ramón's?"

"Who would we ask? Where would we look? Everybody who was alive back then is dead…or soon will be. We don't have anything of Ramón's to try a DNA match with."

"We might get DNA from those bone fragments and compare it to Felipe's," Barbara says excitedly. "Since they were brothers, the tests would be able to verify his story."

"Do *you* want to ask poor Felipe for a blood or saliva sample?" Saldano counters.

"You're right, you're right. It would be like saying we don't believe him." Barbara sighs. Her blue mood returns.

"Trying to prove that the shooting was accidental or that

Ramón's death was a suicide...well, I'm not sure it's worth more effort," Paul murmurs. "Whether it's a murder or a series of unfortunate events doesn't matter. No one's demanding justice. I'd just as soon leave this one die." Saldano drains his soda glass. "What do you think? Do you want to keep going with it?"

"I wish we could find out what happened to Stanley," Barbara says. "In a way, I want to think of him like Felipe's story of Ramón and Flavia...out there somewhere in his old age, drawing pretty girls."

Paul and Barbara sit quietly and stare at their empty plates until Lisa pipes up. "Hey, guys, there's, ya know, a great movie at the Casino tonight. Why don't we go, and you two can stop thinking about, ya know, that murder thing."

The adults smile and nod. But their smiles are strained. Paul knows that when they abandon the case, they'll only have their own futures to contend with.

They sit in the dark theater, holding hands. Paul whispers in Barbara's ear. "You can stay with me tonight if you want. Lisa will be safe by herself at the hotel."

"No, I'd better not. I left her alone all day and...and I'm terribly tired."

I'm glad she said that, Saldano thinks. *Our adventure tomorrow is starting to screw up my mind...if my idea doesn't work we...we could be done...shit, I wish I had a bottle.* It's well after midnight before he finds sleep in his stuffy apartment, clutching the bed sheets to inhale Barbara's sharp, diminishing scent.

CHAPTER 34

It's Easter Sunday, and Saldano feels guilty that he isn't attending mass at St. Catherine's. But then he hasn't been to church since returning stateside from Desert Storm. He rises after nine o'clock, checks the watch reports at the station even though he's off duty, and climbs the stairs to Room 211 at the Pavilion Lodge. The second-floor rooms look out onto a courtyard of manicured green lawn, swaying date palms, and tall white Bird of Paradise. A housekeeping cart crowds the landing outside 211's door. In a panic, Saldano pushes inside and finds a maid changing the bed. There's no luggage in sight.

"*Donde estas las señoritas*?" he asks impatiently.

The maid mutters, "*No lo se,*" and continues her chores.

Paul bounces down the stairs and races through the breezeway onto Crescent Avenue. He spies Barbara and Lisa a half block down, sprints toward them, grabs Barbara, and kisses her before she can speak, clutching her body. She softens to his touch.

Lisa clears her throat. "Come on, you guys," she complains, "get a room, will ya." The two adults part, embarrassed.

"What's wrong, Paul? You scared me."

"I went…to your room…the maid was cleaning…couldn't see any luggage…thought you left on the morning boat…." Saldano tries to catch his breath after his hundred-yard dash and the adrenaline rush.

Barbara tsks, "We just took a walk on the pleasure pier."

Saldano grins stupidly and sucks in a deep breath.

"Paul, I would never leave you like that. Believe me, I

know what it's like." She kisses him again. Lisa groans in mock disgust.

Paul hastily delivers his rehearsed speech. "Look, guys, it's Easter, and the cruise ships will be arriving this afternoon. I thought we'd get away from all that, drive to the West End after breakfast, and explore Two Harbors. What do ya think?"

"You sure you don't want to check in with Al again?" Barbara asks.

Paul makes a funny face at her. "If you must know, I haven't seen her in weeks. She's back in school over town most of the time."

Barbara grins and slips an arm through Paul's. They eat at the Waffle House, a smoky café where the cooks scrape bacon and eggs directly onto plates from sizzling griddles and pour batter into a phalanx of old-style irons lining one wall. The food is heavy but tastes great. The trio collectively vows that they will never eat another waffle.

They wander back to the hotel. Paul leaves them and walks up canyon to Deputy Hanson's house to retrieve her Chevy Blazer. Saldano never needed his own car on Catalina and reluctantly had asked Emily to borrow hers. The loan wasn't without costs.

"So you're going out to Little Harbor to watch the submarine races?" Hanson had cracked.

"Of course not. Barbara's daughter will be with us the whole time. What can you do with a kid in the car?"

"Well, just in case something comes up, so to speak, there are blankets in the back. Anything else, you'll have to bring your own."

Saldano knows the rumor mill would be operating at a feverish pitch when he shows up for work on Monday. *But if this trip fails,* he worries, *the ole rumor mill might be shut down soon enough.*

Paul picks up Barbara and Lisa, drives up Stagecoach Road, and stops at the nondescript turnout from where the bones had first been spotted. Barbara and Paul are quiet. They stare downslope. Paul wonders if the ghosts of those young, desperate ones still roam Catalina's deep canyons, looking for a portal that could lead them back. His Mother believes in ghosts, and for once, Paul wants to also.

At Little Harbor, they watch a weekend yachtsman attempt to tie his cabin cruiser to a mooring. A group of college coeds lay on the ship's deck, wearing thick coats of suntan lotion and little else. Barbara jokes about how challenging Paul's job must be during warm summers, with him armed with nothing but his gun and a pair of high-powered binoculars.

They continue west toward the Isthmus. As before, Paul shifts into low gear and climbs the dirt tract that leads to the ridgeline overlooking Two Harbors. He pulls the Blazer over, and they step out into the calm, warm air. Lisa wanders along the jeep road collecting rocks and wildflowers. Paul and Barbara follow at a distance, holding hands. Paul stops and turns to face her.

"I have someone I…I want you to meet. I don't know this woman well. We've only talked a couple of times on the phone. But she seems willing to talk with you and…and she's expecting us this morning."

"What's this all about," Barbara snaps.

"I've been working on, ah, you know, a way for us to be together. This woman might help."

"A woman?" Barbara says angrily. "You have got to tell me more than that."

Paul shakes his head. "If I do and it doesn't work, you'll hate me even more. Be yourself, and you'll do fine."

Paul heads toward the parked Blazer. Barbara calls Lisa, who trots back with arms full of island things. They drive westward and descend the ridge toward Two Harbors. But Saldano turns the SUV onto a different dirt road and they wind around small hillocks until passing a sign that announces: "University of Southern California Marine Science Center, Catalina Island."

Barbara takes a deep breath and stares at Saldano. Her shoulders shake.

"What's wrong, Mom?" Lisa calls from the back seat.

"Nothing, nothing, I'm fine," Barbara snaps and stares out the windshield.

They pull into an empty parking lot, save for a beat-up Toyota stationed next to the main entrance of a three-story building. The trio climbs out. A woman dressed in jeans and a white lab coat comes out to greet them. She's of medium height, slender, with short-cropped blond hair and a weathered face.

"Dr. Louise Elliott, I'd like you to meet Barbara Spencer and her daughter Lisa," Paul says. The woman extends a hand to Barbara and then smiles.

"Call me Louise, please." She looks into Barbara's frowning face. "The good Sergeant here has been telling me about you. But you know how men can get things confused."

"They're not the only ones, Louise. I'm glad to meet you. Paul has told me nothing about any of this." Barbara glares at Saldano. "I assume you work here at the Science Center?"

"I'm its director, been here thirty years. I started taking Junior Classes out past Bird Rock to survey the kelp forest. But these days, my arthritis keeps me out of the water. You do dive, don't you?"

They enter the building and move down a dark corridor.

"I haven't been wet for three years," Barbara says. "The North Coast is too cold for my Saudi blood. And my diving gear needs an overhaul." Her voice gains strength. "But I have thousands of hours diving in all sorts of locations. I love the quiet and the beauty of it."

"Yes, that's what I miss too. Although having scores of oversexed college boys hanging around provides a full-time distraction."

"You should try living as an Arab woman. It is the men who think we're out to corrupt their morals."

Barbara smiles for the first time. Paul feels invisible. They've come to a set of double doors that lead into a vast laboratory with workbenches, Bunsen burners, and testing equipment scattered everywhere. A large aquarium extends across the back wall.

"Sergeant, I think you and Lisa should explore Cat Harbor. The tide is out and there should be all sorts of sea critters exposed on the mud flats. Barbara and I need to talk for a while. I'll call you on your cell when we're done."

Louise turns and enters the lab with Barbara following. She doesn't look back.

It's the first time Saldano and Lisa have been alone together. *Great, I get nervous when I'm alone with my own daughters,* Paul thinks. *Now, what do I do?*

"Well, kid, looks like they've ditched us," Saldano says. "It's time to go have our own fun."

Lisa smiles, runs ahead and climbs into the Blazer. "Are you going to marry my Mom?" she blurts before Saldano has a chance to fasten his seat belt.

"Well, ah…I think we all need to be together and get to know each other. But…but I love your mother, and that's a good start."

"I haven't seen Mom act like this before," Lisa says, smiling. "She's happy and sad at the same time, but mostly happy. Is that what being, ya know, in love is like?"

"I'm no expert…and you'll find out soon enough." Paul chuckles and starts the car before the conversation can get more personal. They regain the ridge road and descend into Two Harbors. At the Reef Snack Bar they buy soft-serve ice cream, then tour the beach, finding dozens of perfect sea snail shells and strange stones with quartzite and mica streaks in them.

Back in the Blazer, the duo continues along the coast road past Cherry Cove, headed west toward Arrow Point. Since the winter seas have calmed, pleasure boats crowd deep-cut inlets along the inside coast. Saldano catches sight of blue smoke from party fires and makes a mental note to have Emily call the Parks Department to make sure they're on top of the situation.

At Emerald Bay, they turn back toward the Isthmus. Lisa has kept Saldano busy with questions about life in Avalon. But soon enough the conversation has shifted to her excitement about being in Junior High School the next year, about dances and boys, life in San Francisco, and her mother's ex-boyfriends. Paul listened attentively to these last bits of news, wondering what fatal flaws they had possessed.

As they pull into Two Harbors, Paul's cell phone chirps. It's Dr. Elliott. Paul doesn't ask questions, and Louise doesn't offer answers.

They wheel into the Center's parking lot. Saldano takes a deep breath and turns to smile at Lisa in the back seat. She's inspecting her collected treasures happily. When he turns back around, Barbara pushes through the building's door, one hand over her eyes, and walks slowly toward the Blazer.

"Jeez, what's…what's wrong with Mom?" Lisa says. Paul shushes her as Barbara yanks open the car door and climbs in. The trio sits without speaking. Barbara's cheeks glisten with tear tracks. She daubs at her eyes with a crumpled tissue and won't look at Paul.

His heart sinks. *Christ, I never thought that she might fail,* he thinks. *What the hell am I gonna do now?*

Finally, he speaks. "Well, what did Dr. Elliott say? Whatever it was, we can figure something out."

Barbara stares at him, her compressed lips quivering. "I

start work in a month." She throws herself at Paul, who holds her tight. Her soft body shudders in his arms. But the sobs turn to laughter. Lisa bounces up and down in the back seat, giggling. Paul kisses away Barbara's tears.

She struggles for composure. "Lisa, quiet down back there."

"It's all right, Mom. The Sergeant told me he loves you, so it's okay if he kisses you, right?"

Barbara blushes, dips her head, and nods.

"Come on, come on," Paul pleads. "You can't stop there. Give us the details."

"I'm not sure I can remember everything or anything," Barbara says and takes a deep breath, shudders, and settles back in her seat.

She recounts her time with Dr. Elliott. First, Louise had given her a cook's tour of the research labs, the boathouses with their near-shore craft and diving equipment, the library and classrooms. Then, over Earl Gray tea laced with good brandy, they'd talked about Barbara's employment.

"The Center's in a tad of a bind," Barbara says, her voice picking up speed. "They lost one of their best field technicians to an East Coast University…had nobody to arrange the fall term's diving schedule."

"So, are you going to be doing office work or what?" Paul asks impatiently.

"No, stupid, I'll be supervising the dive groups, taking ten to twelve undergrads down in the morning and afternoon, with labs and classroom work in between."

Paul's face turns somber for a moment while he considers his love surrounded by oversexed college kids. Barbara seems too excited to notice his reaction.

"You know, I told Louise I loved the science and diving, but had no real professional experience, except for my work at U of London. I guess we hit it off. Louise has a direct, sardonic way of speaking. We meshed very well. And she thinks I can handle the macho types." Barbara smiles at Paul, who ignores the dig.

"But Mom," Lisa whines, "where will we live, and what about junior high?"

"All right, all right, be patient," Barbara says, laughing. She digs into her jeans and extracts a set of keys.

"The institute provides its staff with partially furnished housing. We can move in at any time…and it's big enough for three." She winks at Paul.

"You don't mind if I live with you guys, do you, Lisa?" Paul asks seriously.

Lisa tries to control her giggling: "Oh yes. I mean…I mean, no. I mean, please stay with us. And take us to our new place."

"Louise also told me that there's a sheriff's station right across the square from the staff housing." Barbara raises an eyebrow. "Could you get assigned there instead of Avalon?"

"Probably not. Frank wants to promote me to Operations Officer and work out of the Avalon station, at least during the season. Maybe I can overnight here but work at the East End during the day…sort of a split patrol. Frank would like more than one resident officer here at night."

Barbara laughs. "That will be fine with me too…so long as it's the right officer. But I've not thought about Lisa's schooling at all."

"She'll have to take the bus into Avalon and back each day," Paul says, "or she could ride in with me."

"Oh no you don't," Lisa complains. "I won't go to school in a cop car. I'll never make any friends."

"Well, I can provide backup in case you miss the bus. How's that?"

Lisa grunts her acceptance of his alternative.

Saldano fires up the Blazer, and they motor into Two

Harbors. Cape Cod-style cottages march across the village's western flanks. Saldano pulls up to one and takes the keys from Barbara. The trio walks up a gravel path, and Paul unlocks the front door. Lisa bolts inside, her excited voice echoing in the empty space. Paul scoops Barbara up in his arms and carries her into the sitting room.

"It's an old American tradition," he explains, "and it's usually followed by an even older tradition that's universal."

Setting Barbara down, Saldano calls Lisa to the front room and extracts his wallet.

"Here's two twenties. Could you go down to the Snack Bar and pick up some hamburgers and fries for all of us? Your mother and I have to talk about…well, about things."

Lisa laughs. "I might check out the video games while I'm there. So don't get, ya know, freaked out if I'm not back right away."

Barbara and Paul listen to her footsteps crunch on the gravel path outside.

"You've done it, Paul, you've done it." Barbara sobs and comes into his arms, her body shaking.

"Are you kidding?" Paul says between passionate kisses. "If anybody could get the job, it's you."

Paul locks the front door and they test the double bed in the master bedroom, their lovemaking joyous and without reservation. They lie in the afternoon sunlight pouring in through un-curtained windows.

Barbara props herself up on an elbow and stares into his face. "Paul, I have questions, ones I never even asked my ex-husband."

Paul lies still and waits.

"I'd love to cook you an authentic Arabic meal. How do you feel about spicy food?"

"You gotta be kidding. My mother's spice rack covered

one whole wall of her kitchen. *Mas es mejor*, no?"

She lies quiet for a moment before speaking. "You must know that Barbara is not my real name. Could you call me Jamella?"

Saldano pulls her into a bear hug. "It's a beautiful name… but you'll have to call me Pablo in return."

Jamella giggles in a decidedly Arabic way. They have just enough time to clinch the deal before Lisa bangs on the front door.

CHAPTER 35

Wavelets slapped against the shore at Pebbly Beach. Stanley struggled to hold onto the bowline of a twenty-one-foot catboat, its single sail still reefed. On the mainland, the morning sun peeked over Mount Baldy and turned the channel an intense shade of cerulean.

George stowed the last of his brother's gear on board, then waded ashore. "You know, you don't have to do this. Father and I can figure out another way and keep our name out of it. Besides, there's no proof of anything."

Stanley ignored his brother. Dressed in a crewneck sweater and dungarees, he studied the sea, the size of the swells, the wind direction, and the clouds sliding eastward over the coastal range. Stan remembered the towering combers from the previous winter's storm that pounded Avalon Harbor, tearing merchant marine and private boats from their moorings and grinding them to pieces against the sea wall. His tiny sailboat wouldn't stand a chance in a Northeaster. But he knew he'd have no chance at all if he stayed on Catalina, or worse, if he returned home.

"Well, at least you know you can come back when all this blows over," George continued his monolog. "Our contacts with the Army should fix the records…so don't worry about…. Are you sure this boat's seaworthy?"

Stan remained silent.

After arguing for two days, the brothers had agreed that shipping out would be the best way to leave the island undetected. A Mexican had eagerly accepted George's money for the battered craft. The brothers spent the night before under the cover of a moonless sky, lugging Stan's gear onboard, the case of art materials being the toughest haul. With the Saint Catherine Eight out getting drunk and the hotel's front desk unmanned, they stole away easily.

"So when you get settled, Stan, drop me a line, and Father and I can plan your return."

"Listen, George, you'll…you'll be lucky if you ever see me again."

"What the hell are ya talkin' about?" George shot back.

"I'm no more a part of your world than you are of mine." Stanley's voice shook, and not only from the morning chill.

"Oh, come on, Stan. You don't need to get melodramatic. When the war is over, and your obsession with art and Mexican women has cooled, you'll be ready to come home. Remember, you're a DeVaul. You can't run from that."

"I'm…I'm not running from anything. I'd rather go it alone without Flavia than go back to Father's estate parties…with those false prophets declaring California ready for redemption."

Stanley looked into his brother's eyes. His voice lost its tremor. "I need to go before the wind changes. Help me shove off."

"Stan…be safe out there. If ya ever need anything…." George took the rope.

Stan pushed through the surf and clambered aboard the catboat. He hoisted its tattered sail quickly and grabbed the tiller. "Let go the rope," he shouted.

George dropped the bowline into the knee-deep sea. The boat came about. Its creased sail snapped taut in the freshening breeze. Stan looped a lead around the tiller and positioned himself quickly over the port side, leaning out above the rushing water. The catboat sliced the ocean, running with the wind and the current. By the time the sun rose high above the coastal mountains, its triangular sail was but a speck on the southern horizon.

The Mexico City Olympics wrapped up, including the defiant raising of fists by the American black athletes. But the people on the outskirts of La Paz had their own drama to contend with. The tall gringo, who'd arrived at the end of the Great War, had died. His driftwood and mud studio on the bluffs overlooking the beach had caught fire overnight. By the time the people scrambled from bed and arrived with buckets and shovels, the flames had destroyed everything. They buried his charred and splintered bones in the churchyard. The priest said a prayer.

The townspeople loved the gringo. He painted portraits of their children in exchange for fish, tortillas, and beans. He'd sat on the beach and drew the women bending in the surf to gather the catch from the nets cast ashore by their husbands and brothers. The women shared their food, taught him Spanish, and flirted with him as they worked, skirts rolled up above their knees in the Sea of Cortez's warm surge. But he never took a wife or an *amiga,* though many had tried to lure him with their charms.

In the years that followed his death, tourists to the area remarked at the wonderful paintings that graced the town's hotels, restaurants, and shops, noting how the style was a strange mixture of Mexican romanticism and something else. The paintings bear no artist's signature and are considered local treasures of immense value.

Terry Sanville lives in San Luis Obispo, California, with his artist-poet wife (his in-house editor) and two plump cats (his in-house critics). He writes full-time, producing novels, short stories, and essays. His work has been accepted by numerous literary and popular journals, magazines, and anthologies, including *The American Writers Review, The Bryant Literary Review,* and *Shenandoah.* He was nominated four times for Pushcart Prizes and once for inclusion in Best of the Net Anthology.

Terry is a retired urban planner and an accomplished jazz and blues guitarist who once played with a symphony orchestra backing up jazz legend George Shearing. His life as a fiction writer began in 2001. Since then, he has written and placed over 330 short stories, including two story collections—"A lot more than Hemingway and Fitzgerald but a lot less than Chekhov," he says, grinning. Other novels include *Face-to-Face* (2020) and *The Misplaced* (2024). He enjoys creating characters with imperfect bodies or minds that somehow make their mark and succeed or fail in memorable ways.

Made in United States
Orlando, FL
05 January 2025

56822850R00146